Sequ .... Stone

A TUMBLED *S*TONE

MARCIA LEE LAYCOCK

A TUMBLED STONE
Copyright © 2012 by Marcia Lee Laycock

ISBN: 978-1-77069-455-2

Word Alive Press
131 Cordite Road, Winnipeg, MB R3W 1S1
www.wordalivepress.ca

WORD ALIVE PRESS
Just Write!

Library and Archives Canada Cataloguing in Publication
Laycock, Marcia Lee, 1951-
    A tumbled stone / Marcia Lee Laycock.
ISBN 978-1-77069-455-2
    I. Title.
PS8623.A944T86 2012   C813'.6   C2012-901071-5

PROLOGUE

THE BOOK'S COVER WAS BLACK. FITTING, SOMEHOW. SHE TOOK THE WHITE pencil crayon and drew on its cover, watching her hand circle an oval pearl, then flow down to make the curve of a lower, smaller one. Two parts of the same whole, one elongated but perfect in its shape, like a tear; the other more delicate, hanging alone.

She didn't realize she was crying until she saw the stain, a streak on the dull black surface. She stared at it as though it had come from some other source, somewhere outside herself. She wiped it away with the heel of her hand and felt satisfied. There. No more tears. She opened the book.

This diary belongs to _____

She traced the line with her finger. The name had only been in her mind until now. She had never spoken it, never written it. She took a blank piece of white paper and practiced on it. Pearl. Baby Pearl. Pearl Drop. Tear Drop. She copied the names over and over, then crumpled the paper and threw it on the floor. She pulled the book toward her and wrote.

This diary belongs to Baby Pearl.

CHAPTER ONE

A farm on the Saskatchewan prairie

ANDREA WAS WOKEN BY THE BANGING OF THE STABLE DOORS. SHE JERKED the covers away from her legs and leaned into the window, the glass cold against her outstretched palm. The yard light strobed around the painted red stable as wind lashed the trees and drove the rain sideways across the yard. Her big Paint gelding, Peso, raced from one end of the corral to the other, tossing his head and flicking his tail. The light flashed on his white blotches, making them glow.

Andrea swore under her breath and immediately felt guilty about it. She had forgotten to put him in for the night. No. That wasn't true. She just hadn't done what her foster father had told her to do.

She threw on her housecoat, pulling the long belt around her waist as she raced down the narrow stairway into the kitchen. There was no truck in the driveway. Edna and Earl were still at their prayer meeting. Of course.

Andrea jumped as the stable door slammed again. It would be blown off its hinges if she didn't get out there. She tugged on a pair of boots and gripped the door handle, feeling the cold bite of it on her hand. She flipped the latch.

The wind caught the door as soon as she opened it, almost yanking her off her feet. She slammed it shut and turned toward the stable. Drenched the minute she left the stoop, her long black hair clung to her face and neck in tendrils, her robe threatening to trip her up as she ran.

She reached the stable and secured the door, then dashed to the corral. The rope latch was swollen from the rain and hard to force up over the post. Peso snorted and stomped while she fought with it. When it finally came free, she shoved the gate open just enough to squeeze through and stood still for a moment. She knew if she ran to the big Paint, she'd only spook him more. She tried to calm herself, feeling her way along the stable wall, the rough wood catching at her clothes.

When she got close to Peso, she put her arms out, calling over the wind and rain. "Whoa, boy. Whoa now, Peso. It's going to be okay. Whoa, now."

Please, she thought. *Please, let him listen to me. Just this once, let him respond to me.*

Peso's wild eyes flashed toward her, but he dashed to a far corner. Andrea moved another few strides toward him, hoping he'd stay in the corner, hoping he wouldn't throw his head when she reached for his halter.

She was close to him, now. His eyes were on her, but his ears lay flat. She could feel the hot breath from his nostrils, the panicked snorting filling her ears. She extended her arm, talking softly. Her hand was only a few inches from his head when her sopping robe wrapped around her legs as she stepped into a hole, pitching her into the mud.

Andrea cursed out loud. Her hands slid through the gritty sand as she struggled to get up. On her feet again, she flinched at the crack of a lightning strike and groaned when the big Paint lunged past her. Her attempt to grab his halter just left her with a fist full of coarse mane hair.

The beam of a truck's headlight shot across the corral, spooking Peso even more as Andrea moved toward him again. She heard the slam of two doors, and in a moment her foster father was in the corral with her, calling to the horse, moving slowly but purposefully. Peso responded immediately, his ears perking forward, the wildness in his eyes fading. His head dropped. Earl had his hand on the halter in a matter of seconds and led the big animal toward the stable.

Andrea stood shivering, watching until Earl looked over his shoulder.

"Get into the house, girl, before you catch your death."

Edna was filling the kettle at the kitchen sink, her thin face pinched into a tight frown.

"I told him it was a mistake to buy that horse," she said.

She slammed the kettle down on the counter and turned on her foster daughter, her angular face made more severe by the knot of graying black hair pulled tight at the back of her neck.

Andrea mopped at her face with a dish towel.

"Look at you. Soaked to the skin and covered in mud. Honestly, Andrea, sometimes you act like you're ten years old, not nineteen."

Edna's eyes drifted to Andrea's belly. The girl's hand tried to cover it, then dropped away.

Edna turned back to the sink. "Get yourself dried off before you go up those stairs. You'll drip all over the place."

Andrea turned away and fled up the stairs without a word.

"Andrea! Did you not hear what I just said?"

Andrea thought Edna might follow, but was relieved when the kitchen door banged and Earl came in, Edna's voice pouncing on him. Their voices boomed up the hall, but she couldn't hear the words. The tone was enough to tell her that Earl was trying to be conciliatory but Edna didn't want to hear it. Andrea was glad when one of them closed the door at the bottom of the stairs. The words turned to a muffled murmur.

She went into the bathroom, peeled off her wet clothing and threw the clothes onto the floor, liking the slapping sound they made when they landed. She stepped into the shower, twisted the tap to the hot position, and let the heat sink into her bones. When she was finished, she stepped over the wet clothing and stared at the heap. Edna would rant about it tomorrow.

Andrea sat on her bed and toweled her hair, then stood and let the towel fall away as she walked by the mirror. The swell of her belly wasn't really obvious yet when she was dressed, but she could see the slight curve of it now, in her reflection.

She pulled a pair of pajamas out of a drawer and thought for a moment about dealing with the wet clothes, but she couldn't make herself do it. There were so many things she couldn't make herself do anymore. So many times she made choices that only made everything worse.

As her eyes flitted open the next morning, Andrea groaned. Sunday. Church. She sighed and lay in bed until Edna's voice made her head jerk up.

"Time to get up, Andrea. We'll be late."

She let her legs drop to the floor, then pushed herself off the bed.

"I'm coming," she answered and opened the door to the closet. She pulled her Sunday dress from its hanger, threw it on, and fought with her hair as she clomped down the stairs.

They were already waiting in the car.

She settled into the back seat and watched the prairie landscape flow by, the barren fields waiting to be ploughed, the stubble of last season's crop yellow in the early morning light. She released her grip on the front of her jacket and flexed her fingers to relieve the cramping. She wished she could get out and walk, just walk away and not have to face anything normal. Nothing should be normal now. But the car hummed steadily, the gravel loud under its tires as they sped toward the church.

She saw the long line of evergreen trees that marked the west side of the parking lot. It was already almost full. The car slowed and she watched the women in their dresses and the men in their dark suits all moving toward the church as though drawn by some invisible magnet. She gripped her jacket again and stared at the back of her foster parents' heads. Andrea's stomach churned. Edna and Earl. Andrea had begun calling them that in her mind a few months ago. Not Mom, not Mother. Edna. Not Daddy, not Dad. Earl.

As her foster father opened the car door for her, she heard familiar music spilling out of the small white building. A few people stood in the doorway, chatting. They turned when they saw the family approaching and called out greetings. Some just nodded. Andrea tried to keep her eyes up, tried not to look guilty as she stepped passed them into the foyer.

"Nice to see you, Andrea."

She turned to face Mrs. Norsely, tried to smile.

"I hear you're going on a trip?"

"Yes, um, to visit my aunt." Andrea was sure her old Sunday school teacher would see through the half-truth.

"What a blessing to be able to travel. You young people have so many opportunities these days. But I hope you'll come back soon and stay with us? We'll be needing a teacher for the kindergarten class in the fall."

Andrea nodded and opened her mouth to say something just as her foster mother took her arm.

"Time to sit down," Edna said.

The sermon was all about judgement, as usual. Andrea tried not to listen. Her back began to ache and she shifted on the hard wooden pew, tried to relax into it, without success.

She peered around at the people she had known for so long, people who only smiled when you did things right. There weren't any others Andrea's age; they had all gone off to the city, most of them right after graduation last spring. Andrea wished she had done the same. If she'd had the money, she would have. If she hadn't been offered the job in town, she would have. If she hadn't met Cory... so many "ifs" that would have changed everything.

But she was here now, her insides quivering with fear and guilt no matter how much she told herself she didn't care what they all thought, didn't care about any of it anymore. Her head pounded and, as the organ droned with the chords of the final hymn, she hung her head and massaged her temple.

They didn't linger after the service, Edna making excuses as they headed for the door. Dinner in the oven. A sick calf to care for. Andrea heard the lies spilling out and almost laughed as she thought of the expressions on the faces of Edna's friends if they had discovered she wasn't telling them the truth. Then she thought of their expressions if they ever discovered her truth, and the laughter stopped.

No one spoke on the ride home. She hurried to her room, pulling at the pins that confined her long hair as she climbed the stairs. She changed quickly, tossing the long Sunday dress into the laundry basket. She had always hated that dress. She'd be glad when it no longer fit. She pulled on a pair of jeans, noticing the top button was a bit tight. Already.

Edna called her to set the table for dinner, but she lingered in her room, staring out the window at the barren fields. It looked so desolate that she wondered if the land would remain barren this year. The spring had been slow to arrive. Large patches of snow still lingered in shaded areas and the days were still cool. The horses hadn't yet begun to shed their shaggy winter coats.

Maybe we've stepped over some kind of boundary, she thought, *and spring will never come. Like the land of Narnia. Always winter. Never Christmas. Maybe I'm the ice queen. Only an ice queen could think the thoughts I've had lately.*

She heard Edna call again. She sighed and slowly went downstairs. The table was already set. Andrea slumped into her chair, the smell of bacon and eggs turning her stomach. She watched Edna serve the plates, watched Earl as he bowed his head to pray. She dared look at his face when his eyes were closed, dared to study the broad forehead and weather-burnished skin. Was she imagining it or were there new lines, worry lines, on his face? She knew he was aware something had changed. She saw it in the way he didn't look at her or Edna over breakfast, lunch, or dinner. He said the same blessings over the food, said the same "Thanks, hon" when he was finished, but he didn't look at them.

Perhaps because he knows the change cannot be undone.

"Eat, Andrea." Edna's voice was flat, without expression.

Dutifully, she put a forkful of egg into her mouth, chewed and swallowed. Once the action was begun she could continue. When the meal was over, she helped clear the table and do the dishes, Edna giving her direction as though she were a five-year-old. When she was done, she folded the cloth and hung it on the oven door as always, then moved quickly to the stairs.

"Have a nap." Edna's voice followed her. "You'll feel better."

In her room, she opened the drawer on a small desk and drew out a notebook she had bought long ago. She had a stack of coil-bound notebooks in which she had written stories and poems and all the other work her high school teachers had so often encouraged her to do. But this one was different. This one was bound like a normal book, but it was black, inside and out. She picked up the white gel pen that had come with it.

Names had been flitting through her mind for days. She'd suddenly realize she'd been listing them, filing some as possibilities, discarding others. But she had never spoken them, never written them. She put the gel pen down, picked up an ordinary pen, and found a blank piece of white paper.

She wrote the list in alphabetical order. Alyssa, Brandilyn, Cameron, Destiny. She scratched lines through that last one, continued the list for a while, then crumpled the paper and threw it into the garbage can by the door. She pulled the book toward her, switched to the gel pen, and turned to the next blank page.

Dear Diary, I wonder if my birth mother ever had these thoughts I'm having. She gave me away, so obviously she didn't want me. Why didn't she just abort me? I guess back then it wasn't so easy. It is now. I heard two girls at school talking about it in the washroom. They didn't even care that I was there. One girl knew a lot about it—how to get the doctor to make a referral. "Just mention suicide," she said, and there would be no problem. "It's just a tiny blob right now," I remember her saying, "but don't wait too long. Waiting complicates everything."

Waiting. I feel like I've been waiting all my life. But for what?

The pen hovered for a moment, trembling. She let it drop and put her hand over her mouth to hold back the sob that threatened to rip from her throat. She had to get out of this room, out of this house.

She grabbed a jacket and slipped quietly down the stairs, out the back door and across the yard to the yellowed field beyond. She strode along the fence line toward the creek, her ears perked for its sound, her eyes peering steadily ahead until she saw the thin line of scrub brush where the land suddenly fell away. Her eyes found the brown scar on the bank where she so often climbed down into the gully. She stood still when she reached it, staring down the incline to the creek. It was swollen with the spring's runoff, its water muddied and full of debris. Part of the far bank had fallen away, exposing the roots of old poplar and spruce trees.

Andrea stared at the churning water. She wanted the peaceful trickle of midsummer, the small sound of flowing water that so often soothed her. There would be no comfort here today.

She stared down at the steepness of the path. If she fell… tumbled over and over…

A crashing sound made her start. A young poplar had yielded to gravity and plunged into the creek.

She turned away and wandered along the bank, feeling the bite of wind not yet warmed by the sun. She had stopped crying. She felt dry, hollow inside, and wondered at the feeling. Shouldn't she feel full, with a baby inside her?

Sitting on an old fallen cottonwood, she put a hand on her stomach. She should feel something. But there was only numbness now, even when she thought about Cory. What would he do if he knew she was carrying his baby?

She could still hear the rushing water in the creek. The wind had increased and seemed to punish the trees. She pushed herself up and headed back toward the house, each foot crushing the ground in front of the other. She could feel the stubble under her shoes like blunt needles trying to break through.

The back door swung silently as she opened it into the kitchen. Earl had fixed the squeak. He was always fixing things, quickly, before they became a bother.

But he can't fix this.

Edna was standing at the sink. Andrea watched her fold the washcloth over the faucet and knew by the slight stiffening of her back that she was aware of her. But she didn't turn; she just stared out the window at the barrenness of the landscape—the land she always said she loved, perhaps too much.

Can anyone love too much? Andrea wondered. *The land, perhaps. An inanimate thing that can't love back. But that's so much safer than loving those who should love but never do.*

Edna's long hand rested on the cloth on the tap. Andrea could see the curve of her high cheek bone, a moistness to the curl of her pale eyelashes as her head turned and dropped almost imperceptibly.

Andrea wanted to scream, "Speak to me. Look at me!" For a moment she imagined Edna turning, a smile quick to her lips, her eyes beaming approval of her only daughter, her "chosen one." Andrea had longed for that look for as long as she could remember. But then a cloud blocked the light like a heavy curtain, dim reality returned, and Edna didn't move. Andrea stepped across the doorway and past into the hall, slowly climbing the stairs to her room. Her legs felt like heavy logs, but her feet made no sound.

Maybe I'm invisible already, only a phantom whose footsteps can't make the floors creak.

Back in her room, she picked up the book and pen.

I'm sitting on my bed now, staring at the small suitcase partly hidden on the floor of my closet. Edna brought it up from the basement yesterday so I could get ready. She's arranged everything with her sister, she said. A sister I've never met. I'm to leave on Friday, go away for a few months, a year maybe, then I can come home, after, and no one will know.
But I've decided. Tomorrow I'll take that small suitcase and walk away.

A sound on the stairway made her freeze. She closed the book and stood up, leaning toward the door to hear what might be beyond. But there was no sound.

She pulled a box of old books from the closet. Edna had discovered it in the basement the week before and brought it up to see if any of the books were worth reading. But Andrea didn't feel like reading much lately. She lifted a stack and slid the diary beneath them, then shoved the box back.

CHAPTER TWO

The Yukon River, downstream from Dawson City, Yukon.

ALEX PERRIN MADE THE FINAL STEP UP OVER THE LIP OF EMBANKMENT ABOVE the river and stared at the place that had been his home. It seemed strange not to be greeted by the cacophony of barking huskies.

He noticed one of the dog chains was still wrapped around a tree, half-buried under bits of decaying branches. Dry brown evergreen needles layered the ground between exposed roots, their gnarled lengths bending up and down, in and out of the hard ground. The spring rains didn't do much to make anything here look alive. The ground simply absorbed the moisture, the roots of the spruce trees drawing it up into themselves like enormous wicks. Their branches hung in short clumps, stunted by the press of others around them. Brown dying parts clung close to the trunks as though trying to hide themselves and pale grey tendrils drooped in the stillness. Here and there, a bit of green moss clung to greying wood. The yard smelled of dampness and rot.

Alex turned as Kenni came up behind him. He held out his hand to help her up over the lip, then turned back and faced the cabin, his eyes scanning. The note he'd nailed on the door months before was still there, faded and ragged on the edges. The log walls were black with age, the plank door weathered to a dull grey. Strange that he'd never noticed before how dark it all looked. George had called it his "hidey hole." The words were apt.

Alex drew in a deep breath. He might have spent his whole life here, slowly driving himself further and further into bitterness and anger, obsessing over a revenge he would never take. And in the end, this place would probably have been his tomb. The death of him, emotionally, spiritually, perhaps even literally.

He felt Kenni's soft hand slip into his. Her touch warmed him but he didn't turn his head. Time to close this door. He moved ahead of her toward the cabin, the hard-packed trail unyielding as his feet thudded upon it.

Inside, the chill of abandonment made both of them shiver.

"Does the sun ever touch this place?" Kenni's voice was hushed, not a whisper exactly, but low, as though she were trying to keep it from some outside ear.

Alex shook his head. "Not much."

Slipping the backpack off his shoulder, he moved toward the bed, bending low to pull two boxes out from under it. There were a few old t-shirts, some socks, and a baseball cap in one. He pushed it back under the bed and pawed through the other, lifting out a pair of jeans and two sweaters. He folded them into the backpack and looked up at the shelves on the wall. He scanned the books, selected a few, and dropped them on top of the sweaters. Using the empty box, he took a few tools, held the axe in his hands for a moment, then fitted it back onto the nails in the wall.

Kenni fingered the utensils in a tray near the table, glanced at the warped coffee pot on the stove, and grinned at him. "Don't think you'll want to pack these out."

Alex shook his head again and shifted the box to his hip. "This is it." Glancing around, he mumbled, "Nothing worth coming back for, really."

Except the closure it brought to see the place again one last time.

They started to leave, but he turned back, set the box on the table and opened the door to the barrel heater. A layer of dry ash made his nose twitch. Kenni stood at the open door as he retrieved the axe and quickly split a pile of kindling. Grabbing some old newspaper from the wood box nearby, he crumpled it, laid the kindling on top, and then two larger pieces of wood on top of that. He shoved the door closed and let the heavy iron latch drop into place.

Straightening, he placed a baggie of matches on the table and hefted the box again.

"Let's go." His boots made a heavy thudding sound across the floor.

They covered the distance to the edge of the embankment in a few quick strides. When they stepped down onto the trail to the river, Alex didn't look back. But as the boat motor roared and he felt the wind tangle his thick black hair, he looked around at the river, breathed in the smell of it, and knew he would miss this. He would always miss the river.

He winked at Kenni, who was watching him. "How 'bout some of that coffee now?" he yelled.

She nodded and dug in a pack for the thermos, poured a cup for him first, turning her back to the wind. He cradled it in one hand and scanned the river ahead. The ice hadn't been out that long and there was a lot of debris still floating in the water—bits of vegetation, chunks of wood, even whole trees. Alex knew hitting something hidden at the speed the boat was moving could be dangerous. And being thrown into the water would be deadly.

A movement on the bank caught his eye. He touched Kenni's knee and lifted his chin toward it. A small black bear scrambled to get away from the noise of the motor.

He'd miss that, too, being part of the wildness of this place. He caught Kenni's blue eyes on him again and raised the cup of hot coffee to his lips. The warmth of it made him smile. They'd come back to the river from time to time. It would be enough.

* * *

Alex settled into the leather seat next to his wife and buckled his seatbelt. He let his head fall back and sighed.

"You okay?" Kenni asked.

Alex opened his eyes and nodded. "Yeah. It feels good to have those loose ends tied up. But I'm anxious to get back and keep going with the search."

They stopped talking as the engines powered up and the plane started to move. It would take three hours to get back to the city. Alex sighed again. He wished he could just snap his fingers and be there. He was more than anxious to continue the search for his sister; he was boiling with an urgent need to find her. The detour to the Yukon had been a necessary delay.

There was so much he had to find out. He'd learned that the Donnellys had brought them both to Vancouver from Seattle, so what had happened to her after that? Had she gone into foster care, too? Or had she been adopted? How could he get access to the information he needed?

He stared out the window as the landscape fell away. The plane banked to follow the river. From this height it looked smooth and inviting, but he knew its true nature. There were swirling eddies and looming deadheads in that water. The strength of its current carved out its banks and its temperature could kill you in minutes. But as he watched it flow beneath them, he longed to be down there, in a boat that made him feel as though he was the only man alive.

He felt a strong pang of regret. Leaving the Yukon seemed almost a betrayal. But there were things needing to be done, things he couldn't run from anymore. He had come to terms with his past as a foster kid. Finding his sister would be another step toward healing. He hoped.

He felt Kenni's shoulder touch his as she leaned in to look out the window.

"We'll be back," she said.

Alex nodded without looking at her, then turned and grinned. "Maybe when we find Andrea we should plan a canoe trip. It'd be a good way to get to know her, real quick."

"What makes you think she'll like camping?"

"She's my sister."

"Siblings can be very different."

Alex turned back to the window. "Yeah, but… I don't know, I just have a feeling she's like me in a lot of ways."

"Ornery and stubborn?"

Alex twisted in his seat and grinned at her. "I was thinking more the strong silent type."

"Ah. And what if she's all girl, pink bows and high heels?"

"Then I guess you two will have a lot in common."

Kenni poked him. "I can do the camping thing."

"Uh-huh, as long as you have your shower and indoor toilet five paces away."

"Well, that's just being civilized."

"My point exactly." He shifted and gave her a quick kiss on the cheek.

She leaned into him but pretended to pout. "I can do camping."

Alex looked down at the curve of river below them. "I hope you get the chance to prove it."

CHAPTER THREE

EDNA SHOOK THE PLACEMATS OUT OVER THE SINK, REPLACED THEM ON THE table, and smoothed them down again. Andrea had come in, stopped for a moment, but then gone up to her room without a word. Just as well. Words only got between them now, like strands of a beaded curtain meant to conceal but only partly succeeding.

She stared out the window without taking comfort from the landscape that usually calmed her. Across the fields, over the hill where a small stand of tall poplar waved their branches as though beckoning—out there on the edge of their land—she had left it. But it would not leave her.

She stared at the pile of potatoes in the sink, their red skins encrusted with black dirt. They made her remember a day not long after the—what should she call it... the incident, the black day?—when she had gone to the garden to dig up some potatoes for supper.

The earth had been dark and loose, the mounds easy to dig. She had pulled the tubers out, shaking the dirt from their skins and dropping them into a small bucket, one at a time.

She had straightened up but then saw one still in the ground, so she took the spade and raised it. It was large, with one rounded end, small at the top, like a head tucked in. She lifted it and the weight felt familiar. She placed it gently on top of the others, took them to the kitchen, and washed and peeled them slowly. All but that one. That one she had scrubbed and dried and taken to her room.

She'd found one of the tiny flannel blankets she had made, wrapped it firmly, and tucked it under the pillow. It hardly left a lump. Earl wouldn't notice.

That night she pulled it to her, the blanket soft and smelling fresh. She had curled around it and fallen asleep.

Edna shook herself. The memories were surfacing more and more now, with Andrea's "problem." They were landmines to be avoided, skirted around. She knew they would explode if she allowed them to, flooding her mind with their poison. So she tried to stay on the edges of them, diverting her mind with other thoughts, remembering instead the day their old dog died.

Her husband had wrapped him in a burlap sack and took him out into the fields, way out by the slough. The day had been bright, with a soft breeze and the sound of red-winged blackbirds singing in tall reeds on the edge of the water. When they had reached the spot, Andrea had wanted to put a cross over the hole but Earl said, "No marker. It's only a lump of fur and bone. Not worth marking."

She needed that steel in her heart now.

Not worth marking. Not worth remembering. Put it away and go on.

But she had remembered the small pile of palm-sized stones that marked the place the next time she walked by it.

It was almost noon the next day before she went to Andrea's room. She was going to urge her to go for a walk again. The girl needed to get out, to act normal, for Earl's sake. For all of them. She would insist on it.

But Andrea wasn't there. Her bed was made, everything neat and tidy. Edna almost turned away, thinking the girl must have gone out quietly.

Then she noticed one of the drawers to the dresser was partly open. When she moved to close it, her hands froze on the two small knobs. The drawer was half empty. She opened the closet. Empty hangers dangled on the rod.

Edna's hand flew to her mouth. She hurried toward the door, saw the crumpled ball of paper sitting in the garbage can, and stopped to pick it out. She held it in her hand for a moment, then slowly pulled it flat. When she saw what was written on it, her hands began to tremble.

She was sitting at the kitchen table with the paper still in her hands when Earl came in. He stood in the doorway for what seemed a long time before she felt his shadow over her.

"What?" he said.

Her shoulders slumped and tears slipped silently down her cheeks. "Andrea's gone."

"Gone where?"

"I don't know. She's just gone."

Earl glanced toward the stairs leading to Andrea's room, his face blank. He took a step toward the stairway, then stopped. Edna noticed his shoulders stiffen. He didn't turn around when he spoke again.

"Why was she going to your sister's, Edna?" When she didn't answer, he turned and stared at her. "Why?"

"She's pregnant, Earl. And now she's run off."

Later that night, after they had decided not to call the police, Edna took the piece of paper out to the burn barrel and watched the writing shrivel on the page.

* * *

This was the third bus she'd been on and Andrea wasn't even sure which direction she was going anymore. But she knew she was going away from her home. That knowledge thrilled her and made her want to wail with loss at the same time. But she would not wail. She wouldn't allow herself to cry.

She stared out the window, watching the prairie flow by. The sun was setting, a stretch of cloud reflecting a strip of pale orange across the horizon. Sunset would come later and later, now, as the spring grew into summer, but she wouldn't be there this year to see the crops ripen and hear the chirp of crickets in the heat.

She took a deep, slow breath. This was the only landscape she had ever known—a landscape where the sky overwhelmed the land and the mind could reach forever and never come to an end of it. But she would have to come to an end somewhere. When would it be far enough? She put her forehead on the window, its coolness bringing her fully awake.

Cory's words played in her head again, like a loop of sound blaring into empty space, echoing back again and again.

"We're too different, Andrea. I'm sorry. It just wouldn't work. We're just too different."

The deep pain of that rejection still twisted in her stomach. It always happened. She just wasn't good enough, not for her birth parents, not for her foster parents, not for the church, not for the "friends" she had tried so hard to connect with at school. She didn't know why she had thought it would be different with Cory. She had dared to hope and now there was only the wracking ache of longing to be loved. Again.

She closed her eyes and willed herself to keep the pain buried deep. She would follow the plan and let no one know.

Her stomach growled as they pulled into Regina. Andrea dug into her purse for some money, aware that she didn't have much, then elbowed a place into the line of passengers getting off.

The building in front of them was tall and grey, but it looked somehow friendly.

Andrea glanced at the sign above the door as she stepped inside. Evie's Rocky Road Diner. The place beamed with warm light and seemed full of stones. There were geodes and fossils of all kinds on high shelves behind the counter, large jars of pebbles decorating the partitions between the booths, and the floor had been painted to look like large stepping stones leading down the length of the room.

The hum of customers' voices and the crash of plates and cutlery made Andrea relax a little. She had worked in a place like this all through high school.

Well, minus the stone decor, she thought.

She saw the "Help Wanted" sign in the window as she pulled herself up onto a stool at the counter and ordered a bowl of soup.

The woman bustling back and forth looked harried. She was a big woman with bright red hair piled into a messy knot on the top of her head. It was the kind of colour you didn't have to guess about.

As Andrea sipped her soup, she watched the woman work her way down the line of customers. She scribbled on the pad in her hand as she took orders, then bellowed them out as she stuck the slips of paper on a metal wheel in the middle of the slot that revealed a slice of the kitchen. Andrea could see only one cook, moving at a pace that made her wonder if the food shoved across the counter was even cooked.

When the woman took the man's order right beside her, Andrea studied her face. She looked tired but didn't snap. She raised her eyes to each person as she took their order. And her eyes remained kind. When they shifted to her, Andrea took a deep breath.

"Do you need some help?" Andrea asked. "I'm a good waitress."

"Praise God, sweetie. You come on back here and I'll put you to work."

Andrea hesitated, the woman's response gripping her throat like a vice. But she needed to make some money. "I'll need a place to stay," she said.

"No problem. There's a room upstairs." Evie grinned. "If you make it through this rush."

Andrea slid off the stool and went behind the counter.

"What's your name, honey?" the woman asked.

"Andrea." It came out automatically and she immediately chided herself for giving her real name, but it was too late.

"I'm Evie," the woman said, handing her an apron and nodding to the booths on the other side of the restaurant. "I'll handle them if you can keep things under control here. I've taken the orders. Just deliver the plates with the bills." She peered at her as she backed away. "Okay?"

Evie was already moving toward the end of the counter but the cook was ringing the bell again. She turned, picked up two plates, and handed them to Andrea.

"Joe growls, but he won't bite."

Andrea nodded and took a deep breath. "Okay." She turned toward the counter to deliver the food.

It seemed like she had worked for only a few minutes when the bus driver hollered for the passengers to board and the diner began to empty. Andrea followed the flow, retrieved her suitcase, and went back into the restaurant.

Evie was clearing a table. She turned and gave Andrea an up-and-down inspection that made the girl hold her breath. But the woman smiled.

"You handled that crowd well. I think you'll do just fine." Then she hollered to Joe that she was going upstairs. Joe gave a wave from the kitchen.

"Come on, hon. I'll show you your room."

As they mounted the narrow stairway, Evie kept up a lively banter. In the few moments it took to reach the second floor, Andrea learned that the restaurant opened at six in the morning and the coffee had better be ready or their regulars would grumble. Buses arrived at about ten, four-thirty, and eight. They closed promptly at ten but always cleaned the place for another hour. Her room and board would be taken out of her wage, which was meagre, but Andrea didn't comment.

"I like my counters gleaming and my floors the same," Evie said.

Evie took a couple of deep breaths, her broad chest heaving from the exertion of the climb, then opened a door and waved Andrea through into a small room with a single bed pushed up against one wall, a small bedside table with a vintage lamp, and an old scarred dresser on the other side of the room. A slit of window looked out onto a brick wall across the alley.

"My room's down at the end of the hall," Evie said. "There's just the two of us on this floor. Joe and Benny live upstairs. Allan, our afternoon cook, doesn't live here." She gave Andrea another up-and-down glance. "Well, I'll let you settle in. No need to clean tonight, but I'll expect you to be downstairs at five-thirty. There's a few uniforms in the closet. Should be at least two that will fit. Hope you're a morning person, 'cause once you're trained, I'll be sleeping in."

Andrea nodded. "I have no problem with early mornings."

"Good. There's a key to the room and the back door—make sure you keep it locked—in the bedside table," she said, nodding toward it.

She seemed to hesitate then, and Andrea had the feeling the woman was going to ask a question she wouldn't want to answer. But Evie just nodded and smiled. "See you in the morning then."

Andrea stood in the middle of the room for a moment. It smelled old but not unpleasant. She looked around at the small space.

Good enough, she thought as she put her suitcase on the bed and started unpacking, laying her clothes neatly in the dresser drawers.

When she was done, she started to close the suitcase, then frowned. She ran her hand into the large pocket on the lid, feeling for the notebook. She remembered digging it out of that box of old books in her closet, but what had she done with it then?

Whirling, she rifled through the clothes in her dresser. She felt something hard and sighed with relief, lifting the book out of its wrapping of t-shirts.

It wasn't until she sat on the bed that she realized the notebook wasn't the same one she had written in a couple of days before. The cover was black, but faded and rougher. She flipped it over and frowned. There was a smudged drawing on the cover. It looked like it had been done with a white pencil crayon.

Andrea touched it with her index finger, circling the shape of a small upper pearl, then flowing down to make the curve of the lower portion. It looked like an earring, the old clip-on kind. She remembered discovering one like it in Edna's dresser drawer one day. It had shocked her. She had never seen her foster mother wear earrings. The church would not have approved.

Andrea cocked her head as she opened the book. The handwriting inside was flowing and elegant. Andrea's breath caught. This was Edna's handwriting, her foster mother's writing.

Dear Baby Pearl: this diary belongs to you.

Andrea's frown deepened. Had Edna fostered another kid before her, a baby?

You will never see it, never read it. I suppose I'm writing it because of my own need. I need to say so much to you, to get rid of the pain. Some will say that's why I did it, to get rid of the pain, to get rid of the pain of you. You were painful, Pearl. I screamed you into existence.

Andrea's hand flew to her mouth.

Then there you were, so tiny, too tiny, but whole and perfect. I could hardly believe it, after everything that had happened. I expected you would be marred, somehow deformed. How could something so beautiful come from my sin? I'm ugly, Pearl. But you… oh, you were so beautiful! You would have been so easy to love.

Andrea suddenly realized she'd been holding her breath. She flipped the book closed and stared at the cover again. Was this saying what she thought it was saying? No. It couldn't be. She knew her foster mother wasn't able to have children. She'd been told that. It was why they had decided to take her in as a foster kid. But the handwriting was unmistakable.

Andrea opened the book again and read the first page. A chill raced through her. Edna had given birth to a baby girl.

She turned the page.

I know God is punishing me. And I deserve it. My sin is beyond measure and can never be forgiven. But why did he punish you, Little Pearl? It was all my fault. You were innocent. Earl said it was for the best, that now we can go on with our lives. Put it all behind us. But how can I forget? How can I pretend that everything is just as it should be?
It will never be right with Earl and me again. God forgive me. God forgive me. God forgive me. Maybe if I beg long enough. Maybe if I write those words over and over again, like writing lines for doing something wrong in school. Maybe it will happen. But forgiveness is only for those who repent. I can't repent of you, my Baby Pearl, or of the love I finally found. I won't.

Andrea put her hand to her mouth again as she read the last paragraph on the page. It was written in red ink.

"There is no one righteous, not even one... their throats are open graves; their tongues practice deceit... ruin and misery mark their ways... There is no fear of God before their eyes" (Romans 3:10–18).

Andrea shivered again. When had this happened? What had happened to that baby? Was it Earl's child or...? Questions flooded her mind.

She caught her breath. Where was her diary? She must have left it in that box and grabbed this one by mistake. Slumping down on the bed, she clenched her fist. Stupid. What if someone found it? Her heart raced at the thought—her whole life was in that book.

She stood up and paced, trying to calm herself. If Edna found it, read it... Andrea started to shake. She had said so many things that would hurt her. They were the truth, her true feelings, but Andrea had never intended that Edna should read them.

But what did it matter now? She'd never see Edna again. The thought sank in like a poisonous stone lying at the bottom of a deep well.

But this is what she'd wanted, wasn't it? To leave everything behind and start a life of her own? She sank back onto the bed. Then why did she feel so guilty and so empty, like there was just a huge hole inside her now?

The scripture she had just read flowed through her mind. Andrea closed her eyes, bile rising up in her throat. Fear of God. That's all they knew, all she knew. Would she never escape it?

* * *

Evie poured a thin line of water into the dish that held a small African violet. She almost let the water run over, but caught herself in time. She was thinking about Andrea, the latest in a fairly long line of strays the Lord had brought to her door. The girl was an answer to prayer. She seemed to be a pretty good little waitress.

Evie smiled as she put the watering can down. She knew God was way ahead of her, as usual. He hadn't just brought her there to be a waitress, Evie was sure of that.

"Give me wisdom, Lord," she prayed. "And all the love and mercy you can spare."

CHAPTER FOUR

A LEX SAT IN THE CAR, STARING AT THE SMALL BLUE BUNGALOW ACROSS THE street. He wondered what kind of reaction he'd get from the man who lived there. Only one way to find out.

He pushed open the door and stepped into the street. His sneakers made no sound as he strode across the pavement. In a few long strides, he was on the doorstep.

Hesitating for only a moment, he rang the bell. Heavy footsteps thudded inside.

Suddenly, Alex was face to face with the tall blond man who had tried very hard to put him behind bars.

By the way Stan Sorensen's bushy eyebrows shot up, Alex knew he had recognized him. His mouth went dry and he forgot the opening line he'd rehearsed.

Sorensen smirked. "Well? Donnelly, isn't it? You going to stand there all day or are you going to tell me why you're here?"

Alex took a deep breath. "It's Perrin now. That's my real name."

Sorensen stared but said nothing.

Alex cleared his throat. "You were pretty good at tracking me down."

Sorensen nodded. "'Cause I believed you were guilty as sin and I wanted you off the streets."

"But you were wrong."

The tall man shrugged. "It happens now and then." He frowned and tilted his head. "Is that what you want? To rub my nose in it?"

Alex shook his head hard. "No. I need help."

Sorensen started to close the door. "I'm not a social worker."

Alex took a step forward and raised his voice a notch. "I need a good detective."

Sorensen hesitated. "I'm not a detective either. Not anymore. I'm retired."

"But I'm betting you're still pretty good at finding people."

"What people?"

"My sister."

Sorensen's blue eyes stared at him so long Alex started to fidget. Then the former detective took a step back and swung the door wide.

"Come in."

They stepped through a small foyer into a living room furnished with a shabby hide-a-bed along one wall and a recliner facing a large-screen TV. A computer was set up in the far corner on a good-sized desk. There was only one file lying beside it.

Good, Alex thought. *He's not overloaded with work.*

He glanced sideways at Sorensen. "So, how's retirement?"

Sorensen waved him to the sofa. "Got everything I need. Computer, TV, cable—every channel full of every kind of garbage you can imagine. What more could a man ask for?"

"Sounds fulfilling."

Sorensen grunted. "Let's just say tracking down your sister sounds a lot more interesting. What's the story?"

Alex leaned forward, slipped the photo from an inside jacket pocket, and stared at it for a moment. His own eyes squinted back at him, a little boy with his baby sister. He handed it to Sorensen.

"This was in a safety deposit box I discovered a few months ago," Alex said. "Until then I thought I was an only child. I've been able to find out that my sister and I were adopted together when my parents died, then moved to Vancouver. My adoptive parents died there and that's when things get hazy. I ended up in foster care but I don't think she went to the same place. At least, that's what I'm guessing."

"Adoptions are tricky. They don't like to release the records."

Alex nodded. "Tell me about it. I've been knocking my head against the bureaucracy wall for months."

"This will take time." Sorensen raised his eyes from the photo. "And money."

"Money's no problem."

Sorensen gave a nod. "Flat rate to start is five thousand. I'll invoice all expenses on top of that. When I find her, that'll be another five."

Alex extended his hand. "Deal," he said.

Sorensen wrapped his huge hand around Alex's and nodded again. "I'll need all the names you know, places, dates. Don't leave any detail out."

"Got a pen?"

* * *

A fine spring rain had polished the street into a mirage grey that shimmered under the street lights. Andrea watched her reflection passing in each store window as she hurried to a small pharmacy a block away from the diner.

A blast of heat drove the dampness away as she pushed the glass door open. Scanning the signs above each row, she found the stationary aisle.

There was a display of journals with decorative covers in a rack at the end of the long shelf. She looked at them for a moment, checked the price on a couple, then continued down the aisle until she saw a stack of spiral notebooks. That would do. She chose a pack of pens as well, paid the clerk, and hurried back to the grey building that was now her home.

Back in her small room, she picked up the black book for a moment, tempted to read more, but changed her mind and slipped it into a drawer. Then she turned to the spiral notebook. She thought about trying to rewrite the last entry she had made in the other book, but decided there was no point. The words weren't intended to be read. They were just for her. For her own therapy.

Interesting word, that. Therapy. She said it over in her mind several times, glanced toward the dresser that held the small black book, then began to write.

I've discovered Edna had a child, but something happened, something she needed forgiveness for. Was Earl the father?

As soon as she wrote the question she knew the answer. Earl would have been happy to have a child. Unless the child wasn't his.

I can't believe she would have done something... something so "sinful." That word she uses all the time. And all the time, it applied to her. It's strange, but it makes her seem more human to me. I wish I'd known long ago.

Andrea clicked the pen in her hand. What had they done with that baby?

* * *

Earl lifted the sledgehammer above his head and slammed it down onto the top of the iron splitter buried in a large birch stump. He'd been working away at this old stump in the corner of the backyard for over a year, slowly breaking it down. He aimed and brought the sledge down again, feeling each blow course through his arms and chest. He didn't try to reason out the rage he felt. He just let it build, then explode when the hammer struck. He hit the splitter over and over with such violence that finally a huge chunk of the stump split and fell away.

Earl stared at it, then let the heavy hammer slip from his hands. It hit the ground with a dull thump and he staggered back, his torso heaving from the exertion, his arms shaking. Andrea's face floated in front of him—her slow smile and the tinge of sadness that always seemed to linger in her eyes. He had wanted desperately to make that sadness go away. But he knew he would never be able to accomplish that. All he could do was watch as she turned to other things, other people for the happiness and love he couldn't give her. Just like Edna had.

He slumped down beside what was left of the stump and buried his head in his hands.

God, what can I do to fix this?

* * *

Andrea woke to the buzz of her clock, swung her legs over the edge of the bed, and silenced the alarm. The room was dark, only a sliver of pale light showing through the small window. She clicked on the lamp beside the bed and sat very still for a time. She hadn't slept well. Nightmares had woken her twice and she had stared into the darkness for long hours.

She scrubbed at her eyes and stood up. Evie hadn't said anything about a washroom, but there had to be one somewhere. She pulled on her bathrobe, clutching her toiletry kit in one hand and a towel in the other, and opened her door a crack.

The hallway was dim and silent. There were no other doors she could see so she slipped out, moved quietly toward the end of the hallway, and glanced around the corner. There was a door at the end and another just to her right. That must be the bathroom, she thought.

Just as she took a step toward it, the door flew open. Evie stepped into the hall, towelling her hair and almost bumping into Andrea.

"Oh, I'm sorry, hon," she said. "Didn't see you there. I'm done in the bathroom if you want it now." Her voice was loud in the quiet hallway.

"Thanks."

Andrea stepped into the steamy room and closed the door. She stared at her face in the mirror above a small square sink, then down at the slight curve to her belly.

What are you going to do? she asked herself, then answered in a whisper. "Survive. That's all. Just survive."

She finished her ablutions without another glance in the mirror. A few moments later, dressed in a green and gold uniform that was a full size too big, she descended the stairs to the diner.

There weren't any customers yet, so only the lights in the kitchen were on, giving the place a warm glow. Andrea looked along the length of the counter, at the stone-patterned Formica spotless under the dim light and the condiments, set in shining chrome holders, spaced at even intervals. At the far end, a glass case was angled toward the front door. It was full of stone jewellery.

The dark green booths along the wall looked like they had just been freshly polished. For some reason, Andrea thought of the creek near her home, where the water rushed over layers of tumbled stones. A longing for home surged up inside her, but she swallowed hard and tried to ignore it.

Evie was scooping coffee into paper filters, piling one on top of the other. She turned when Andrea approached.

"This takes two scoops each, rounded, see?" She held the scoop full of coffee for a moment, then dumped it and put the filter on top of the previous one. "I like to do a few of these in the morning so we don't fall behind during the rush. But don't stack them too high." She patted the side of the coffee machine. "This old boy is a little iffy sometimes, so if you don't see the water start to run in a minute or two, wiggle the cord." She swung her considerable bulk around. "Next thing is to check all the receptacles—sugar, jam stacks—make sure they're full. Then put a bowl of creamers on each table. You'll find 'em in the small fridge in the kitchen."

Andrea stared.

"You can do that now."

"Oh, okay." Andrea stepped through the swinging door into the kitchen, expecting to see Joe. Instead a boy who looked a little younger than her leaped back.

"Whoa," he said as he dodged the swinging door.

Andrea stopped short. "Sorry."

He focused on a spot over her left shoulder. "You're supposed to sing out when you come through."

He was a few inches taller than her, and stocky. His shoulders were broad but slightly hunched. She stared at him but he said nothing more. Then Andrea remembered why she was there.

"I, um, I need to get the creamers from the small fridge."

He stepped aside and gave a bow, sweeping his arm down with a silly grin. "Be my guest, princess."

Andrea looked past him and saw the fridge. There wasn't much room between him and the long counter stacked with pots and pans. He was bowing slightly from the waist, the silly grin still on his face but his eyes on the floor. She stepped forward and was about to slip by him when he leaped out of the way. His grin had vanished. When she turned from the fridge with four bowls of creamers in her hands, he blocked her way.

"I'm Benny," he said, staring at the ceiling. His round face and thick neck were covered in red splotches. He raised his eyebrows. "And you are… you are a princess." The grin returned.

"My name is Andrea."

He still didn't make eye contact.

She dropped her eyes. "Evie's waiting for these."

He stepped to the side. She felt him watching her and was glad when the door swung back into place. She was still staring at it when Evie came up behind her.

"Did you find them?"

Andrea jumped, spilling a couple of the creamers onto the floor. She stepped back as Evie bent to retrieve them. The large woman looked from the girl's face to the kitchen doors and back again.

"Oh dear, I'm sorry, hon. I should have told you about Benny." She peered into Andrea's face. "He didn't scare you, did he?"

"Well, not exactly."

"He is a little odd, I know, but he's the best busboy I've ever had." She leaned in closer. "And he's harmless. Really. Please don't quit on me."

"Quit? No, I'm not going to quit."

"Oh good." The relief on Evie's face was plain. "My last two girls just couldn't handle working with him." She sighed. "But he really is harmless, I promise," she repeated.

Evie swooped through the doorway into the kitchen without another word. Andrea heard her talking quietly to Benny but couldn't make out what she was saying.

For the next half hour, she followed Evie around, trying to put all the instructions into a memory vault and not let her eyes flick to the slit in the wall where she could see Benny and Joe moving around in the kitchen. Then Evie led her through the kitchen to a small back room that held a chrome table and three chairs. One end of the table was stacked with papers and an old adding machine.

"Joe will cook us some breakfast now, but eat fast. The morning crowd will be here in half an hour."

The customers soon began to arrive and the morning flew by. Andrea had just served a family of six when Evie came up behind her.

"You'd better go take a bit of a break before the lunch crowd hits, honey. Help yourself to something to eat."

Andrea stepped into the kitchen. Joe was busy with a large frying pan and didn't look up. She opened the small fridge quietly and took a couple of slices of tomato and ham to make a sandwich.

When she turned around, Benny was behind her. Close behind her. She backed up and almost dropped the plate.

"Evie said I could get something to eat," she blurted.

Benny grinned. "Okay. Don't take that bacon. Joe has plans for it."

Andrea realized the door to the fridge was still open. To close it she would have to step toward him. So she stayed where she was. Benny grinned and opened his mouth just as Evie's head appeared in the slit below the order wheel.

"Benny, I need you to mop under table three."

He ducked his head and moved toward the counter, calling "Comin' up" over his shoulder.

Andrea took two slices of bread from a bag and headed to the back room. She was glad for the chance to sit down but had just settled when Benny slid into the chair opposite her.

"So, where's the princess from?"

Andrea frowned. "West of here a ways."

"Aha, west of here. I've never been west of here. So…"

They heard Evie call his name from the kitchen.

Benny jumped up. "No rest for the wicked," he said, giggling.

Andrea tried not to look at him but he just stood there so she finally raised her head.

He winked at her. "To be continued."

It was her turn to sigh. Something was obviously not quite right with Benny, but like Evie said, he seemed harmless. She finished her lunch and went back to work.

It was busy, so there was no time to think. The end of the shift came and she trudged up the narrow stairs to her small room. She was more tired than she ever remembered being before. So tired that she didn't think about a shower or what would come next. She just slumped down on her bed and fell into a deep sleep.

* * *

Benny first noticed the girl at the bus stop. He couldn't help staring at her, staring at her enlarged belly. She pulled her coat across it and turned away from him, her spiked red hair making him think of a porcupine. But he slid closer.

"Babies need protection," he said.

She nodded. "Yes, they do."

He smiled and nodded back. "I learned that word from my dictionary. Protect. Protector. Protection. Protection," he said again. "That's a good word."

The bus arrived and she got up quickly to board. He didn't follow, just sat on the bench, nodding. He noticed she sat with her back to him, but she looked over her shoulder as it drove away.

Benny saw her approach the bus stop again the next day, but then she crossed the street and kept walking. It was only three blocks to the next stop. He hurried and when she arrived he was sitting there, waiting. She didn't sit beside him, just stood in line at the pole.

"I know a safe place for babies," he said, coming up behind her.

She didn't turn or answer him.

"It's warm and safe."

The bus arrived and she almost leaped inside.

"Stay away from water," he called after her.

He went back to sit on the bench, watching. There were other girls who were having babies. Soon he would find one to protect. That was his job now, to protect the babies.

* * *

Sorenson stared at the sheet of paper in his hand. Then he looked up at the young man sitting across from him.

"So they won't give you any information at all?"

Alex shook his head. "No."

"That means she wasn't adopted."

"How do you know?"

"It's the system here. If she had been adopted, you could at least request the government's help in finding her. But if she was in the foster care system, they won't help. How old would she be now?"

"Nineteen."

Sorenson nodded. "Okay. So she would have aged out of the system by now. That'll make things even more tricky."

Alex sighed.

Sorenson looked up. "But not impossible."

"When can you get started?"

The tall man glanced at his almost-empty desk. "Well, I've got quite a backlog, as you can see."

Alex grinned. "Right."

"I'll get on it right away, starting with finding out more about your parents."

"Anything else I can do?"

"Not at this point. I'll keep you posted."

"I'll keep praying."

Sorenson's eyebrows shot up. "Whatever turns your crank."

* * *

Andrea's hands trembled as she picked up the diary. It felt wrong to be reading it, but she couldn't stop herself. She opened the cover and turned to the page she had last read, then turned to the next.

I don't know how it happened. No. That's not true. It began when I was a teenager, sneaking off to a friend's to read the magazines she hid in her parents' barn. They were full of romantic stories about true love. That was the seed of my sin. And when I saw Roy—he was so handsome—the kind of handsome I saw in those magazines, the kind a young woman dreams about.

I remember the day he arrived at the farm. Earl told me his name, that he'd hired him to work during the harvest. Then he waved at me and said, "This is the missus," and turned away as though I were dismissed. But Roy pulled the cap from his head and smiled while looking at me—really looking at me—and I knew. I ran from it then, my face crimson I'm sure. But I knew, and eventually I gave up trying to deny it.

"Chemistry," they called it in the articles in those magazines. Earl and I never did have chemistry. We just had duty. I married him because my father told me to and because I thought I probably should take what I could get. I don't know why he married me—perhaps for the same reason. I was a suitable match, after all, capable of all that a farm wife has to do, and not too pretty. But Roy looked at me as though I were beautiful.

The first time he touched me—and it was a simple touch on my arm— nothing that could lead to anything, yet it thrilled me to my very soul. Earl had never touched me like that, in a simple ordinary gesture that said he cared. Never.

I shouldn't blame Earl. He is what he is. And it should have been good enough, I know, but when Roy looked at me that day, nothing was good enough—it just wasn't, not anymore.

> "Then, after desire has conceived, it gives
> birth to sin; and sin, when it is full-grown,
> gives birth to death" (James 1:15).

Andrea let the book rest in her lap. So this was the secret that was always between them, always a wall that couldn't be scaled, couldn't be acknowledged.

No wonder, she thought. *No wonder.*

She closed the diary and glanced at the clock. She was five minutes late. Groaning, she forced herself out of bed, pulled on her uniform, and headed for the washroom. A quick splash of water on her face would have to do.

CHAPTER FIVE

BENNY STOOD JUST BEHIND THE SWINGING DOORS AND PUSHED ONE OPEN enough that he could see, then shifted so he could watch Andrea through the crack. She had been helping Evie for about two weeks. The longer Andrea was here, the more he liked watching her. She was filling the sugar canisters, being careful not to spill, he could tell. When the last one was full, Benny saw her hand slip down to her abdomen and rest there for a moment before she lifted the tray of dispensers and walked away.

Benny let the door ease back into place. He smiled, remembering how his mother had touched her stomach that way and made him promise not to tell. Benny was good at keeping secrets.

* * *

Andrea's routine was going well. The hectic pace kept her from thinking about her problem and how to solve it. The need to be polite and even congenial with the customers kept her mood up. She got along fine with Joe, and Benny seemed to attach himself to her like a puppy to its mother. She wasn't quite as tired anymore when her day was over. In fact, she decided it was time to take a walk and see what the neighbourhood looked like.

It was obvious that the diner was not in an upscale area of the city. The shops lining the streets had been there a while. She smiled at a small stuccoed building with a big handwritten sign in the window that read "Shoe Repair. Recycle Your Old Friends." There were a couple of pawn shops that made her think about crossing the street and a Chinese restaurant that had only one English word, "Eat," flashing in neon above the door.

She turned down a side street and found herself moving away from the business area. Tall trees lined each side. The houses were small bungalows, some neat and trim, but most looked as though the residents hadn't been home in a while. Garbage cans lay on their sides and the grass needed mowing. It all made her sadness surface, like a large bubble that had been churning under the surface of a calm lake. As she circled the block, weariness flooded through her and she headed back to the diner.

She glanced into the kitchen as she passed it, but Allan didn't seem busy. There were only a couple of customers in the back booths and Evie was nowhere to be seen, so she climbed the stairs to her room. She wasn't hungry anyway. She just wanted to sleep.

* * *

Andrea woke in darkness, rolled over, and then scrambled up as whatever was in her stomach came up into her throat. She covered her mouth with her hand and fumbled for the lamp but only succeeded in knocking it over. Then she remembered where the door was and lunged for it just as her stomach erupted. At least it landed on the linoleum hallway, not the carpet in her room.

She leaned against the wall for a moment, shivering, then made her way to the bathroom, found a towel, and started to clean up the mess. She was on her hands and knees when Evie came around the corner.

The big woman's eyes bulged for a second, then she charged toward her.

"Are you okay, honey?"

Andrea got to her feet. "Yeah, just a touch of flu, I think."

"Oh dear. Well, you'd better get back into bed then."

Andrea nodded. "Maybe it was something I ate."

"Not here, I hope."

Andrea gave her a small grin. "I have kind of a sensitive stomach sometimes."

"Oh. Well, just take it easy this morning. I'll take your shift and come check on you later."

"Sorry, Evie."

She waved her hand. "No problem. Just get better quick."

Andrea stepped back into her room, righted the lamp, and headed for the bed. As her head hit the pillow, her mind spun.

I have to find a clinic. Tomorrow.

The word seemed to hiss in her mind. Tomorrow.

Yes, she thought. *I can't wait any longer.*

* * *

She woke a few hours later. The room was dim and for a moment she didn't know where she was. She flicked on the small table lamp and saw the spiral notebook beside it.

Memories of Cory suddenly crowded her mind. She pushed herself into a sitting position, picked up the notebook, and read what she had written the night before.

I don't know why I believed Cory loved me. I guess I just needed it so much, needed to feel loved. I think Edna and Earl tried to love me. Maybe I was the one at fault—maybe I'm just totally unlovable. My own mother obviously didn't love me. If she didn't, how could anyone else? Maybe that preacher back home is right. Maybe everyone is full of lies. Including me. Most of all me.

She threw the book to the floor, curled into herself, and tried to go back to sleep, her tears leaving a damp trail on the pillow.

She had just started to doze when a sharp rap on her door jerked her wide awake. She jumped up and tried to smooth her rumpled clothes as she opened it.

Benny stood with a blanket over his arm and the familiar grin on his face

"Hey. Evie said you weren't feeling good." He stared at the floor. "So c'mon, I'll show you my favourite spot." He turned on his heel and strode down the hall, not waiting or turning to see if she was following.

Andrea grabbed a sweater and strode after him. She turned the corner in the hall just in time to see him squeeze his bulky frame through the window at the end. She hesitated a moment and glanced over her shoulder. There was no sound from Evie's room, no noise from downstairs. She stuck her head out the window. Benny was gone.

She looked down the long fire escape but saw no one below. Then she heard a short whistle and looked up. The bottom of Benny's feet hung over the top rung of the ladder for a moment, then disappeared. Andrea squeezed though the small window and looked up again.

Benny's head appeared. "Not afraid of heights, are ya?"

Andrea answered by taking hold of the ladder and climbing. He reached for her arms as she reached the top, helping her over the lip of the roof. A stiff wind blew her sweater open, making her shiver. Benny led her across a grey pebbled surface and around a small wooden structure that reminded Andrea of the chicken coop at home. They stepped to the other side of it, blocking the wind.

Benny spread the blanket down over the rough surface and dug around in his pockets until a sudden flurry made Andrea jump. Benny laughed.

"My friends," he said, pulling a bag of bread crumbs from his coat pocket. "They aren't very patient."

As he unfolded the bag, four large grey and blue pigeons paced at his feet. Another white one roosted on his shoulder. Benny fed that one first.

"This is Toby—he's a rare one, but he has no manners at all."

Andrea smiled and watched as he fed the others, almost laughing at their competitive cooing and flapping. Benny watched them for a moment, then flapped his arms and shouted, "Shoo birds, shoo."

The pigeons reacted with a flurry of flight. Andrea watched them go, then realized Benny was watching her.

He grinned and reached for the edge of the blanket, giving it a tug to straighten it. He stepped aside and bowed low, offering her a seat. She lowered herself onto it and shook her head when he offered her some of the broken bits of bread.

"Sorry," he said, looking ashamed. "Benny didn't bring a plate."

"It's okay. I'm not hungry."

"Not at all?"

"No."

He pursed his lips, then laughed. "So you're a rare bird, too."

She smiled. "Not where I come from."

Benny's eyebrows shot up. "Where is the princess from? Does she live in a castle?"

Andrea laughed. "No. I'm no princess, Benny. I'm just an ordinary girl."

He shrugged. "Benny is… incurably curious." He smiled. "My mom always said that." He looked away suddenly, his face so sad that Andrea wanted to put her arms around him.

"Where are you from, Benny? Around here?"

He snorted. "No. No." His eyes narrowed slightly. "But it's nice here. Evie's a nice lady." He stared at the blanket. "Kinda like you."

Andrea looked away, but she was aware that he had slid down the wall of the small coop to sit on the opposite corner of the blanket. She heard him rattle the bag as he ate some of the bread.

His voice was soft when he spoke again. "I like it up here," he said.

Andrea peered around them. It was grey and dismal. "Why? Because of the pigeons?"

Benny put the bag down, scrambled to his feet, and waved his hand, beckoning her up. They stepped out from behind the shed and the wind made Andrea grab the front of her sweater. He led her toward the edge.

"Benny likes the view," he said.

The city spread out around them, tall buildings gleaming in the sun as it began its slow slide to the horizon, the short ones looking like stumps in a forest. Lines of traffic flowed like columns of ants in organized formation. Here and there, people moved in clumps from corner to corner as traffic lights flashed green, yellow, and red. Andrea found herself mesmerized until Benny spoke.

"There's something fascinating about it." He turned to her. "Benny likes that word." He grinned and looked down at the view again. "Fascinating. Fascinating. Fascinating." He swayed from side to side.

Andrea looked down at the city. "It's like watching one of those ant colonies in a terrarium. We had a big one in the school I went to when I was a kid. I would've spent hours watching that thing if they'd let me. I liked that there was pattern and order to it, you know? It looked like chaos, but it wasn't—each ant had a purpose and each one did what it was supposed to do."

Benny clapped his hands. "If an ant gets separated from its colony, it can't join another one." He nodded his head for emphasis.

Andrea shook her head. "I didn't know that."

"It has something to do with scent. Each colony has a smell and if a strange ant tries to join, they know instantly and they won't let it get close."

"Kind of like people, sometimes," Andrea mumbled.

Benny didn't respond, but she knew he was watching her.

"Where do you learn all these things, Benny?"

"Books," he said. "And TV programs about animals and things." He frowned and looked down at the streaming traffic. "I remember a lot, but some things I just don't get right. I don't know why."

Andrea smiled. "But you know a lot, Benny. I'm impressed."

"Impressed. Impressed. That's a good word." Benny nodded and swayed.

Andrea turned away and strode back toward the shed.

He followed and crouched down to retrieve the bag of bread. He stuffed the rest of the crumbs into his mouth, then looked up at her.

She pulled her sweater tight. "I'm chilly, Benny."

He jumped up. "Princess shouldn't get cold. Cold could hurt the baby."

Andrea froze. Benny was nodding, staring up at the sky.

"What do you mean? What baby?"

Benny started to hum to himself but said nothing.

"Benny, how did you know about the baby?"

He shook his head hard. "Benny knows about babies. Babies are good."

"Benny, this is important. I don't want you to tell anyone, okay? Not even Evie. It's a secret. A very important secret."

Benny clapped his hands again. "Secrets. Everybody has secrets."

Andrea watched him for a moment. "Promise me you won't tell, Benny. Promise."

"Benny can promise. Benny knows about secrets."

Andrea tossed out a short prayer that he wouldn't tell, then realized even if there was a God who cared, it wasn't likely he'd grant any of her requests.

* * *

Back in her room, Andrea opened Edna's slim black book and found the place where she had left off.

Sometimes I feel Earl watching me, when I'm caring for baby Andrea. I'm not sure if he's disapproving or not. I'm afraid to look at him. Afraid of what I might see in his eyes. He hasn't held her yet, hasn't helped care for her at all. But he watches us.

I walked out to the slough the other day. I'm almost afraid to do that, too, afraid someone will see me. But there's no one to see, no one for miles around, and even if there was, who would care about a woman walking? They couldn't know what we're hiding.

Sometimes I wonder what Roy would have done, had he known about the baby. Would he have insisted I leave with him? Would he have cared?

Earl's plan was best. Best to just put it away where no one would ever know. But I know. I know because of the emptiness I feel, the coldness. And the dull look in Earl's eyes. He can't forget either. I killed something in him that will never come back. It's all my fault. All my fault. And God will never forgive me.

Andrea closed the book and stared at the cover.

CHAPTER

IX

Kenni glanced at Alex out the corner of her eye. It was past closing time and even the lawyers were gone, but as usual she had stayed to work for a couple more hours. Kenni had thrown herself into volunteer work at the small law office her dad had recommended. Alex had encouraged her, at first, and gotten involved at a youth centre nearby. For a while, it had been enough, for both of them, but then Alex had gotten moody, restless, and defensive.

He'd been sitting beside her desk for over an hour, not moving, just staring into space. She closed the file she'd been working on and stood up. He didn't seem to notice.

"Alex?" She frowned when he didn't respond, then moved toward him and repeated his name.

He glanced up, but his eyes didn't seem to focus on her. She sighed, pulled a chair up beside him, and touched his arm. "Alex, you have to snap out of it."

He stared at her for a moment. "Snap out of what?"

Kenni cocked her head. Alex dropped his.

"Okay, so I've been a bit distracted lately," he said.

"Lately? Alex, you haven't really been here for weeks."

Alex turned his head away. When he finally spoke, his voice was low. "I miss the Yukon. And I just feel kind of lost, Kenni. Like I don't belong anywhere, like nothing I do has any point."

"But you know we're doing important work here, work that matters. I'm helping people who can't afford lawyers. You're helping kids at the centre. I thought that's what you wanted."

Alex nodded. "I did." He stood up suddenly. "I do. I know it's important and I know you love what you're doing. And I… I do like the work at the youth centre, but it's… it's just not me." He sighed, picked his baseball hat off the desk, and pulled it down over his eyes. "I'm going to go see Sorensen."

Kenni shook her head. "He'll only tell you the same thing. There's nothing new and he'll call you when he finds something."

"But it's been three weeks. He should have found some trace by now."

"It takes time, you know…"

"I can't stand doing nothing," he blurted.

Kenni stood up and moved toward him. "But you've done all you can." She watched his shoulders tighten.

"It's not enough. I need to find her. I need to find her soon."

Kenni touched his arm. "You're going to drive yourself crazy, Alex." She grinned a little. "Not to mention driving your wife to distraction."

Alex pulled the cap off his head and ran his hand through his thick black hair. She'd seen him do that so many times she knew the signal. She prayed for the right words to give him peace.

"Let's pray about it," she said.

Alex whirled away from her. "I have prayed! I haven't stopped praying!"

Kenni didn't move until she saw his shoulders slump. She moved into his arms.

"I'm sorry," he said as his arms tightened around her.

"I know it's hard." She squeezed tighter. "But I really think you need to try and distract yourself with something else."

"Like what?"

"How about making a plan about what to do with the rest of that money your mother left you?"

Alex shook his head. "I can't think about that right now. All I can think about is finding Andrea. Any plan should include her."

Kenni sighed. "Okay. Let's go see Sorensen."

"He'll yell a lot."

"I know," she said with a grin. "But with me there, maybe he'll keep the expletives to a minimum."

* * *

Sorensen opened the door before Alex rang the bell. "Come in," he said, and disappeared around the corner.

Alex glanced at Kenni, then moved aside for her to enter first.

Stan stood over his small desk, an envelope in hand. Alex and Kenni waited for a moment, then Alex stepped forward.

"You have something? Something about Andrea?"

"No, not yet, but I do have this."

The envelope Stan handed him wasn't very big. As Alex opened it and started to scan the report, Stan told him what it was.

"They were killed in a fluke accident. Your dad owned a small construction company and they were both on the site of an apartment building that was about half done. A crane collapsed into a wall. They and one other man were crushed when the wall caved in. It was the noon hour, so your mother may have been there to meet your dad for lunch."

Alex frowned. "I always thought they'd been in a car accident of some kind. That's what I was told."

"That information wasn't correct." Stan was quiet for a moment. "Your mother was a nurse, worked at a small walk-in clinic near the site. From everything I could see, they were good people, Alex. Your dad's business was doing well. There was an investigation and they ruled that no one was at fault. It was just an accident."

Alex nodded and looked up. "Anything else?"

Stan shook his head. "No. I wasn't able to get any medical information. But with their ID cards, you can request their medical records yourself. The easiest way to do that is to go to a doctor and ask him to do it through the medical channels. Otherwise it could take a while. The privacy act has made things complicated, as you know."

"Thanks, Stan. I appreciate your help."

Stan grinned. "No problem." He slid another envelope across the table. "Here's the bill."

Alex grinned back and stuck out his hand. "Thanks," he said again.

* * *

Alex had read Stan's report six times and kept coming back to what Stan had said about the medical records.

"I guess I should do that," he mumbled.

Kennie turned from the kitchen stove. "What's that?"

"Get my parents' medical records. I should do that soon."

"Yes," Kenni agreed. "Especially…"

Alex looked up when she didn't finish her sentence. "What?"

She took a few steps toward him, waving a spatula. "Medical information could be important when, if…"

Alex frowned. "If what?"

Kenni sat down beside him on the sofa. "If we decide we want to have kids someday."

Alex stared at the paper in his hands. "Right. Yeah, I guess it could be important."

When he remained quiet, Kenni went back to the kitchen.

* * *

"This is Evie's secret," Benny said, grinning as he pushed the door open.

Andrea stared down into the dark cellar. Benny giggled and started down. Andrea hesitated only a moment, then followed.

The wooden stairs creaked under their feet. She kept her head down, watching each smooth, rounded step give a little as she put her weight on it. She imagined how they would sag under Evie's feet.

Benny reached the bottom and stopped. When Andrea's eyes adjusted to the dimness, she saw a line of light under a door to the right. Before she could stop him, Benny charged toward it and flung it open. Andrea arrived in time to see that Evie was surprised but not upset. She waved them in with a warm smile.

"I didn't mean to barge in, Evie." Andrea's eyes darted to Benny, who was grinning again. "Benny said this was your secret."

Evie laughed and winked at Benny. "Not really, hon. This is just the place where I like to escape now and then." She waved her hand toward a long bench. "This is my hobby."

Andrea stepped closer. Two large gooseneck lamps shone down onto a bench littered with stones of every description, some round and smooth, others rough and angular. There were pails filled with dusty stones, jars filled with colourful chips of stones. Evie stood in front of two machines that looked like grinders. A third machine that looked like a small drum sat at the far end and the wall behind the bench held an array of chains, lengths of different kinds of twine, and coils of silver and gold wire.

"I'm a closet lapidary fanatic… quite obsessed, I'm afraid."

Andrea looked from the bench to Evie's face.

The woman beamed. "I love stones."

"Evie makes pretty stones," Benny said from over her shoulder.

Evie smiled at him. "And sometimes Benny helps." She turned back to Andrea. "I use some local rock and it's amazing what I've found in this area. I don't get out to find them as much as I used to, but I've probably got enough right here to last years."

She picked up a fist-sized rock from the bench and turned it over, revealing a flat surface that had been cut and polished. It looked almost like the rings of a tree but was a deep purple. Evie handed it to her.

"And I get some from suppliers that get them from other countries. Like amethyst," Evie said, nodding at the geode. "It comes from Brazil."

"It's beautiful." Andrea slid her thumb over the smooth surface, put the rock down, and picked up another that was a rich red colour. "What do you do with them?"

"Some I just like to have around. You might have noticed that." She grinned. "But some I cut and polish and make into jewellery."

Andrea's eyebrows shot up. "The jewellery in the case. You made all that?"

Evie nodded, pushed a large wooden case toward her, and opened the lid. Andrea sucked in her breath. It was full of stone pendants, polished and shining, some flat and set into gold or silver, others round with clasps attached or swirls of silver wrapped around them, ready for a chain or loop of twine. She reached in and picked up a large stone encased in silver. It was a deep green, shot with lines of white. She traced the silver edge.

"This is what I do on Saturdays, in the summertime," Evie explained. "I go to the farmers' market over on Centre Street—it'll be opening soon—and there are a couple of shops downtown that sell for me, so it adds up to a little extra income."

"Could you teach me?" Andrea watched the expression on Evie's face, gauging her reaction. She smiled when Evie nodded with enthusiasm.

"Of course. Benny and I would love that, wouldn't we, Benny?"

Benny clapped his hands. Evie reached up to a shelf to the side of the bench and handed Andrea a book. "You can start with this. It tells you everything you'll need to know."

Andrea took the book, sat on a stool at the end of the counter, and flipped through the pages.

"Looks like there's more to this than meets the eye."

Evie nodded with a grin. "But it's worth the effort."

* * *

Edna went through the motions of making dinner. Meat and potatoes, as usual. The roast was in the oven, though she didn't remember putting it there. The carrots were peeled and sliced, though it seemed someone else must have done it. The potatoes lay in a heap in the sink. She stared at them, at the large oval one on top, and suddenly the kitchen faded away.

She heard a rushing sound in her ears, like fast flowing water. She gripped the edge of the counter to keep from sinking to the floor, then staggered back and sank into a chair. The sobs made her whole body shake. She couldn't stop, couldn't even think. Only one word surfaced.

Andrea. Andrea. Andrea.

She didn't realize she was screaming it until she felt Earl's hands on her arms, shaking her. She looked into his face and stopped breathing.

"What have I done?" she whispered.

Earl raised her from the chair and held her. "Nothing," he said. "Nothing we can change. Let it go."

Edna pulled away from him, shaking her head. "I can't." She gripped the edge of the sink. "I won't, Earl. Not this time." She turned to face him. "I'm going to find her."

Earl's shoulders sagged. "And then what?"

"Bring her home."

Edna knew the unspoken thoughts in his mind. If Andrea came home, everyone would know. Was that what he was worried about? Or was he worried she'd resist?

"Yes. I'm going to bring her home." The resolve in her own voice gave her courage. She turned and ran up the stairs, pulling clothes from her dresser and tossing them on the bed.

She felt Earl standing in the doorway watching her for a while, then he left and returned a few minutes later with a suitcase in his hand.

"Where will you look?" he asked. "You don't even know which direction she went."

Edna sank onto the bed and buried her face in her hands.

God, she prayed. *Please. Please.*

Earl sighed. "I'll call the bus depot. Maybe they'll remember seeing her and know where she went."

She heard the suitcase hit the floor with a thud, and his footsteps descending the stairs. She took a deep breath, pushed herself to her feet, and followed him.

CHAPTER SEVEN

ANDREA BLINKED AT THE SOFT TAPPING ON HER BEDROOM DOOR. SHE PUSHED the covers away, pulled on her robe, and opened it a crack. Evie's smiling face looked like it was glowing.

"Benny and I are getting ready to go to church, Andrea, and I wondered if you'd like to come with us."

Andrea frowned. "Well, I… I'm not even dressed."

"Oh, there's lots of time. I was just going to make us some breakfast downstairs, then we'll go. It's a short walk from here."

Andrea hesitated. Would Evie fire her if she said no? She had to keep this job, at least for a while. She nodded.

"Okay. I'll be down in a minute."

Evie beamed. "Wonderful."

As she dressed, Andrea groaned to herself. *Church. Why did I have to pick a place where the owner went to church?*

She was pulling her jeans on when she realized she should wear a dress. Maybe that would be enough of an excuse. Maybe Evie wouldn't want her to come in jeans. She hoped so, but Evie just waved her hand when Andrea explained she didn't have a dress to wear.

"No worries, hon. Lots of people come as they are." She plopped a plate of eggs and bacon in front of her.

Benny clapped his hands. "Andrea will like church," he said.

I doubt it, she thought.

* * *

The church didn't look like one. It was in a large community centre. The service was held in the gym, everyone sitting on small uncomfortable plastic chairs. That wasn't the only reason Andrea felt uncomfortable. Some of the music was familiar, some of it new and a lot more upbeat than what would have been allowed in her church at home, but the words were what got to her. These were songs about loving God, about him loving them.

Right, she thought. *In your dreams, Andrea.*

The pastor was young, his brown hair was spiked, and he was wearing jeans. Andrea didn't realize he was the pastor until he started to preach, or rather, talk. It wasn't like any sermon Andrea had ever heard, though he did begin with the Bible, telling everyone to turn to the book of Matthew, chapter nine. Evie leaned toward her a bit and pointed to verse fourteen. The pastor started talking about new wine and old wineskins. Andrea didn't quite understand what he was trying to say, until he moved on.

"Now look at verses twenty to twenty-three," he said, scanning the congregation. "Here was a woman with a problem." His eyes were suddenly focused on Andrea. She looked away.

"This is such a brief encounter with Jesus," he continued, "yet one of the most powerful in terms of faith and in terms of healing. The woman had been bleeding for twelve years. Twelve long years. In that culture, that meant she would have been ostracized for all that time, unclean, not allowed to go to the temple, not allowed to associate with others. But she sought out the healer, this Jesus, believing that just touching his clothing could change her life. What faith! What audacity! In that culture, Jesus would have had every right to spurn her, to send her away, even to punish her. But look what he says. 'Take heart, daughter.

Take heart—be encouraged, have hope.' Daughter. An endearment. 'Daughter, your faith has healed you.'"

The man paused. Andrea suddenly became aware that tears were slipping down her face. She ducked her head and swiped at them, glancing sideways to see if Evie had noticed. The big woman's eyes were closed. She was smiling and swaying slightly, her head nodding.

"And another life was changed," the pastor continued. "Another life healed. What healing do you need here today?" He smiled as his eyes roamed, then seemed to settle again on Andrea.

She stood up abruptly. She had to get out of there. Now.

Pushing past Evie and Benny, she whispered, "Excuse me."

Evie caught her arm and whispered, "Are you okay?"

She nodded and pulled away. "I just need to find the washroom."

The cold water felt good on her face, but her heart wouldn't stop pounding.

* * *

Alex stopped breathing when he saw the name on his cell phone. Sorensen. His hand shook a bit as he pressed the call button and said hello.

"We may have something," Sorensen said. "Can you come over?"

Alex broke the speed limit getting there and didn't bother to knock on the door. Kennie followed him in and saw Stan staring at a small piece of paper as Alex charged into the room.

"You have a lead?" Alex leaned toward him.

Sorensen hesitated. "Maybe."

"Well?"

"I have this friend." He glanced at Kenni, then back to Alex. "I emailed a packet out to a bunch of guys, you know? Guys I thought might be able to help with a lead, any lead. I sent your photo, too." He scratched a spot behind his ear where his thinning blond hair was turning white. "Don't know why I did that, now that I think of it." He stared at the sheet for a moment, then continued. "But maybe it was providential. This friend—he used to be a good PI, worked some big cases. Then he had some kinda breakdown and wandered off to a small town out on the prairies to lick his wounds."

He held out the sheet of paper to Alex.

Alex read it and frowned. "What's this mean?"

Sorensen shrugged. "Don't know. But my gut tells me it means something."

Kenni cleared her throat. "Um, sharing is good, gentlemen."

48

Alex turned to her and read. "It says, 'If you believe in God, or even fate, get on a plane. Call the number when you land.'" He looked at Sorensen. "This could be about anything. It could be a waste of time."

Sorensen nodded. "But he wouldn't have contacted me unless he'd received the packet and, like I said, my gut says go."

"Why not call him first?" Kenni asked.

"Tried. That number connects to a guy who says my friend can't be reached. He's out in the boonies. Cut himself off from everything. I'm surprised the email got to him."

Alex handed the note back to him. "So you're going."

Sorensen nodded. "Was just about to book the flight."

"Then I'm going with you."

"That wasn't the deal. I work alone."

"I can't sit back and do nothing. We have to find her. And find her fast."

Stan frowned. "Why the urgency?"

Alex pushed a hand through his thick hair. "I don't know. I just know it's important we find her as soon as possible."

Sorensen stared at him for a moment, then gave a quick nod. "Make the flight arrangements. It's all on your dime anyway."

* * *

Andrea woke to a soft tapping on her door. She opened her eyes and squinted at the flood of light as the door squeaked open.

"How are you this morning, hon?" Evie's tousled head popped into the room.

Andrea pushed herself up on one elbow and nodded. "Okay. I think."

Evie moved into the room, switched on the small bedside lamp, and set a steaming cup and saucer beside it. "Brought you a cup of tea. It always helps me when my tummy's upset."

Andrea smiled her thanks.

Evie seemed about to leave, then stepped back into the room. She brought the small chair close to the bed and sat down.

"I think we need to talk," she said.

Andrea took a sip of the tea and waited, holding her breath.

"It's been over three weeks now and you've been sick almost every morning." Evie's eyes didn't waver, but they were warm and caring. "Are you pregnant, honey?"

Tears sprang to Andrea's eyes almost instantly. She turned her face away. Evie's large hand massaged her shoulder.

"You are, aren't you?"

Andrea nodded into the pillow.

"And you're running away? From the father?"

Andrea shook her head. "He doesn't even know. He left before I discovered it."

"What about your family? Do your parents know?"

Andrea shifted and sighed. "My parents are dead. My foster mother—she knows. She was going to send me to a relative who would arrange an adoption… then I was supposed to go back and pretend nothing had ever happened." She sniffed. "So they could keep up appearances for the neighbours and…" She almost sneered. "And for their church."

Evie was quiet for a time. Andrea peeked at her to see her reaction. She was staring at the floor, a deep frown creasing her face.

Finally, Evie looked up. "What are you planning to do, then?"

Andrea sniffed. "I… I don't know, exactly."

Evie sighed. "Well, one thing's for sure, you can't work the morning shift."

Andrea held her breath. If she had to leave, where would she go?

"So we'll switch," Evie said. "You can handle the afternoons, I'll do mornings. Till the morning sickness is gone at least. You'll have to learn the dinner menu and I'll warn you, Allan is harder to please than Joe."

"You're not going to fire me?"

Evie took her hand and patted it. "You're a good little waitress. And Benny likes you. That's a big checkmark in my book." She smiled briefly, then became serious again. "But we're going to have to find you a doctor."

"A doctor?" Andrea pushed herself up and shook her head, but Evie kept talking.

"Yes, a doctor, and I know just the one—"

"But—"

Evie stood up. "No buts. We need to make sure everything's okay, hon, and this doctor—"

"But I can't have this baby!" Andrea's voice was shrill in the quiet room. She sank back onto the pillows. She should have found a clinic weeks ago, like she'd planned.

Evie sat back down. "Talk to me, sweetie."

Andrea gulped for air between sobs. "How can I have a b–baby? I have no money, no place to live." Her fist struck the pillow. "And why should I have it? It'll only hate me."

Evie leaned forward and wrapped her arms around the girl as she sobbed into the blankets. "Oh, honey, why would it hate you?"

"Be… be… ca… cause everyone else does."

"No, no, no," Evie crooned. "Not everyone. Not me, not Benny. And not the good Lord. We all love you, Andrea. Truly."

As Andrea's sobs ebbed, Evie picked up the teacup. "Have a sip," she said.

Andrea sat up and did what she was told. The sweet hot liquid calmed her.

Evie watched her drink, then sighed. "Maybe you don't believe this, sweetie, but I do believe that Jesus brought you here for a reason. He knew you needed us and we needed you."

Andrea frowned. "You needed me?"

"Yes, desperately." Evie smiled. "And not just as a waitress. You've made a world of difference in Benny's life already."

"I have?"

"Most people don't know how to handle him. So they just pretend he isn't there. You didn't do that and it's made a difference."

Andrea sniffed again. "He's a little hard to ignore."

Evie chuckled. "I know. But when he's rebuffed, which most people do, he's like a little turtle that draws in his head and legs and hides from the world. You've given him courage. And that's something, Andrea. Something big." Evie sat up. "So I'll call that doctor in the morning and make you an appointment. Okay?"

Andrea squinted, stared at the cup, then nodded.

Evie patted her arm. "Okay. You rest now." She pushed herself up and left the room.

Andrea thought about what she'd said. Was God directing her life?

She tugged the blankets up to her chin and closed her eyes. She didn't want God directing her life. He'd made a mess of it so far. But he had brought her here, to a place that seemed safe, and she was thankful for that. Maybe she should try praying.

But no prayers would come, only the other words.

Get rid of it. It's not too late. Get rid of it.

CHAPTER EIGHT

Kenni peered out through the round window in the small plane. The land below was a geometric pattern of squares. Most were a tawny colour, some already ploughed into a dark brown. Roads cut through them at evenly spaced intervals. Here and there a cluster of newly sprouting trees surrounded a farmhouse and scattering of barns and sheds. There weren't many. It all looked designed, a giant plan organized for a purpose.

She shifted in her seat as she felt Alex lean toward her. "What's the name of this place, again?"

"Carson's Corner," he answered, then grinned. "I couldn't find it on the map. We'll be landing at a small airstrip nearby."

"I wonder why someone who had a thriving business would run off to such an isolated place."

"I can think of a few reasons."

Kenni gave him a knowing look. "You think he's running from something."

Alex shrugged. "Maybe." He peered passed her to the landscape below. "Or running to something."

The plane banked steeply and Kenni grabbed Alex's arm as the ground seemed to slip a lot closer. Stan leaned toward them from the seat across the aisle. "We'll be putting down in a few minutes," he said.

Kenni tightened her seatbelt as the plane levelled off and began to descend. She always held her breath on landings, especially in small planes like this one, when the whole thing seemed about to shake its bolts loose. She tossed up a quick prayer as the dirt airstrip came into sight. Then there was a bump and the whole plane complained as the wings shook and the engines powered down.

They stepped out onto the flat prairie. A man in his mid-thirties pushed himself away from a pickup truck and walked toward them. Sorensen stepped forward to meet him, turned, and did the introductions. Ted Blacker was a tall man with thinning brown hair that showed a distinct ring when he pulled his baseball cap off as Sorensen introduced Kenni. His hand felt thick and calloused when he put it in hers. He then turned away to help the pilot unload their luggage into the back of his truck. Alex and Stan climbed into the crew cab's back seat. Ted held the passenger door open and took her elbow as she climbed in.

"Beechum said to take you right out to his place," Ted explained. "But maybe you want to go to the hotel first?"

"No," Alex answered quickly from behind Kenni. "Just take us to him."

Ted nodded and put the truck in gear.

Kenni's curiosity got the better of her. "Do you know Mr. Beechum well?"

Ted shook his head and answered without taking his eyes off the road. "Not at all, really. I do errands for him now and again, take groceries out, handle the mail when there is any. He pays good. But he doesn't talk much." He looked at her out the corner of his eye. "Kinda like me."

Men, Kenni thought as she turned to look out the window.

The prairie streamed by in a blur of yellow stubble. Here and there she saw plumes of dust, marking the spots where huge machines worked the land.

She tried again. "How was the harvest last year?"

Ted loosened his grip on the wheel. "Good. It was late, but most got a good crop off. The weather held, thank God. 'Course, the price of a bushel was low. Still is. Canola's paying not bad. Barley's holding on this year."

Kenni could smell the earth as he spoke. "You farm, then?"

"Nope. Gave it up a few years back. Make more fixin' machinery and runnin' errands."

His thumb thumped out an imaginary beat on the wheel. The broad nail was chipped and yellowed, a black line visible under its rim. Now she could smell the oil and grease of a mechanic's shop. She shifted her feet and looked down at a piece of some kind of machinery on the floor.

They drove in silence for about an hour.

Ted suddenly broke it as a long line of poplar trees came into view. He pointed. "That's Beechum's place. I'll drop you. Got a delivery to do, then I'll swing back this way. Be about two hours."

Sorensen leaned forward from the back seat. "That'll work. Do you have a cell in case I need to call you?"

Kenni was surprised when he rhymed off the number.

"Reception's not great out here," he said, giving a snort. "Even though there's nothin' around to block the signal."

The truck bumped down a narrow lane between two rows of old spreading poplar and came to a stop in front of a small frame house with a dormer above the door and a porch along the front. It hadn't been painted in years, but Kenni thought it looked welcoming somehow.

Ted sped away the moment they were out of the truck.

Alex made it to the front door first, and knocked. He rapped harder when there was no answer, then turned the doorknob when that got no response. Kenni and Stan stood behind him as he hollered a hello into the large kitchen. No answer. Alex glanced at Stan, who shrugged his shoulders and stepped around Alex into the room.

The three of them heard the tractor at the same time and hurried back out the door. The large machine came to a halt at the side of the house. A short man in a green flak jacket lowered himself down, pulling a Tilley hat off his head as he strode toward them. Kenni was surprised that he was smiling. The man extended his hand to Stan as though he were a long lost friend.

"Good to see you, Stan, good to see you." His voice rang with welcome as he pumped Stan's hand and invited them into the house, striding to the coffeemaker as he told them to sit at a large wooden table in the middle of the room. "Sorry to be so cryptic with that note, Stan, but I had a teenager breathing down my neck at the library in town. And I figured it might take a little intrigue to get you to fly all the way out here into the boonies."

"Why did you send it, Mr. Beechum? Do you have information about my sister?" Alex leaned forward in his chair.

"Call me Bennett." He hit the start button on the coffeemaker and turned away, striding out of the room without another word.

Alex frowned at Sorensen. Stan extended his hand, palm down, and pushed air as he lowered it. "Slow down, Alex. He'll get to it."

Alex sighed in exasperation. Kenni thought he was going to leap out of his chair when Bennett returned with a large manila envelope.

"I've taken up a new hobby since coming here," Bennett said, laying the envelope on the table in front of Stan. "Old style photography. There are some great faces out here on the prairies." He put his hand inside the envelope and drew out several black and white photos. "The minute I saw that picture you sent me of Alex here, I pawed through everything I'd done in the darkroom for the past year. I have a good memory for faces, you might recall."

Stan nodded but said nothing as Bennett handed the photos to him.

"Took these at a church bazaar about a year ago."

Sorensen slid the photos to the middle of the table so they could all study them. There were a few close-ups of weather-beaten farmers and smiling farmers' wives. The others were shots of the crowd. Alex picked one up.

"It's her," Alex said.

Kenni got up and leaned over his shoulder. The photo was of a line of teenaged boys sitting in front of a table full of pies. The boy at the end was turned away, looking up at a girl standing behind him, her hand resting on his shoulder. Kenni let out a small gasp. The girl looked like Alex's twin.

* * *

Edna gripped the handle of her small purse and stared out the truck's windshield, watching as her husband talked with the attendant at the bus stop ticket counter. Earl had insisted she wait in the truck until he had a chance to find out if anyone knew anything about Andrea. The man at the counter shook his head, then nodded and pulled a dirty baseball cap off his head. Edna sighed and prayed he would have some information about where Andrea had gone. She watched Earl shake hands with the man and walk slowly back to the truck.

He didn't say anything as he fastened his seatbelt.

Edna sighed again. "Well?"

"He said he thinks she bought a ticket heading east. That's all he knows."

Edna put her hand on the door handle but Earl caught her arm. "There's no point heading off in some direction they think she might have gone, Edna. You come back home with me, now."

Edna gripped the handle, then slumped back in the seat and let her purse slip to the floor between her feet. Earl put the truck in gear.

She stared out the passenger window as they drove home. The land looked so barren, as barren as that day they had walked to the edge of the slough with that tiny bundle wrapped in a blanket.

She shivered. *No. Don't think about that day. Focus on Andrea.*

East. There were a lot of places to go when one headed east, but Regina would be the logical place. Edna shivered as a hundred "what ifs" flew through her mind. How could she find Andrea in such a big place? Where would she even begin? She slipped her hand up to wipe the tears away, turning her face further toward the window so Earl wouldn't see.

When she turned back to face the front, she saw Earl's hand drop from the steering wheel. It rested on his thigh for a time, then slowly moved toward her. She felt the rough calluses when he placed it over her hand and squeezed gently. More tears came, but this time she didn't turn away.

"Maybe she'll come back, Edna. She's a good girl." Earl's voice broke. "We have to believe she'll come back to us."

Edna withdrew her hand. "God's punishing us."

His hand returned to the steering wheel and his fingers tightened as she stiffened in the silence.

"I'm not sure I even believe there is a God anymore." Earl's voice was low and gruff. "But if there is one, I can't believe… I don't know. I don't know what he'd do." His jaw clenched. "But why would he—"

"Because of what we did, what I did." Edna buried her face in her hands and sobbed. "I th–thought it was all past. I thought… oh God." Her voice dropped to a whisper and she turned her head away. "Please. Please."

She felt Earl's thick hand clutch her shoulder. Slowly the sobs subsided.

"What can we do?" She turned to Earl, pleading with God in her mind that he would give them some kind of answer, but afraid to hope that he would.

"We wait," Earl said. "And I guess maybe we can pray." He put both hands back on the wheel. "At least, you can," he mumbled.

CHAPTER NINE

The photo trembled in Alex's hand as he looked up at Bennett. "Where was this taken?"

"Carson's Corner. It's about twenty kilometres west of here, a small village—just a gas station, restaurant, hardware store, a church, and a few houses. The churches are usually the centre of all the activity in this area." He nodded at the photo. "This was taken at an event they have every spring."

"Do you have any idea what her name is, how we can find her?"

Bennett shook his head. "No, but she shouldn't be too hard to track down. I was thinking if you all want to stay here tonight we'll go to the service at the church in Carson's tomorrow morning and take the photo with us. I'm sure someone there will know her."

Alex sat back. "We're so close."

Stan nodded. "Tomorrow could be the day."

Kenni reached over and put her hand in her husband's. "Tomorrow," she said.

Bennett poured them all another cup of coffee and started pulling things out of the refrigerator. "Anybody else hungry?"

"I'm starved," Stan admitted.

Kenni stood up. "Can I help?"

Bennett handed her a block of hard white cheese. "I was thinking spaghetti. My grandma's sauce is a winner." He rattled the pots and pans in a large drawer and came up with a slightly rusted grater.

Kenni smiled as he handed it to her. "Spaghetti is one of Alex's favourites."

The corner of his eyes crinkled. "I even have a loaf to make garlic bread. We can all breathe on one another over a game of dominoes later."

Alex stood up suddenly and mumbled something about going for a walk.

Stan watched him leave, then glanced at Kenni. "He's wound tighter than a ten-dollar watch."

Kenni nodded. "He's been like this for months. It's more than just wanting to find his sister," she sighed. "But he's not talking about it."

Stan snorted. "It's a man thing."

"Tell me about it."

Bennett chuckled. "How long have you been married?"

"Just over a year." Kenni rushed her next words. "And it's been great, really great, but sometimes…"

"Uh-huh?" Bennett raised his eyebrows.

Kenni hesitated. "Well, we do have our issues, but everyone does." She stood the grater on a plate and pressed the block of cheese across it.

Bennett plopped a head of lettuce in front of her. "You can shred that when you're done with the cheese."

Kenni noticed his large hands were long-fingered and slender. They didn't look like the hands of someone who had done a lot of farm work.

"How long have you been out here, Bennett?" she asked, relieved to be able to divert the conversation.

Bennett shrugged. "About two and a half years."

"It's been that long?" Stan interjected. "Time flies."

"What brought you here, to the middle of nowhere?" Kenni asked. "I don't imagine there are many PI jobs in this area."

He laughed. "You got that right. Nothin' to investigate but the gophers. I kinda like it that way."

"Oh?" Kenni's eyebrows flickered.

Bennett chuckled again. "Seems you have a bit of a PI bent yourself."

"I do have an insatiable curiosity. Sorry, I don't mean to pry."

"No problem. I don't mind telling the story, but maybe we'll wait till after supper."

They all heard the truck at the same time. The chair scraped the floor as Stan stood up and stretched. "That must be Ted, coming back for us. You two seem to have the domestic chores well in hand. I'll tell him we're staying the night."

They heard the truck roar off in a few minutes and Stan returned, bumping the door open with their luggage.

"Kenni and Alex can have the first room on the right upstairs," Bennett called to him. He turned to her. "Sorry, there's only one washroom, but it's right outside your room." He turned back to Stan. "You get to bunk in the room across from me, Stan."

"That'll work," Stan said, heading for the stairs.

Kenni and Bennett worked in silence for a while, but Kenni didn't find it a strain. In fact, she realized she felt very comfortable with this man, in spite of having known him for such a short time. She stole a look at him out the corner of her eye. His chestnut hair was greying at the temples, but he had aged well. His strong jaw gave him an air of confidence, but there was a gentleness in his eyes that she liked.

She pushed a strand of hair behind her ear, finished grating the lettuce, then found a bowl and chopped up a tomato and some celery.

Bennett finished dicing two cloves of garlic and some onion and dropped them in the large frying pan. He stirred them around for a bit, then added a large package of ground beef. He opened the freezer and took out two jars filled with tomato sauce, zapped them in the microwave for a minute, then dumped them into the pan. The smell filled the room by the time the other two men returned.

"Did I mention I'm starved?" Stan's booming voice told them he approved of the aroma.

Alex stood beside Kenni as she stirred the pasta with a long wooden spoon.

"How about you?" Kenni asked. "Hungry?"

Alex shrugged. "I could eat."

Bennett reached into another cupboard and handed him a pile of plates. "Then make yourself useful." When Alex turned away, Bennett gave Kenni a wink. She returned it with a weak smile.

They ate in relative silence, each one relishing the food.

"Best spaghetti I've ever had, Bennett," Stan declared. "Where'd you learn to cook like this?"

Bennett shrugged. "Taught myself using my grandma's recipe box. Cooking has become another hobby—another dimension to life I've been discovering since coming here." He gave Kenni another smile. "It's nice to have people to cook for, for a change."

"Is Grandma's recipe a secret, or will you share?"

"I'll make you a copy."

Stan stood up and took his plate to the sink. "Okay, Bennett, time to spill your story. What made you head for the hills, or, uh, flat lands I guess I should say? I was more than a little surprised to hear you'd quit. Thought you had a pretty good thing going with your PI business."

Bennett nodded. "Too good. That was the problem. I was gone all the time, never saw my family. I shouldn't have been surprised when they pulled the plug, but I was surprised at what it did to me. I fell apart. I'd probably be on skid row right now if it wasn't for a preacher at a street mission who showed me what life is really all about."

Kenni's head snapped up. "You're a Christian?"

"Yup." Bennett grinned. "Bona fide." He picked up her plate. "Alex and Stan can clean up while I tell the story if you'd like."

Stan stood up. "Right. You two cooked. We'll clean." He grabbed a dish towel from the handle on the stove and tossed it at Alex.

Alex tossed it back. "I'll wash," he said.

Bennett poured himself another coffee and sat down.

"Well, like I said, I had a booming PI business, so I tried to throw myself into my work even more when my wife left. It didn't work. Just made me feel more alone and miserable." He stared at the table for a moment. "I don't know how I could have expected Jinny to keep holding the fort while I went off and did my own thing day after day, month after month." He shook his head. "She tried to warn me. We had some rip roaring battles over it, but somehow I really was shocked when she left. I couldn't believe how much I missed her and the kids— the boys were both teenagers, thirteen and fifteen at the time. It was hardest on them, I think."

He stared into space and was quiet for a while, then began again with a sigh. "The drinking had always been part of my life, but it got more intense after the separation. I was living in my office, passing out each night 'cause it was the only way I could sleep."

Stan turned toward them as he dried the dishes. Alex had his back to them, but Kenni could tell he was listening.

"Then I woke up one morning and realized I'd lost a couple of days. Whole days—gone." He shook his head. "I tried to stop after that, but couldn't. I needed the bottle to get through every day, not just emotionally, but physically. I wasn't eating much and that started to take its toll." He wrapped his hand around his coffee mug. "Then the clients started dropping off. My business tanked pretty quick. Nobody wants to hire a PI who can't keep his notes straight." He snorted. "I kept mixing things up—reported to a guy who wanted me to find his daughter that his wife was indeed having an affair." He grinned. "That didn't go over so well."

Stan chuckled. "Don't imagine it would."

"The day finally came when I got evicted from my office. Came back from doing some surveillance to find the door locked and a notice pinned to it. I stood for a long time staring at that piece of paper, thinking, *This is it. I'm done.* So I walked away, found my favourite bar, and drowned my sorrows. I woke up in the gutter. Literally." He took a long drink of his coffee. "That's when Peter found me, dragged me back to the shelter and started talking."

Bennett smiled. "The man was a talker. Talked me right into rehab. That was a process I don't ever care to revisit, I can tell you. But it worked. I dried out and started working at the mission. Met a lot of amazing people there—people with a patience and compassion that I knew could only come from something deep inside. I started listening to Pete's preaching. I had a lot of questions and he was always willing to try and answer them." He looked at Alex's back. "It took me a while, but I finally realized what all those people had inside—it was the spirit of God.

"It's been almost three years now since I let the words affect my heart and gave my life to Jesus." He grinned at Stan. "Bet you never thought you'd hear those words come out of my mouth."

Stan grunted. "You got that right."

Bennett shook his head. "I looked like I was as far away from God as you could get at that time in my life, so I guess it just proves that the people who are furthest away are sometimes right on the edge of being the closest."

Kenni leaned forward. "But why come way out here?"

"My dad left me this place several years ago," he explained. "My grandparents had been gone for a decade and Dad never wanted to come back here to live, so he sold off most of the land but held onto the house and a few acres. It was passed on to me when he died. I was sitting in a park in the middle of the city one day, enjoying the feeling of being in the country, when it suddenly occurred to me that I could be in the country all the time if I wanted to." He grinned. "Minus the trees. It seemed like a good idea at the time, and I'm not sorry I did it. The time alone has been good."

"Do I hear a 'but' coming?" Stan asked.

Bennett nodded. "Yeah, I think my time here is coming to an end soon, but I'm not sure what will be next. God hasn't told me yet."

Stan frowned. "So, you're going to just stay out here in the boonies until God tells you what to do?"

Bennett chuckled. "Yeah, that's pretty much it."

Stan shook his head and opened the cupboard to stack the clean dishes on the shelf.

"Have you been in touch with your family?" Kenni asked, then blushed and stammered. "Uh... I... I don't mean to pry, I just..."

"It's okay." Bennett smiled. "As a matter of fact, I have—both the boys have been here to visit and Jinny and I have emailed a lot." He stood and placed his coffee mug on the counter. "I'm trying not to get my hopes up, but I'm praying that we can reconcile and be a family again. If I can stay sober, we might have a chance."

Alex swished the cup in the water, placed it in the drain, and pulled the plug. Bennett opened the door on a tall cabinet near the door and took out a tin box. He gave the table a swipe with his hand, then dumped the contents out.

"Okay, time for some serious dominoes."

CHAPTER TEN

EDNA WOKE AS A PALE LIGHT BEGAN TO FILTER THROUGH THE CURTAINS OF the bedroom window. She lay on her side and watched the intensity of the light increase, but couldn't bring herself to get out of bed. She heard Earl come in and rattle around in the kitchen. Probably making himself coffee, she thought. She should get up and make him some breakfast like she'd done every morning for so long.

She pushed the covers off her shoulder and shifted her hips. Her eyes fell on the small black suitcase she had packed yesterday. She closed her eyes and pulled the blanket up again. No. She would not serve Earl. Not today.

It was almost noon before she got up, dressed, and went downstairs. The house was so quiet. The quiet of emptiness. The quiet of despair. She pushed the back door open and stepped onto the porch. Peso and the other horses were grazing in the pasture beside the barn.

She took a deep breath. The earth had wakened, releasing its aromas as it burst into life. For a moment her spirits rose as she drew the rich smell into her. Spring always brought a little hope, but hope for what? For something... something more. She sighed. It was a curse. She always longed for something more.

But she did love this place. A flutter of birds suddenly erupted from a tree beside the house. Watching them whirl up into the sky made her ache for something but she didn't know exactly what. Some kind of freedom? She could hear their chickens cackling and a gate creaking somewhere. It was past time she collected the eggs. She went back into the kitchen, grabbed the old egg basket she always used, and headed for the coop.

When she was just a little girl, Edna's mother had taught her to collect the eggs, and she had always loved doing it. She loved clucking to the hens under her breath, moving slowly as she slipped her hand beneath them. The feel of the smooth warm roundness of the eggs made her smile. She stood staring at a large brown egg for a long time, thinking about the tiny life that could grow inside it.

She was halfway to the slough before she realized what she was doing. The wind had come up and the chill seeped into her, still cutting with a lingering memory of winter. She could see the trees, three old gnarled poplars at the crest of the small knoll, barren but beginning to show signs of the greening that would come soon.

As she got closer, she noticed a broken branch hanging down the trunk of one of them, leaving a fresh scar. Yellowed grasses grew tall at their base and a single stone, barely visible, heaved itself up from the earth, marking the place. She moved toward it, thinking of the day that had come and gone so long ago yet still seemed like yesterday.

The stone was cold when she knelt and touched it. Cold and lifeless. She remembered the stiffness of the small body, the cold that went so deep into her that she knew she could never dig it out. She sank onto the ground and let the words flow out again. The same words that seemed always in her mind, words always needing to be spoken.

"Please," she whispered, "please forgive me. Forgive us. Please. Please."

But there was never an answer. A dead baby could not forgive.

* * *

The doctor's office was in an old stone building that had been refurbished. The gold lettering on the glass door listed the names of three doctors and ended with the words, "To Your Good Health."

Evie reached around Andrea and pushed the door open. The receptionist smiled and handed Andrea a clipboard with a long list of questions. She had just stood up to give it back when another woman dressed in bright scrubs called her name and led her down a narrow hall into a small examining room.

She took the clipboard, placed the sheet next to a computer, and smiled. "Dr. Hardisty will be right with you."

Andrea sat in the chair and studied the diagrams on the wall. One, with six photos of the development of a foetus, held her attention. She was still studying it when the doctor knocked and entered the small room. She was what her mother would have called a "big-boned" woman who seemed to fill the space when she closed the door behind her. Her light brown hair was pulled into a knot at the back of her head and everything about her seemed crisp and clean. Andrea pressed her back into the chair.

Dr. Hardisty scanned the sheet. She looked up with a frown. "You've left a lot of your family's medical history blank."

"My parents are dead. I don't know any history, medical or otherwise."

"I see." She turned back to the computer and opened a file, then without looking at Andrea, asked what she could do for her today.

"I'm pregnant," she blurted.

The doctor swivelled in the chair and faced her. "I see," she said again. "Is this your first pregnancy?"

"Yes." Andrea tried not to let the tears start, but they seeped out the corners of her eyes.

The doctor scooted forward and put a hand on her knee. "An unplanned pregnancy?"

Andrea nodded.

The doctor squeezed her knee. "It's going to be okay."

"But I'm not married. I don't even have a boyfriend anymore." Andrea gripped the arms of the chair. "I don't know what I'm going to do."

"Well," the doctor sighed, "there are options."

Andrea waited, but the doctor didn't continue. "I just don't know. I was wondering about... about..."

"Terminating the pregnancy?"

Andrea shivered but nodded again.

"I can't make any decisions for you," the doctor's voice was cool. "But I can help you take one thing at a time. Right now, we need to determine how far along you are. So I will need to examine you, okay?"

Andrea sniffed. "Okay."

The doctor gave her a gown and told her she'd be back in a moment.

The examination didn't take long and when it was over the doctor was smiling. "Everything seems fine. I think you're about four months along, does that seem right?'

Andrea shrugged. "I guess." She looked up at the doctor. "Is that too far to, you know..."

"To terminate?"

Andrea nodded but said nothing.

The doctor's voice dropped a notch. "No, in this country it's not. But I would advise against it. Abortion does have risks, especially after the first trimester."

She turned back to the computer and rapidly typed something. "I'd like you to have an ultrasound, then come back to see me in two weeks. That is," she glanced at Andrea. "if you decide to continue with the pregnancy." She finished typing. "The receptionist will book the appointments for you."

Andrea nodded again. "Okay." Her voice had trailed off.

She felt the doctor's eyes on her back as she left the room.

Evie stood up when she came back into the reception area, carrying a brochure and two slips of paper with appointment dates on them. Andrea let the woman slip her arm across her shoulders.

"How was it?" Evie asked.

"Fine," Andrea answered, stepping ahead of her out the door.

As they rode back to the diner on the bus, Andrea flipped through the brochure. It was a duplicate of the diagrams on the wall of the doctor's office, with explanations under each one. Termination was an ugly word. But she couldn't have this baby, she just couldn't. How would she support herself and raise a child? Others had done it, she knew, but it meant living in poverty for the rest of her life. She'd never get to go to college, never travel, never have all the things she'd dreamed about. No. She couldn't have this baby.

Evie was silent until they got home.

"I'll make us a cup of tea, sweetie. Why don't you go on into the staff room?"

Andrea slumped into the chair and opened the brochure again. She had to admit it was fascinating. The idea that a child was growing inside her had amazed her from the beginning, but the details of its development made her jaw hang open. At four months, it was already over six inches long and could get the hiccups. If something bitter were put into the amniotic fluid, it would stop swallowing. But if something sweet was introduced, it would swallow faster. It would also cover its eyes if a sudden bright light was focused on the womb.

She closed the brochure as Evie put a mug and teapot in front of her and glanced over her shoulder.

"Amazing, isn't it? A miracle for sure."

Andrea pushed the brochure away. "I guess." She peeked at Evie out the corner of her eye as the big woman sat down.

"Every one of mine was a miracle, that's for sure."

"You have kids?" Andrea tried to keep her voice flat.

The woman's face beamed. "Oh yes. I have six."

Andrea's eyes widened. "Six?"

Evie chuckled. "Yup. Four boys and two girls, and most of them doing great. One of my girls just gave me my fourth grandchild."

Andrea stared at the brochure again. "It's weird, isn't it, that it's something so common—millions of women do it every day, but it's amazing, too."

Evie nodded. "The most common miracle on earth."

Andrea sighed as Evie poured the tea.

Evie took a drink, then put her mug down and leaned forward. When she spoke, her voice was gentle. "Andrea, are you still thinking of having an abortion?"

Andrea's head jerked up. "Well, I…" She dropped her eyes, then raised them again in defiance. "What if I am?"

"I'm not judging you, honey."

"That'd be a first. Everyone else does."

Evie put her mug down and leaned back. "You aren't alone, you know. I'm here to help, as much as you need me."

"Even if I decide to abort it?"

"Especially then."

Andrea's took a deep breath. "I thought maybe you'd fire me."

Evie shook her head hard. "No. I wouldn't do that." She put a hand on Andrea's arm. "But I don't think abortion is a good solution."

Andrea's voice had lost its edge. "But being a single mother…" She stared off into the distance. "I just don't think I can do that."

"But there are groups that can help, too. Pregnancy care centres, for instance. There's one not far from here."

Andrea didn't respond. Evie took another sip of her tea. She picked up the brochure with the photos of the foetal development.

"I remember when I had my first baby. I was pretty scared, too."

"You were?"

Evie nodded. "Scared but incredibly happy. I'd been married for six years when I discovered I was going to have a child. I'd thought it would never happen. And oh my, I wanted a baby. All my friends had children and it was like a knife inside me when I looked at them. It was the one thing I wanted above everything else at that time in my life, but I was pretty sure I'd never have it."

"Why?"

Evie sighed and looked away. "I thought God was punishing me because of all the things I'd done in my life that I knew were against God's laws, and because of something that happened when I was about fourteen years old." She paused. "I was hanging around with a wild bunch then. We'd figured out how to use makeup to make ourselves look older than we were so we could sneak into the bars. It was fun for a while, until one night I somehow got separated from my friends. I had no way home, so I started walking. A man came along and offered me a ride." Evie shook her head. "But he didn't take me home. He raped me and dumped me on the side of the road like a bag of garbage."

Andrea said nothing for a moment, but when Evie didn't continue, she asked, "But why would you think God would punish you for something like that? It wasn't your fault."

Evie nodded. "I know that now, but back then, I was really still a child and I thought it was all my fault. I thought God was punishing me for the way I'd been acting. I thought the rape had made me unacceptable, unlovable, especially to God." She looked up. "So I convinced myself God didn't exist. That was better than believing he had rejected me. By the time I left high school, I decided to just live my life the way I wanted to and I ended up living a lifestyle that was, well, you've heard about the sixties, haven't you?"

Andrea nodded.

"Then you get the picture," Evie said. "Like so many other young women, I was looking for love and acceptance in all the wrong places and it gave me nothing but emptiness and misery." She smiled ruefully. "Free love wasn't all it was cracked up to be." She stared at her mug for a moment. "Then one day I discovered I was pregnant. I was about your age and I was terrified. I didn't really have a relationship with the father—it had been one of many times I just wanted someone to be with. I knew my family would disown me if they found out and I was terrified of what my father might do, so I did what all my friends told me was best. I had an abortion."

Evie looked away. "I finally found a man who loved me, but we couldn't have a baby." Her eyes shifted again. "The doctors said there was too much scar tissue. They said it would never happen." Her eyes riveted on Andrea. "I thought God was punishing me. And I thought I deserved it. Why should I have a baby now, when I wanted one, when I had murdered one just because it wasn't convenient at the time?"

Andrea swallowed and stared at her hands.

"Then my husband went on a long haul—he was a freelance truck driver—and he was involved in a really bad accident. Four people died. He wasn't at fault at all, but it really shook him up. He went into a severe depression, could barely get out of bed some days. He lost his job, and then he started to drink. Things got pretty bad.

"We had a neighbour—an elderly lady named Grace. We helped her out sometimes, took her grocery shopping, mowed her lawn, that kind of thing. She would bring us baking and come over to visit now and then, and about that time she started to visit a lot. Well, she started talking about God. I'm not sure how she got me to go to church with her, but one day there I was, sitting in a pew beside her."

"Did you like it?" Andrea asked. "Going to church, I mean?"

"Not at all." Evie laughed and Andrea couldn't help but grin. "I felt terribly uncomfortable. The people were much too nice to me."

Andrea chuckled. "I know what you mean."

"But for some reason I kept going, and things started to make sense. I was pretty scared about what was happening to Jake, and when the people at the church prayed for us, well, that was a real comfort, even though I wasn't really sure who or what they were praying to, at first. They didn't seem to mind that. And they didn't seem to mind trying to answer all my questions."

Andrea cocked her head a bit. "Like what?"

"Things like what God was really like—was he just some kind of cosmic force out there?" She waved her hand in the air. "Or was he a real person you could have a relationship with?" Evie shook her head. "Most of what I believed was pretty messed up. When I pictured God, he was some kind of old man sitting on a big throne, just waiting for me to make a mistake so he could smack me."

Exactly, Andrea thought.

"I remember the pastor telling me to picture the best kind of father I could imagine, and then imagine someone one hundred times better and it still wouldn't be close to who God is. I thought about that a lot and then one day, well, I just sort of gave up, or gave in, or, well, I just asked him to show me who he was, and he did."

Andrea cocked her head. "How?"

"It's really hard to explain." Evie was quiet for a moment. "But it was like I'd been living in a negative for a long time."

"A negative?"

Evie chuckled. "Sorry, I'm dating myself. Have you ever seen those old strips that used to come out of a thirty-five millimetre camera?"

Andrea nodded. "We played around with them in a darkroom in high school."

"Then you know what it looks like—a picture that's black and white and somehow seems all inside-out. It was like I'd been living in that kind of one-dimensional world and then suddenly everything came to life—everything was fuller, richer, and bursting with colour." Evie smiled. "And then I knew I was forgiven—totally, completely, absolutely forgiven. And it was the most wonderful feeling in the world. I couldn't stop smiling and singing, and humming when I wasn't singing." She laughed. "Just about drove Jake crazy."

Andrea leaned forward. "What happened then?"

"About two weeks later, I got up in the morning and I was really sick, but it was weird because after I'd vomited I wanted to eat a big breakfast."

Andrea grinned. "Morning sickness."

Evie nodded. "At first I didn't believe it. I was so sure it would never happen, because of what the doctors had said. Then one morning, after the vomiting had been going on for about a week, I realized I was pregnant and that it was God's gift—his way of proving he loved me. He'd given me the desire of my heart, in spite of everything. My little Lizzie was born just after Christmas." Evie's smile beamed.

"And then Jake started to change. He quit drinking and started looking for work. He was worried at first, about a baby coming, because work was pretty scarce, but once she was there he was the proudest papa ever. Things were hard for a while. Especially when more babies came." She chuckled, smiling. "And kept coming. But we managed and eventually Jake got a steady job and started going to church with me. He started singing, too." Evie laughed again. "We never had a lot of money, but we had twenty wonderful years together, raising our babies, until cancer took him." She sighed. "I wouldn't trade a minute of those years, even the hard times. They pulled us together and they pulled us closer to God."

They were both quiet for a while, the only sound the sipping of their tea. Then Evie slid the brochure across the table and patted Andrea's hand.

"Think hard about this, Andrea. Some things, once they're done, can never be reversed, and they can be awful hard to live with."

* * *

Andrea stared at the scrawled writing in her diary. The ink flowed across the page, word after word, sentence after sentence, paragraph after paragraph. All of it indelible. Just like some decisions, like Evie had said. She clicked the pen and wrote.

I don't want to have an abortion. But I'm so scared of having a baby. I've heard it's the most painful thing anyone could go through. That's what the girls at school said. And then you have this crying, messy creature to take care of all the time, 24/7. And you can't just do whatever you want anymore. You always have to think of the baby. And diapers are really expensive. I glanced at them in the pharmacy the other day. How can anyone afford them? Who would take care of it while I work? I know it's wrong to have an abortion, but I don't see what else I can do. I know Evie will be disappointed in me, but she promised she won't fire me. I have to find a clinic. Soon.

CHAPTER ELEVEN

Kenni watched Alex's profile as he moved past the window. He'd gone for another long walk while she lay awake waiting for him to return. When he finally lay down beside her, she put her hand gently on his chest.

"You okay?"

"Yeah. Just don't think I can sleep much."

Kenni shifted onto her side. "What is it, Alex? I know you're anxious to find Andrea, but there's something else wrong. Talk to me."

When he finally spoke, she could barely hear him. "I'm not sure what it is, Kenni. I'm just restless."

Kenni rolled over with her back to him. She was almost asleep when she felt him squeeze her shoulder and heard the bed creak as he got up.

"Where are you going?" she murmured.

"Go to sleep," he said. "I'm not going anywhere."

She heard the floorboards creak as he went downstairs. A few minutes later, she heard them creak again. Someone had followed him down.

Kenni rolled onto her back and began to pray.

* * *

Alex didn't speak when Bennett came into the kitchen. He watched him move around in the dim light, filling a kettle and turning on the stove. The blue flame seemed to dance too brightly.

"My grandmother used to say tea made everything better. Want some?"

Alex rubbed at his eyes. "To tell you the truth, what I'd like is a few shots of good tequila." He looked at Bennett. "Guess there's no chance you have a bottle or two of that tucked into a cupboard?"

Bennett shook his head with a wry smile. "No chance at all."

Alex dropped his head into his hands. "Good thing," he muttered.

Bennett waited for the kettle to boil before turning on a switch under the cupboards. A pale light flooded the counter. He filled a teapot and set it in the middle of the table along with two mugs and a sugar bowl. The chair creaked when he sat down.

"Guess I'd be in the same state if I thought I was going to be meeting my sister for the first time. How'd you two get separated?"

Alex explained that his parents, and then his adopted parents, had died in accidents and he and Andrea had been placed into foster care.

"I didn't even know she existed until a few months ago. I started searching right away, but all of the leads we've followed have come to dead ends, until Stan got your email."

"Guess I should have told him what was what."

Alex shrugged. "It got us here."

Bennett poured the tea and passed Alex the sugar bowl. "So, foster care. What was that like?"

"All the horror stories you've heard? They're all part of my life story."

"Are? Present tense?"

Alex focused on stirring his tea. "Some."

"Healing doesn't usually happen overnight, does it?"

"So they tell me."

"You have a great wife. Seems like she'd be a real support."

Alex nodded. "Kenni's amazing. I really believe she's God's best gift to me, but sometimes…"

"You feel like you need space."

"Yeah. Or something."

Bennett stood up, opened a broom closet, and retrieved a flashlight. "Bring your tea," he said, walking out the door.

Alex followed, stepping into the quiet summer night. He'd forgotten what the darkness was like in the country—so complete, a darkness that filled every seam and corner. Bennett stopped and shone the pale light across the backyard. Alex followed its path and they stepped through a side door into a three-bay garage. He flicked a switch on, giving them enough light to see a large mound covered with an old tarp.

"Give me a hand, will you?"

Alex put his mug down on a ledge and helped Bennett pull on the tarp. It fell to the floor and revealed a dark green 1952 Chevy.

Alex whistled and ran his hand over the front fender. "Wow. This is a classic."

"Yup, she's a beauty. My grandfather only used it to go to church on Sundays and town on Fridays. She's in mint condition, except for one thing."

"What's that?"

Bennett lifted the hood and switched on a trouble light so Alex could see. He frowned as Bennett pointed to the motor.

"See anything missing?"

Alex leaned in. "No carburettor, no battery. Looks like the starter's missing, too."

"Grandpa kept giving parts away. I have no idea why he didn't just give away the whole car. It was kind of a joke in the family—that we had this great car that just needed a new motor."

Alex chuckled. "So, you're looking for parts?"

"Haven't really had time yet. But yeah, someday I'll track them down. Meantime, I've got this great old classic that could be worth a lot. The outside looks great. The interior's mint, too, and I know the motor would run, but without those essential parts, it's just going to sit where it is."

Alex squinted. "You talking in metaphor now?"

Bennett shrugged. "Well, if the story fits…"

"Yeah, I guess it does." Alex pulled his fingers through his hair. "I'm just not sure where to find the parts to fix it."

"No?"

"I've had counselling. A lot. But the carb still sputters, and some days the starter won't fire at all." He gave Bennett a grin. "To continue the metaphor."

"Maybe there's something you're holding onto."

"Like?"

"That's for you to discover."

Alex sighed. "Yeah, I guess it is."

"But let me give you one more thing to think about, Alex."

"What's that?"

"This old car would have been on the road months ago if I'd had somebody to work on it with me." Bennett gave a jerk of his head and they both stooped over to pull the tarp over the vehicle. "My boys and I will enjoy it someday. I know she'll be a dream to drive once she's been tuned up."

* * *

As Alex's footsteps receded down the hallway, Bennett put the two mugs in the sink and turned off the counter light. He walked into the living room, turned on a small lamp, and sat in his favourite chair, one he remembered his grandfather sitting in for hours at a time. During the day, the view from the window was a broad vista of waving wheat. His grandpa used to say it was like watching the ocean. There was no wheat in the field yet, but Bennett knew it would be there soon, once the seeds germinated, sprouted, and grew to full maturity. He wondered if he would be there to see it happen this year.

What do you have in mind for me now, Lord?

He had a feeling there was something coming, but he wasn't sure what. He knew he didn't want to go back to his old work. Spying on people and finding out all about the dirt in their lives had no appeal anymore. But helping Alex and Kenni find his sister—he'd been really excited about that.

Suddenly, the light went on. There were probably a lot of people out there looking for lost relatives and loved ones. He could get excited about doing that full time. Really excited.

With Stan.

Bennett's head jerked up. Well, it was something to think about, and pray about.

"Thanks, Lord," he said out loud. He turned the light off and went to his bed. He fell asleep praying for Alex, Kenni, Stan, and a young woman he'd never met.

Evie placed the rough stones in the cylinder and nodded to Benny. He poured a liquid slurry on top of the stones, making sure the canister was only about three-quarters full. Then Evie plugged it in. The machine gave a slight shudder and began to spin.

"This imitates the process in nature when the flow of water makes stones tumble over one another in a river. The water and abrasive will grind the rough edges off the stones," Evie explained. "After a few days, when they come out, they'll look like this."

She held out her palm and showed Andrea four stones, all round but looking like they were frosted.

"How do you get them to look like that?" Andrea asked, pointing to a tray of polished stones ready to be made into jewellery.

"We grind them again, and then a third time. Then we test them to see if they'll shine. That takes elbow grease." Evie grinned. "Doesn't it, Benny?"

"Benny is a good polisher," he said.

Evie patted his arm. "Yes, you are. A very good polisher."

Andrea picked up a polished piece of carnelian. Flecks of grey showed through inside the black stone as though small snowflakes had been embedded in it.

"It all takes longer than I thought it would," Andrea said.

"The timing is important," Evie responded. "If you leave the stones in too long, they can get scratched or marred in some way, making them useless for jewellery. But if you take them out too soon, they'll still be rough and too hard to polish." She smiled at Andrea. "Kind of like a baby." She put the stones in her hand back into their compartment. "Kind of like people, too. God is always doing things in our lives, but it takes time. He knows exactly when to take the pressure off or increase it. He knows just how much tumbling we need."

Andrea let her thumb slide over the surface of a polished piece of brown agate. "I guess some of us need more tumbling than others."

Evie smiled. "All of us get our share, dearie, believe me. We all get our share." She took the stone from Andrea's hand, threaded a black cord through the loop attached to it, and slipped it over Andrea's head. "For you," she said, "for any time you feel like God isn't there. Just remember that it's a process, like tumbling stones."

Andrea slipped her hand under the stone and lifted it. The stripes of amber and brown made her think of the land around the farm where she'd been raised.

A sudden homesickness rose up inside, but she smiled at Evie and gave her a hug. The woman responded by wrapping her ample arms around her.

Benny wrapped his huge arms around them both until Andrea squirmed. "Too tight, Benny," she said.

Benny smiled, then frowned at her. "Benny likes to hug Andrea and his baby. Benny has to protect them."

Andrea shook her head at Evie, who was about to say something. She patted Benny's arm. "But this is my baby, Benny, and hugging too tight makes it hard for the baby, and me, too. So just do little hugs, okay?"

Benny nodded. "Little hugs for Benny's baby. Okay."

Andrea opened her mouth to correct him again, but then changed her mind. She knew Benny was harmless. And it was kind of sweet that he thought of the baby as his own.

She felt a sudden coldness that seemed to drill through to her bones. It wasn't Benny's baby. It wasn't *anyone's* baby, and maybe it never would be.

CHAPTER TWELVE

THE CHURCH WAS EXACTLY AS ALEX EXPECTED—SMALL, WHITE, WITH BLACK trim and a tall spire at the front. A large sign read, "Established by the work of our hands, 1902." Organ music was already pouring out. He stood by the car and watched the people file in until Kenni came up behind him and put her hand in his. He put his arm around her and gave her shoulders a squeeze.

"Sorry I've been such a jerk lately," he said.

"Do you miss the Yukon that much?"

"Sometimes, but it's more than that. I just feel like I should have my life all sorted out by now, but instead it feels like it's all unravelled."

"So, it's more than a river trip on the Yukon would fix?"

He grinned. "I'm afraid so."

Kenni leaned into him. "I understand, but I do wish you'd talk to me, or to someone. Even if you haven't figured out what's going on inside you, I think talking about it would help."

Alex nodded. "You're right. And I will. Just… it might take a little time."

"Okay." Kenni sighed. "I'll try to be patient. You try to talk. Deal?"

"Deal." Alex planted a kiss on the top of her head and they walked hand in hand toward the church.

They both scanned the congregation for a young woman with dark hair but couldn't find anyone who looked like she might be Alex's sister. They settled into a pew at the back, Bennett and Stan flanking them.

Kenni sang heartily to the old hymns, but Alex stumbled through them. He was more familiar with the choruses they sang in their church than the more traditional hymns, but he listened to the words and liked what he heard. He also liked hearing Kenni sing.

The sermon was nothing dynamic, but Alex felt refreshed at the end of the service. He noticed Kenni looked more relaxed, too.

When it was over, Bennett and Stan worked the crowd outside, showing everyone the photo as they headed for their cars. It was all Alex could do to keep himself from charging the pastor after the service, but he waited to the side as the congregation filed out, some shaking the man's hand as they went. Alex was thankful that not many stopped to talk. At last they were the only people left and he made his move.

He greeted the pastor and handed him the photograph. Alex didn't realize he'd been holding his breath until he saw the man shake his head and frown. Then it felt like a balloon had been let go. All the air went out of him.

"This looks like it was taken at our bazaar last spring," the minister said, "but I'm afraid I don't know her. She must have been visiting. There were a few church groups here that day."

"What about the boy? Do you recognize him?"

The pastor stared at the photo. "Maybe… it's hard to tell with his face turned away, but I think it could be Cory Jacobs."

"Is he here today?" Alex stepped forward, glancing out the door at the vehicles already leaving the parking lot.

The minister shook his head again. "No. You won't find Cory in church anymore." The frown deepened. "His father used to drag him here when he was a boy, but now, well, these young people get caught by the world and then they're gone. I think I heard Cory's been working the rigs for some time. I haven't seen him since about the time this photo was taken." He handed the photo back. "I'm surprised he was here. He's too old for the youth group."

"Is his father here?" Alex asked.

Another shake of the head. "No, I didn't see him or his wife today."

"Where can we find them?"

The pastor frowned. "What is this about?"

Stan had come back inside. He stepped forward, flashing his identification. Alex noticed it looked as official as his police ID had.

"We're in the middle of an investigation and need to talk to this young woman as soon as possible," Stan said in his most officious voice. Alex noticed he didn't say what they were investigating.

The pastor was still frowning, but Alex guessed that wasn't unusual. He was relieved when the man gave them directions to the Jacobs' farm.

They didn't waste any more time talking.

* * *

Mrs. Jacobs was a chatty woman who invited them in for tea, but she couldn't tell them who the girl was. She seemed embarrassed.

"Cory left to work for an oil company two years ago. I'm sorry, but I'm afraid our son hasn't been very communicative in the past few years. He doesn't tell us who his friends are. He lives his own life and doesn't let us into it very often. I have no idea who that girl is. She must live in another county."

She willingly gave them the name of the company her son was working for and a phone number where they might be able to reach him.

"But don't hold your breath," she cautioned. "The last time I called, the phone was out of service."

Alex groaned out loud.

"What about the other boys?" Bennett asked.

She studied the photo again, pointed to the boy beside her son, and said his name was Jesse Lovette. "The Lovettes live about fifteen kilometres east of here, on Range Road 268."

After thanking her, Bennett gave her his phone number and asked her to tell Cory to call him. As they drove away Alex commented about dysfunctional families living in the country as well as the city.

The story at the Lovettes' was similar. Jesse didn't live there anymore. He'd gone into the army right after high school and was deployed to Afghanistan. But he did call home now and then. There was no phone number they could try.

The ride back to Bennett's house seemed interminably long. Alex's leg started to jump, but he didn't notice it until Kenni put her hand on his knee. He stared out the window for most of the ride, holding back an urge to curse.

Once at the house, Bennett headed for the coffeemaker while Stan called the number Mrs. Jacobs had given them. Kenni found a frying pan and started making a lunch of bacon and eggs. Alex stood close enough to Stan to almost hear the phone conversation—if there had been one, that is. The number had been disconnected. Alex mumbled that word he'd been trying not to use.

Bennett set the table and poured coffees all round.

"What now?" Alex asked.

"We start in the nearby towns and counties." Stan slumped into a chair. "I know this is disappointing, Alex, but we have the photo. We'll find her."

Alex sighed and pushed his hand through his thick hair. "Patience has never been one of my virtues."

Stan snorted. "No kidding."

That got a grin.

"You're welcome to stay here as long as you like," Bennett offered.

Stan nodded at him. "That's appreciated, Bennett, but Alex here is footing the bill and he can afford a hotel. We don't want to impose."

Bennett shrugged. "Up to you, but I don't think you'll find the hotel in town is exactly up to your standards and I sure don't mind the company. Besides, if you don't object to an old alcoholic PI being on the team, I'd be glad to help cover the ground."

Alex sighed. "We need all the help we can get." He looked at Stan. "I think it would make sense to stay here." He glanced at his wife. "If it's okay with you, Kenni."

She nodded. "Fine with me."

"Good." Bennett slapped his cup down. "It's settled then. This will be home base until we find her."

Kenni put a platter of bacon and eggs on the table. "Let's pray that will be soon."

* * *

Andrea pushed herself out of bed and dressed slowly. Her shift didn't start for another few hours but she was hungry, again. Evie had told her to eat whatever she wanted, whenever, and Andrea was thankful. It seemed she was hungry all the time.

She put her hand over her stomach. It had started to swell a lot more, almost immediately after the doctor's appointment, as though taking that step had made it a reality. There was a baby growing inside her and it was active. She still sucked in her breath every time she felt the watery tickle. It seemed this baby liked to swim.

Just like me, she thought.

She pulled on a loose-fitting shirt and looked in the full-length mirror. Evie said she didn't really look pregnant yet, but it looked obvious to her and she felt fat, especially when she wore loose clothing. She was conscious of the pregnancy every minute of every day. Her world now revolved around that fact, and around her swirling thoughts about termination. That's what the doctor had called it—termination—but Evie had used the word "murder."

Andrea shivered. She wouldn't think about that. She couldn't think about it any more than she could think about what it would be like to hold her very own baby in her arms. She gave a long sigh, ran a brush through her hair, and headed downstairs.

Benny stood at Joe's elbow at the grill and gave her a wide grin when she waved. The smell of the grease threatened to turn her stomach, so she kept going and squeezed into a booth at the back of the restaurant. Evie smiled at her and put a finger in the air to indicate she'd be there in a minute. There were only two other booths occupied, so Andrea didn't feel too guilty about taking up Evie's time. She ordered a grilled cheese sandwich and a bowl of chicken soup.

"Good choice, sweetie." Evie winked at her. "Calcium and Vitamin C. Good for you, good for baby."

Andrea frowned back. "I'm starting to feel guilty about how much food I'm eating, Evie. Maybe you should stop paying me for a while."

Evie waved her hand in the air. "Not to worry. The excitement of having a baby around in a few months will make up for it. I just love babies!"

Andrea didn't smile as she watched her lumber away.

Benny brought out the bowl of soup first and sat across from her. His eyes focused on her stomach, but he didn't say anything. Evie had explained about the baby, but Benny was having a hard time understanding.

Andrea absently put a hand on her tummy.

"It's getting bigger, isn't it?" Benny asked.

Andrea nodded but said nothing.

"Are you sure it's a baby?"

"What else would it be?"

He shrugged. "A basketball?" Then he looked up and she couldn't help but laugh.

Evie brought her the sandwich, nudged Benny over, and squeezed in beside him. Andrea told her what he'd just said.

"Benny! You know ladies have babies when their tummies get big, don't you?"

Benny shook his head and started batting his ears. "Babies have to breathe inside. Mothers can't fall down. Can't fall down."

Evie put her cup of coffee down and took his hands gently in hers. "It's okay, Benny. Andrea isn't going to fall down. It's okay."

He nodded and smiled at Andrea. "Benny will take care of this baby."

They looked from one to the other. "Andrea, what do you think about taking Benny with us when you have the ultrasound this afternoon?"

Andrea frowned. *No,* she thought. *I don't think that's a good idea.*

Benny looked at her. "What's that? I want to go, too."

"It's a machine that takes a picture of the baby inside Andrea's tummy," Evie explained.

Benny clapped his hands. "I want to see the pictures. I want to see the baby."

Evie reached over again and stopped the clapping, raising her eyebrows at Andrea.

"I don't know," Andrea said, still frowning.

"Benny wants to come, too. Benny has to come to be with his baby."

Andrea gave Evie a pleading look, but she seemed oblivious.

Evie smiled at Benny. "I'll tell Joe you won't be here for your regular shift. He'll just have to manage without you."

Benny started clapping again.

Andrea sighed but couldn't bring herself to object again.

* * *

With Evie and Benny squeezed into the small room, there was barely enough space for the technician. The woman frowned when she saw Benny and looked like she was about to ask him to leave, when he gave her a wide grin that seemed to change her mind.

His eyes widened, too, when he saw Andrea's bare, swollen abdomen. Andrea saw Evie take his hand. He leaned forward as the image appeared on the screen. The technician pointed out the head and feet. Benny mumbled something, but

Andrea couldn't make it out. Then the baby's hand flashed across the monitor. Benny jumped up and down and started waving back.

"He waved at me, Evie! He waved at me!"

Evie chuckled. "Yes, he did, Benny. He surely did."

"He?" Andrea asked, craning to see the monitor more clearly.

"Well, that's a little hard to tell," the technician said. "What are you hoping for?"

"It doesn't matter." Andrea's voice was almost a whisper.

"Another few weeks and we'll be able to tell, if you really want to know," the technician said.

Andrea leaned back but said nothing.

Evie patted her arm. "Being surprised is part of the experience."

"Well, you can make that decision next time," the technician added.

If there is a next time, Andrea thought.

"Everything looks okay, though?" Evie's voice rose a notch.

"I'm not allowed to make that call," the young woman said. Then she smiled and patted Andrea's hand. "But I'm sure the doctor will tell you everything's perfect." She winked.

Andrea turned her head away.

* * *

Back at the diner, Evie dished up three large pieces of her famous lemon meringue pie. Benny made them all laugh again when he forked a huge bite into his mouth, leaving a ring of meringue around his lips.

"Are we celebrating Benny's baby?" Benny asked.

"Andrea's baby," Evie said gently. "It's Andrea's baby, not yours, Benny. You'll see her, or him, when she or he comes, but not for a while." She lifted a forkful of pie. "But yes, this is to celebrate. Five and a half months." She winked at Andrea. "You're more than halfway there."

Andrea swallowed the lump in her throat as she nodded, smiling weakly at Evie. Five and a half months. The ultrasound had shown her what she'd been having a hard time denying. There was a baby growing inside her. Not a mass of tissue. A baby. And in just a few more months, it would be born. What would she do then? How could she care for it?

Oh God, she prayed, *if you're really there, help me know what to do.*

* * *

84

Benny smiled to himself as he went back to work. He would keep the words inside him. Sometimes words had to be kept secret. Benny's baby. He liked those words.

CHAPTER THIRTEEN

Bennett tugged the dish towel from Kenni's hands. "You cooked. Stan and I will clean up." He jerked his head in Alex's direction. Kenni took the hint and approached him.

"Hey. Feel like a walk?"

Alex took her hand and stood. "Yeah. Sounds good."

Once outside, Kenni breathed in the summer air. It had rained a bit and the air had a fullness to it, a ripeness that Kenni knew one could only feel in the country, away from the concrete and noise of the city.

A chorus of frogs seemed to follow them as they walked.

"I do love it in the country," she said. "Maybe we should consider moving out of the city."

Alex's eyebrows rose. "Music to my ears. You'd really consider it?"

She nodded and squeezed his hand. "Yes, I would."

"What about living in the Yukon?"

"Don't push it."

Alex chuckled.

"A trip up north now and then would be fine, but not for settling down. Somewhere in the country but still civilized could work. Of course we'd have to pray about it—a lot."

"Right." He sighed. "I've been kind of lagging behind on the prayer scene lately."

"Why is that?"

Alex shrugged. "I guess, maybe because God doesn't seem to be listening or responding, and I'm kind of mad at him about that."

Kenni waited, knowing he would go on. They walked in silence for some time.

"Maybe my expectations were off."

"Expectations?" she asked.

"Yeah. I think I sort of expected that everything would just fall into place once I became a Christian. I didn't think there'd be so much struggle. I figured we'd find Andrea right away. I thought that's what God would want."

Kenni chuckled. "Welcome to the real world, the fallen world. We still have to live in it and somehow cope."

"Exactly."

Kenni stopped and faced him. "But the Lord will get us through, Alex, as long as we hang onto him and take all the struggles to him. He'll come through. He always has for me."

Alex's chest rose as he took a deep breath. "Yeah. I guess I just want it to be easier. I mean, why couldn't he have made it easier to find Andrea?" He waved his arm in the air. "Why give me such an urgency to find her and then take us through all this?"

Kenni was quiet as they started walking again. "Maybe we're just not ready," she said softly.

She glanced at Alex out the corner of her eye to gauge his reaction. He was frowning, but said nothing for a few minutes.

"So, what do you think I have to do, to be ready?"

"I don't know, Alex. I just know that God's timing is always right." She hesitated. "And maybe it's not you. Maybe it's Andrea who isn't ready. Maybe God is doing things in her life that we'd mess up if we found her right now."

Alex sighed. "So it all comes down to trust again, doesn't it?"

"It usually does, in one way or another."

They strolled along for a bit before Alex put his arm around her. "Bennett's right," he said with a grin. "Carburettors are a lot more fun to fix when you have company."

Kenni frowned up at him. "Huh?"

Alex shook his head. "Just trying to say I love you."

"Oh." Kenni laughed. "It must be a guy thing."

They circled back to the house and found Stan and Bennett hunched over a large map spread out on the table. Bennett smiled when they came in, still hand in hand.

"We thought we'd split up and cover the next county to the west." Stan tapped the map. "There are two small towns, a lot of farms, and four churches. I thought it might be a good idea to focus on the churches first. She was at a church function, so maybe she's connected to a congregation close by."

Alex nodded. "Sounds good to me, but, uh, who's going to go in the tractor?"

Bennett chuckled. "I have a half-ton and a Toyota in the barn. Stan and I will take the truck and cover this quarter." He covered an area with his hand. "You and Kenni can take the car and head further north." He handed Alex another map and a copy of the photograph. "Show this to as many people as you can along the way. Sooner or later we'll find someone who knows her." He turned to the counter and tossed Kenni a paper bag, then handed Alex a large thermos. "Munchies in the bag, coffee in the thermos. Good luck."

Alex stopped just as he started for the door, looking first at Stan, then at Bennett. "Uh, would it be okay if we prayed before we go?"

Bennett stretched to his full height. "More than okay with me."

Stan just shrugged. "Can't hurt, I guess."

Alex took Kenni's hand again and bowed his head. Before he could begin, Bennett's booming voice filled the room, asking God to direct them, asking him to keep them all safe. Kenni added a prayer for Andrea, that he would prepare her for receiving the news that she had a brother. Alex opened his mouth to pray but choked on the words.

They stood in silence for a while until Bennett said "Amen" and they headed for the vehicles.

* * *

The first few farms seemed deserted, except for a few dogs. Alex braved it a couple of times and went to the doors, but no one answered.

"Where is everyone?" Kenni asked as Alex returned to the car.

Alex shrugged. "Farming's hard these days. When the men aren't in the fields, they sometimes get jobs working in nearby towns. So do their wives." He sighed and turned the ignition. "I guess we just keep going until we find somebody."

At the fourth farmhouse, they struck gold—an elderly man and wife who had lived in the area all their lives. They didn't recognize Andrea, but they provided detailed directions to all the farms and churches nearby, along with names and cautions about which dogs might be a problem. The coffee and pie were a bonus.

Alex charged toward the car when they were able to pull themselves away. "There's a church five kilometres down the road. Let's check it out next."

They spotted the long row of spruce trees and turned into a large parking lot. There were three trucks parked side by side.

Alex tried the front door, but it was locked. They heard a noise coming from the back of the building and discovered three men on ladders painting the outside wall.

One of them climbed down to talk and Alex showed him the photo.

"Sure. That's Andrea Calvert," the man said. "Lives on Range Road 294." He scratched his head, leaving a streak of white paint. "Haven't seen her for a while, come to think of it."

Alex was halfway back to the car when the man called out, "Look for a red mailbox with a tractor painted on it."

Kenni waved and hurried after Alex. They said nothing as they sped along the dirt road, gravel striking the steel around them.

* * *

Edna lifted the last plate from the hot soapy water and set it in the drain rack. Earl rattled the newspaper behind her. She turned and was about to suggest they go to town for some groceries when they both heard the vehicle. Earl got up and went to the window, leaning forward to look.

Edna leaned over him. "Who is it?"

Earl shrugged. "Never saw the vehicle before."

He opened the back door just as Alex raised his hand to knock. Earl stared. Edna gasped.

Alex finally spoke. "Mr. and Mrs. Calvert?"

Earl nodded. "Yes?"

Alex stuck out his hand. "My name's Alex Perrin. This is my wife, Kenni." His eyes shifted to Edna's face for a moment. "Uh, do you have a daughter named Andrea?" He pulled the photo from his breast pocket and held it up. "A foster daughter?"

Edna pushed in front of Earl. "Have you found her? Is she all right? Please tell me she's all right."

"Found her?" Alex frowned. "No. We've been looking... I mean, we were hoping she was here."

Earl stepped aside. "Come in," he said, taking Edna's arm. "Edna, some coffee."

Edna stared at him.

"Coffee, hon."

She nodded and moved to the counter. Alex and Kenni sat at the large table. Edna didn't take her eyes off Alex's face as she put a mug down in front of him.

"You're related to her, aren't you?" she asked.

"I'm Andrea's brother," Alex answered.

Edna gave a soft groan and sat down hard. "I didn't know. We weren't told she had a brother."

"I'm sorry to barge in like this. I know it must be a shock, but do I understand you correctly that you don't know where Andrea is?"

Edna's hands fluttered from the table to her face and back again. "She left—it's been several weeks now. No, we don't know where she is."

Alex groaned.

Edna glanced at Earl. "We know she headed east," he offered.

"You look so much like her," Edna said, staring at Alex. "Were you... are you twins?"

"No. We're a couple of years apart." Alex put the photo on the table. "But yes, we do look a lot alike. That's how we've been able to track her down. A friend took this photo last spring."

Edna picked it up and nodded. "Yes, at the church bazaar in Carson's Corner. I remember she went over there with some other young people from our church." She frowned. "Who is this boy?"

"We think his name is Cory Jacobs. That's all we know."

"Jacobs," Earl said, taking the photo from Edna's hand. "There's a Frank Jacobs lives south a ways past Carson's. That his boy?"

Edna frowned at the dark look on Earl's face. "Could be."

"Mrs. Calvert, could you… would you tell me a little about Andrea? Do you have pictures? Anything? I've been waiting a long time to meet her."

Edna jumped up. "Yes, of course. We have albums of photos. Come into the living room."

For the next two hours, Kenni and Alex poured over the albums while Edna talked. She told them Andrea was good in school, that science was her favourite subject, and that she loved to swim. Edna pointed out pictures of her daughter with her first horse and proudly displaying a ribbon she'd won in a calf breeding competition in 4H. Her fingers traced each successive school photo—pictures of a shy but seemingly happy young girl with curly black hair and eyes that had grown more and more like Alex's as the years went on.

When the last album was closed, Kenni asked the question none of them wanted to hear, the question they had all been avoiding.

"Mrs.Calvert, why did Andrea leave?"

Edna clutched the album to her. "Because…" Her eyes flicked to Earl's face for a moment, then back to Kenni. Her voice dropped. "Because she was pregnant."

Alex sank deeper into the sofa.

Edna's eyes darted from one to the other. "We had arranged for her to go away, to stay with my sister. We thought it best if she had the child and then gave it up for adoption." Edna felt the tears seep out from the corner of her eyes. "Then she could come back to us." She swiped at her face with the back of her hand. "I don't… we don't know why exactly, but she left before that could happen, without saying a word to us."

Kenni took her hand. "We'll find her. Don't worry. God led us here and he'll guide us to her."

Edna's head snapped up. "You're a Christian?"

"Yes." Kenni looked up at Alex. "Both of us are."

Alex looked at Earl. "Do you have any idea where she might have gone? Have you checked with friends? Does she know people in any towns nearby, people she might stay with?"

Earl shook his head but Edna answered. "No. Andrea was a shy girl. Her only friends were at our church and at school." She stood up suddenly and came back with a high school yearbook. "This was Andrea's last yearbook. She graduated just over a year ago." She opened the book to Andrea's class page and pointed out Andrea, then another girl. "That's Carolynn Chisholm. She and Andrea have been friends since kindergarten."

Kenni looked up from the book. "Have you talked to her?"

Edna glanced at Earl, then stared at her feet. When she responded, her voice was low. "No," she said. "We haven't told anyone that Andrea ran away. Everyone thinks she went to my sister's, as we'd planned."

"Do you have this girl's phone number?" Alex asked.

Edna looked at Earl again, remaining silent.

"Mrs. Calvert?"

Edna watched Alex struggle to control his anger.

"It's very important that we find Andrea, and soon," Alex said.

Edna's heart fluttered. "Why?"

Alex sighed. "I don't know. But it's—it's just a strong feeling I have. So please, any information you have that might help…"

Edna stood up. "I'll get Carolynn's phone number."

When she came back, her hand shook as she held out a small piece of paper. Alex reached for it, but she drew it back. "No. I'll do it. I'll call her right now."

Alex sat back into the sofa as she left the room again. Her hands shook as she dialled the number. Carolynn's mother seemed concerned, but Edna didn't offer any information. She just asked her to call if Carolynn saw Andrea.

When Edna returned to the living room, they were all sitting in silence and the room felt tense with disapproval. She glanced at Earl but turned to Alex.

"Carolynn has been away at college for the past year. Her mother said she didn't think the girls have been in touch since she left, but she said she'd ask Carolynn if she's heard from her. If so, she'll call me."

"Are there any others? Other kids she might have talked to?"

Edna shook her head, embarrassment colouring her cheeks. "I don't think so. And most of these kids are gone. They all go off to college or work in the cities. Not many of them stay after graduation. In fact, I think Andrea was the only girl in her class who didn't leave."

Alex sighed. "Then it's going to take some time to track them down. Can you give us a list of those we should start with?"

Edna nodded and handed Alex the slip of paper with Carolynn's home number. Then she pointed out three other girls they should talk to.

"What about boys?" Alex asked.

Edna shook her head. "Andrea was shy," she repeated.

Alex frowned. "So, you don't know who her boyfriend was?"

Edna dropped her head and shook it.

Kenni leaned forward. "Mrs. Calvert—"

"Please, call me Edna."

"Edna, I hope this isn't too personal a question. Was… is Andrea a believer? Does she know Jesus?"

Edna wrung her hands and frowned. "Of course. We raised her to go to church. Every Sunday."

She saw Kenni glance at Alex, but was comforted when the young woman covered her hand with her own.

Edna gave her a weak smile. "Please find her." The words were almost a whisper.

Kenni squeezed her hand. "We will."

Alex stood up. "Thank you for your help, Mrs… uh, Edna. Can I keep this for a while?" He held up the yearbook.

Edna hesitated, then nodded. "Yes." Her eyes lingered on it. "But I want it back."

Kenni stood and handed her a slip of paper with their cell phone numbers on it. "Don't hesitate to call anytime," she said.

Edna saw Kenni watching her through the rear window as they drove away. She stood at the door until their car disappeared into the dust.

CHAPTER FOURTEEN

ALEX CALLED STAN AND TOLD HIM THEY HAD FOUND ANDREA'S FOSTER parents. They agreed to head back to Bennett's place immediately and regroup.

Kenni sensed Alex's disappointment, again. She put her hand on his arm. "How you doing?"

Alex patted her hand. "I'm okay. Trying to think positive. We're close. It might take a while, but at least we're on the right track now."

Kenni nodded and settled back into her seat. "She must be so confused and scared. I've been praying for her continuously."

"Me, too. I just hope…"

"What?"

"I hope she doesn't do something that she'll regret, before we can reach her."

"You mean an abortion?"

Alex nodded. "She's gotta be thinking about it."

"Yes, but I don't think... she's been raised in a church..."

"Raised in one, yes, but, well, it might make a difference, but maybe not."

Kenni sighed. "We'll just have to keep praying." She glanced at Alex. "You know, really, it's amazing that we're here—amazing that Bennett connected you to the photo he took. Amazing that we found the Calverts. God is directing us."

"Yeah. I know." He grinned and turned to her. "I just wish he'd direct us a little faster."

She grinned back. "Have you prayed for patience lately, by any chance?"

"Why?"

"Because if you did, maybe God's giving you the chance to develop it."

Alex chuckled. "Could be."

Kenni sat back. "Like in that crazy movie we watched a while ago—the one about the guy who started turning into Noah and was sure God was telling him to build an ark. Remember?"

"Yeah... what was it called? *Evan Something,* wasn't it?"

"*Evan Almighty.*"

"Right."

"Do you remember the scene in the diner, when Evan's wife and kids have left him, and Morgan Freeman, who's God, tells her that God doesn't just go 'poof' and make something happen?"

"Vaguely," he said.

"She prayed that their family would be closer, so God put them in a circumstance that would make that happen. He didn't just go 'poof' and make it so."

"Right. I get it. This is a patience-building circumstance."

"Yes. I think so."

Alex nodded. "Patience and trust." He put his hand in hers. "It just never quits, does it?"

Kenni smiled. "God never quits. He's always working on us."

Alex ran his hand through his hair. "And some of us are made of harder stone than others."

* * *

Alex could see Andrea clearly as she climbed a long staircase made of black stone. She was almost to the top. His heart beat wildly as he lunged toward her, using his hands at times to scale the steep stairs, panting from the exertion of the climb. No matter how fast he tried to go, he knew he wouldn't reach her in time. He could feel the heat from the fire on his face and wondered how she could stand being so close.

He looked up and saw that she had stopped. She turned and glanced back, their eyes meeting. Hers looked glazed, unseeing. She looked down and Alex realized she was carrying something in her arms. She took another step forward, then opened her arms and let the bundle fall into the flames.

Alex woke up screaming, "Noooo!"

Kenni's arms were around him then, her voice soothing, calming him. He sank back onto the bed, panting.

"What was it, Alex?" Kenni asked, her cheek on his chest.

"Andrea," he said. "We have to find her, Kenni. We have to find her fast."

* * *

Edna heard the vehicle and leaned into the window to see who it could be. A big pickup with extended fenders stopped near the back door and a young man got out. Edna waited for the knock, then opened it.

"Mrs. Calvert?"

"Yes."

"I'm… my name is Cory Jacobs. I'd like to talk to Andrea."

Edna took a step back. "She's not here."

"Can you tell me when she'll be back?"

Edna shook her head hard. "No."

Cory's shoulders dropped. "I really need to see her."

Edna's eyes narrowed. "Andrea's gone. She doesn't live here anymore."

"Where did she go?"

"I don't know. I'm sorry, I have things to do…"

Cory took a step closer. "Please, when you're talking to her, ask her to call me."

Edna closed the door on his last word and went back to the window. She watched him get back into the huge truck. A cloud of blue smoke billowed from the back when he turned it on.

Earl stood in the doorway of the barn, wiping his hands on a rag. Gravel spit from under the truck's tires as it sped out of the yard. Earl stared after it, then at the house. He turned and went back into the barn.

He knew who the boy in the big fancy truck was—the father of Andrea's baby. He knew it in the pit of his stomach, the way he always knew when a sick calf was going to die.

He gripped the top of a stall door, leaned hard into it, and struggled for control. He hadn't allowed himself to cry since he was a boy. The last time was the day his favourite horse had broken his leg and needed to be put down. His father had put the rifle in his hand and told him it had to be done and that he was the one who should do it. It was like putting a bullet into his own head. It killed something in him.

That something had been awakened again when he met and married Edna. God, how he had loved that woman. Had? Was it all past tense? He gripped the stall door so hard that his knuckles went white. He still loved her, God help him. But she had long ago shown that she didn't love him. He still wondered why she'd stayed with him. But she had. All these years, she even cooked his favourite foods, desserts she knew he liked. Was it only because she felt guilty? Maybe if he had shown her more tenderness somehow, maybe they could have mended the rift between them.

It always seemed to be there between them, the unspoken words, unspoken accusations, unspoken confession. He'd heard the expression, an elephant in the room, and he knew what it meant. Their elephant had been living with them for twenty years. He had waited for her to admit it, but she never did, so he had not told her he'd forgiven her. He had, long ago, but he didn't know what to do with that forgiveness. He had hoped that bringing Andrea to their home would bridge the gap somehow, show her that he had forgiven her. It had helped but not healed the wounds.

He followed Edna out to the slough sometimes, watched her sit there and rock back and forth, mourning that child even after so long. He couldn't feel anything for it. He knew it wasn't his. God help him, its death had been a relief to him. It had saved them having to lie to everyone, pretend that everything was fine. But then, they were doing that now, every day, living a lie. And it had cost them the only spark of joy they'd ever known. Andrea.

* * *

Cory eased up on the accelerator once he was well away from the Calverts' farm. Something was going on. His mother said that a man had called asking about Andrea, but now Andrea's mother wouldn't give him the time of day.

He tugged the piece of paper out of his pocket and looked at the number written on it. He shoved it back into his pocket and let his foot slam down on the accelerator. He should stay out of it. Far out of it. But his curiosity nagged him.

He'd heard a rumour that Andrea was missing. He did like her. She was a sweet girl, though so naïve it used to make him laugh. God, she hardly ever left her own backyard. What could have happened to her?

He tugged the phone number out again, set it on the seat beside him, and took his Blackberry out of his shirt pocket. As he dialled the number, he hoped he wasn't walking into some kind of mess.

* * *

Bennett's phone startled him and he grabbed it quickly. There was silence for a few seconds after he said hello. Then a young male voice asked if he could talk to Bennett Beechum.

"That's me," Bennett said. "Who's this?"

Silence again for a minute, then the hesitant voice. "Cory Jacobs. My mom said you were trying to reach me?"

"Yes. Yes, Cory, I was. Where are you calling from?"

"I'm on my cell."

"I'm near Carson's Corner. Are you nearby? Can we meet?"

The pause was longer this time. "What do you want?"

"I need to talk to you about Andrea Calvert."

"What about her?"

"It would be really good if we could talk face to face, Cory."

Bennett heard a deep sigh.

"Okay. Meet me at the Prairieland Café in Carson's. I'll be there in about half an hour."

"Good. Half an hour."

Bennett hung up and prayed. He knew this wouldn't be an easy conversation.

* * *

Cory Jacobs was a slim boy who looked fifteen, but Bennett knew he was a few years older than Andrea. He sat hunched over in a booth, a baseball hat pulled down hard over his eyes and a hoody hanging limp on his slim frame. Bennett approached slowly. The young man didn't look up until he said his name. He gave a quick nod, avoiding Bennett's eyes. Bennett slid into the booth and ordered a coffee.

"Cory, I need to know if you've had any contact with Andrea Calvert in the past couple of months."

The boy shook his head. "No. I haven't seen her or talked to her since a few weeks after I left for the oil patch." He finally looked at Bennett. "Why?"

"Did you know she was missing?"

"Missing?" The boy frowned at him, then his eyes went wide and his back stiffened. "Hey, listen, if you think… I told you I haven't seen or talked to Andrea for months and I wouldn't, I would never take her, or hurt her, or anything."

Bennett raised his hand, palm out. "That's not where I'm going, Cory. Do you have any idea where she might have gone? Does she have friends anywhere close by?"

Cory sat back and shook his head. "No. She never mentioned any. She never mentioned wanting to go anywhere. She was pretty much a stick-at-home kinda chick."

"Did you know she was pregnant?"

Cory's head jerked up. "What?"

"That's why she left."

The boy seemed to have stopped breathing. His eyes darted around the room.

"You're the father, aren't you?" Bennett asked.

Cory made a fist and cursed. "I don't know. I guess… I could be. She didn't tell me. She didn't say anything about being pregnant." He grabbed the visor of his hat with both hands and groaned. "I swear, I didn't know. If I'm the father, why wouldn't she have told me?"

"What did you say to her the last time you talked to her?"

"I told her I was seeing someone else. Like I said, that was about three weeks after I left. She stopped calling after that." He scratched the side of his head. "She should have told me. What do you want me to do?"

Bennett shook his head. "Do whatever you can to help us find her."

"Us? You mean her parents?" His eyes shifted. "I don't think they'll want my help, especially now."

"Andrea's brother and his wife are trying to find her, too."

"Her brother? I didn't know she had one."

"She doesn't know—it's kind of a long story."

They were silent for a moment. Bennett let it linger.

"Regina," Cory mumbled. "I guess that would be the logical place to..." Cory turned his face away.

"To what?"

Cory's voice dropped. "To get rid of it."

"You think that's what Andrea would do?"

He shrugged. "That's what other girls do, isn't it?"

"Not always."

Cory stared at the table. "Yeah. Andrea was, sweet, you know? Maybe... I guess maybe she'd want to keep it." He groaned again. "God, what a mess. My dad'll kill me if he finds out."

"If Earl Calvert doesn't do it first."

Cory's face went pale. "Does he know? Does he know it was me?"

"I took a picture of the two of you at the Carson's Corner Church bazaar last spring. We showed it to Earl and Edna. I imagine they'll put two and two together."

Cory pulled the hat off his head. His sandy hair stuck out in all directions. Under different circumstances, Bennett would have smiled.

"God," Cory groaned again. "I'm sorry, but I'm involved with someone else now, you know? I can't... there's nothing I can do."

Bennett finished his coffee and stood up. He handed Cory his card. "Call me if you hear from her, or hear anything about her."

Cory nodded. "I will."

Bennett started to turn away, but Cory stood up and caught his arm.

"Mr. Beechum, if I am the father, I should... I want to know."

Bennett nodded. "I'll call you if we hear anything."

Cory pulled a pen out of his pocket and wrote on the napkin. "This is my cell number," he said. "If you talk to her, tell her to call me, okay?"

Bennett glanced at the napkin and stuck it in his pocket. "I'll let you know," he repeated, then left the café.

* * *

Edna hadn't been into Andrea's room since the day she'd discovered her daughter was gone. She pushed the door open and stood still for a time, staring at the bed, so neatly made, the dresser tidy and clean, a small jewellery box sitting on top. It was so like Andrea. Everything had to be in its proper place. She sighed and stepped in. Alex and Kenni had suggested she look for anything that might tell them where Andrea had gone.

She went to the small desk and touched the books one by one, then opened the drawer and moved things around, but there was nothing there, no notes, no letters, nothing to give her any clues. She went through all the drawers in the dresser, but they only contained some of Andrea's clothing—things she had left behind.

She was about to leave the room when she noticed the box sticking out of the bottom of the closet. She pulled it out. It was the box of books she had brought up from the basement. Andrea had been planning to go through it before they took it to the church for the rummage sale.

She moved some of the books around. Then her hand hovered and began to shake. The diary. *Her* diary. Oh God, she had forgotten about it. She had intended to burn it. How had it gotten in here? Had Andrea noticed it? Had she read it?

She lifted the black book out and frowned. No. This wasn't her diary. Hers had the drawing of the earring on the cover, one just like the pair Roy had given her. Edna sat on the edge of the bed and opened the cover. Her hand trembled, so she steadied the book on her lap and began to read.

I wish I had a cell phone. I told Cory not to call here, but that makes it hard to stay in touch. I'll see him at work tomorrow, of course, but I want to talk to him. All the time. I want to be close to him, as close as I possibly can be. It's a wonderful feeling, but terrible at the same time. I feel as though I'm not whole anymore—or maybe I never was. Twelve long hours before I can see him again.

Edna skipped ahead to the last few pages.

I know God won't help me now. I've broken all the rules. And the things I'm thinking about... If I do what I'm thinking about, that will be it with me and God, me and my parents, me and everyone. I'll have to leave, start a new life, become a different person. Maybe that wouldn't be so bad.

The last few pages were full of Andrea's words to the baby she knew she was carrying. They wrenched Edna's heart until the tears became sobs. She should have been there for her daughter. She should have talked to her, helped her, instead of becoming a cold statue that couldn't respond, couldn't offer anything but a heartless solution.

She closed the book, put it on top of the dresser, and left the room. At least she knew one thing: Andrea had been planning to have an abortion when she left here. That meant she would probably head for Regina.

But she couldn't tell anyone that. Especially Earl. It would kill him if he knew.

No. She just couldn't tell anyone.

* * *

A light rain fell, dampening the sidewalks and leaving puddles on the road that sprayed up as the cars passed, but Andrea didn't notice. She stared at the building across the street and frowned. This was the address, but she couldn't see any sign that told her where the entrance to the clinic was.

She scanned the front of the building again and noticed a narrow door to one side with a small sign on it. She was too far away to read what it said, but as she stared a young girl came out of the door and stood on the step for a moment. She clutched the collar of her jacket, peering up and down the street. Andrea could tell she was crying.

A small car pulled up and a young man got out. He approached her and Andrea thought he was going to put his arm around her, but she stepped away from him before he could, then went around the car and got inside. The boy got in after her and drove away.

Andrea was soon standing in front of the door, staring at her hand as it rested on the doorknob. She saw the knob turn and the door open. She saw the grey stairs and her hand sliding along the metal railing.

A woman smiled at her from behind a desk. "Can I help you?"

Andrea didn't respond.

"Would you like to talk to someone today?"

Andrea nodded.

The interview didn't take long. The woman asked a few questions and, when Andrea told her how far along she was, the woman put the clipboard down.

"We can only do the procedure up to sixteen weeks." The woman's eyes looked sad. "But we can refer you to a clinic in another province."

"Oh." Andrea stood up, suddenly filled with an urgency to leave.

"Is that a problem for you?"

"No. I… I'll come back," she said, whirled around, and ran from the room.

She sat on a bus stop bench, panting as the wind whipped the driving rain around her. As she tugged at the neck of her jacket, her fingers touched the black cord. She pulled it out and wrapped her hand around the small brown stone, remembering the day Evie had given it to her. Suddenly the day seemed real again, the cold biting through her jacket.

She climbed onto the first bus that came along and rode it for over an hour before she realized she was heading in the wrong direction. She pulled the cord, asked the driver for a transfer, and clung to the pole by the door until the bus pulled into a stop. Then she ran to the other side of the street and climbed into the first bus that would take her back to the warmth of the diner.

* * *

Back at Bennett's, Kenni and Alex listed the names of the kids in Andrea's class and broke them into two groups. The next morning, they headed for the high school in Meadow Bend. Alex prayed all the way that the principal would be cooperative and willing to give them the contact information they needed.

When they arrived, Stan's ID proved useful again. And again, Alex thought how ingenious it was to make it look like police ID.

The principal was hesitant at first, but he gave them the information they needed and they started calling. Some of the parents refused to give them phone numbers for their kids, but some didn't hesitate once they were told why the information was needed. The parents remembered Andrea as a sweet girl and seemed anxious to help when they heard she was missing.

They spent all that day on the phone but got no further helpful information.

Alex slumped into a kitchen chair and ran his hand through his black hair. "What now?"

Stan poured himself his tenth cup of coffee and joined him at the table. "The Calverts said they know she took the bus east. We'll talk to the ticket agents and see if they remember her and where she might have gotten off."

That strategy proved a little more fruitful. One of the agents remembered seeing her and remembered that she had bought a ticket on a bus heading south. "I don't remember if the ticket was all the way to Regina, but it was definitely in that direction," he said.

"Looks like we need to book a flight," Stan suggested.

Alex was on the phone before he finished his sentence. It took him a while, but he managed to charter another small plane to pick them up at the airport the next morning.

"I'll keep knocking on doors around here," Bennett said. "I was thinking I'd go talk to Andrea's pastor—see if maybe she talked to him at all."

"Good idea," Stan said. "Any details, no matter how small, may help."

Bennett nodded. "I'll call if I discover anything."

CHAPTER FIFTEEN

ANDREA SHIVERED AS SHE WATCHED THE RAIN SLIDE DOWN THE SMALL window in her room. She pushed the pillows behind her back and tucked the quilt around her. The small lamp made a halo of light that was enough to write by. Or read.

Her eyes fell on Edna's diary. She opened it to the page she had last read and continued.

I'm sitting in my favourite chair in the living room. The sun is warm today, promising summer days to come. I've been reading my Bible a bit lately— mostly the Psalms. Reverend Castor doesn't approve of his flock reading the Bible on their own. "Too much room for error," he says. But I love the Psalms and I don't see how it could hurt to read them. They help sometimes.

But today I went further, into the New Testament. I almost felt as though I were doing something wrong, but I felt compelled to read it. I didn't get much out of the first part of Matthew, but then I came to the ninth chapter, verses twenty to twenty-two.

Andrea held her breath. That was the same passage the pastor in Evie's church had preached on.

I've heard the story before, but today the words seemed to almost flash like neon lights. When I read them, my heart started pounding and I started to cry. I am that woman, a woman haemorrhaging for years, a woman needing to be healed. If only I could have that same kind of faith. If only I could touch the hem of Jesus' cloak now as that woman did thousands of years ago.

Andrea's hands trembled as she brushed the tears from her eyes, put the book down, and turned out the light. Such sad words. *If only.*

* * *

Evie was sipping a cup of tea with one hand and tapping numbers into a calculator with the other when Andrea walked into the staff room. Evie smiled and cleared a spot on the other side of the table.

"Want some tea, hon?"

"No thanks, Evie." She plopped down in the chair across from her boss.

Evie took another sip but didn't take her eyes off Andrea's face. The girl looked tired, dark circles under her eyes making her look older than she was. "You okay?"

Andrea nodded. "Just trying to decide some things."

"Ah."

Andrea pushed her hair behind her ear and sighed but said nothing more.

Evie shifted the pile of papers in front of her. "Where did that brochure go?" she muttered. "I know it's here somewhere... ah, here we go." She held the brochure in her hand for a moment, then slid it across the table. She held her breath.

Andrea stared at it before raising her eyes to Evie's face.

"I don't mean to push, Andrea, but I really think it would help to talk to these people. They've helped a lot of young women in your situation." She leaned forward a bit. "I'd be happy to go with you, if you like."

Andrea picked up the brochure. It had a picture of two women on the front, one a little older than the other. The older woman was leaning forward, her face full of deep concern.

Andrea sighed. "I'll think about it," she said, putting her hand on the table and pushing herself up out of the chair.

Evie grabbed Andrea's hand. "Don't just think. Promise me you will. Please?"

Andrea sighed again. "Okay. I guess it won't hurt to talk to them."

Evie spent the better part of the next hour praying that Andrea would keep her promise.

* * *

Two days later, Andrea told Evie she was going out for a walk. The brochure for the pregnancy care centre was folded deep into her pocket. "I won't be long," she said.

The pregnancy care centre was only a few blocks away, in a small house on a side street away from the busy traffic of downtown. Andrea stood outside for a while, staring at the front of the building. It was a cute house, with flowers edging the walk, the kind of place that looked like a family might be living in it, a family with small children. She brushed her tears away with a quick stroke.

She got as far as the corner. She had promised Evie she'd talk to these people and she had to keep her promise, but she didn't have to take their advice. She just had to talk to them. She put her hand on the curve of her stomach, took a shuddering breath, then walked toward the front door.

The woman at the desk smiled and gave her a form to fill out. It didn't take long before another young woman called her name and led her into a small room. The walls were pastel-coloured and a loveseat in a floral pattern sat across from a large overstuffed chair that looked big enough for two. On the opposite wall was a table with a TV that had a DVD slot built into it. A selection of magazines about caring for babies lay scattered across a small glass coffee table. The woman waved Andrea toward the loveseat and sat down in the chair.

"I'm Nicole," she said. "How can we help you, Andrea?"

"Well," Andrea began. "As you can see, I'm pregnant. I'm not married, don't have a boyfriend, and I work as a waitress. So I guess I wanted to ask you, how can you help me?"

"Are you planning to keep the baby?'

Andrea sighed. "I don't know. I kind of… I don't see how I can." She dropped her head and stared at the floor. "I was thinking…"

"About an abortion?"

Andrea shrugged. "Sort of, but it's probably too late now, anyway, isn't it?"

"Have you read any information about abortions, Andrea? Do you know what they involve?"

"No. But my doctor gave me a brochure about the baby's development and I know all about that. I know it's a real baby, not just… not just a ball of tissue." She looked at the magazines on the table, with pictures of smiling babies and mothers, then looked away. "But I can't… I just promised a friend I'd talk to you people first."

Nicole reached over and touched her hand. "Good for you. That's a brave decision. Have you thought about adoption?"

Andrea nodded. "That's almost as hard to think about."

"I know." Nicole's head tilted a bit. "But there are good things to consider. The baby will be with a family that truly wants it and can care for it."

"How do you know that?" Andrea's voice was sharper than she'd intended. "There are lots of kids who get dumped with people who don't even like them," she said more softly.

"That's true, but those people don't usually go looking to adopt. There are many people waiting for babies, wanting to give them a good home."

Andrea was quiet for a while. Nicole seemed willing to wait.

"Can I pick who would get her?"

"There are different options you can explore. One is an open adoption, so yes, it might be possible to know the couple and be part of the baby's life. But that isn't the most common scenario. Many parents don't want that. We can help you find an adoption agency that will explain everything."

Andrea's voice went quiet. "I understand."

Nicole sat back. "Tell me a bit about yourself, Andrea. You said you're working?"

Andrea nodded and told her about Evie and the restaurant. Slowly and gently, Nicole drew her out and soon she found herself talking about her family, her childhood, and even Cory.

"Have you talked to your parents? Do they know?" Nicole asked.

Andrea hesitated. "My mom—my foster mother knows."

"But she isn't supportive?"

Andrea looked away and shook her head.

"Do they know where you are, Andrea?"

"I don't think they care anymore."

"I don't know them, but I can tell you in all the experience I've had, most parents, once they get over the shock, do come around. Most parents do care. And I've found it's best if everyone is kept informed as much as possible." She paused. "Will you think about calling your mother?"

"I'll think about it," Andrea conceded, "but I don't think I'll do it."

When Nicole glanced at her wristwatch and said they would have to stop, Andrea was shocked to realize they had been talking for over an hour. She was even more shocked at the information she had given this young woman. It felt good to have let it all out, though.

When Nicole asked if she'd like to book another appointment, Andrea hesitated but said yes.

* * *

Bennett sat in the cab of his truck and said a quick prayer. He had heard a bit about this church and the minister and none of it was very complimentary. But he tried to keep an open mind. Maybe the gossip wasn't true. It wouldn't be the first time.

He knocked on the door of the small house tucked into some poplar trees to the side of the church. A small neat-as-a-pin woman opened it and invited him in. She turned on her heel and led him down a short hallway, tapped on a door, and opened it a crack. She stuck her head into the room and said something in such a soft voice that Bennett couldn't hear the words. Then she stepped back and opened the door wide, keeping her eyes on the floor. She had not smiled once.

Reverend Castor stood but didn't come out from behind his large desk. Bennett had the feeling the man shook hands only because Bennett had extended his first. He sat down in the small chair offered and got right to the point.

"I'm here to talk about a young woman in your congregation, Reverend Castor. Her name is Andrea Calvert."

The reverend frowned. "Yes, I know the Calvert family."

"Did you know that Andrea has disappeared?"

"Disappeared?"

"Well, her parents think she ran away, actually. She has been gone for a few months now."

The reverend pursed his lips. "I was not aware of that."

"I wondered if you might have had any contact with her before she left?"

"Contact?"

"Yes, you know, did she come to talk to you or ask for counselling?"

"No. Is there a reason she should have?"

Bennett hesitated, then made a decision. "I'm not at liberty to say."

"These people are in my flock, Mr…"

"Beechum."

"Mr. Beechum. If something is going on, I should be made aware of it."

Bennett stood up. "Then I suggest you talk to the Calverts, Reverend."

The reverend's eyes narrowed. "Yes, I will. Be assured, I will."

Bennett nodded and headed for the door. "Thank you for your time," he said over his shoulder. He didn't offer to shake the reverend's hand a second time.

When he got back into his truck, he said a second prayer for Andrea. With that man as her pastor, Bennett was pretty sure her picture of God was distorted.

Bennett was about to turn south and head home when he decided to pay a visit to the Calverts. He'd just stuck his nose in their business and maybe caused them more grief. They deserved to be warned.

* * *

Edna had just made a fresh pot of coffee and put a large piece of Saskatoon pie in front of him when Bennett sat down at the kitchen table. It made him feel even guiltier.

"As I said," he began, "I've been helping Alex and Kenni and talking to people about Andrea." He looked at Earl. "I'm afraid I might have just made things more difficult for you folks."

Earl frowned. "How so?"

"I thought perhaps Andrea would have talked to your pastor about what was going on in her life, so I went to see him." He heard Edna take in a short breath. She was gripping the back of a chair. "I didn't get the impression… well, I think he's going to be calling you."

Edna went pale. Both were silent for a moment.

Earl sighed. "I suppose we knew we couldn't keep it secret much longer."

"Reverend Castor didn't know anything about Andrea. That kind of surprised me."

Earl snorted. "He'd be the last person we'd tell."

Bennett sighed. "I'm sorry."

Earl waved his hand, then looked at Edna. "It's okay. It's all okay. I've been stuck for a long time and all of this has been kind of like a crowbar prying me out of a tight place." He took a swallow of his coffee. "I'll talk to the reverend when he calls. And I'll tell him we'll no longer be attending his church."

"But Earl…" Edna began.

Earl held up his hand. "I've been coming to this point for a long time, Edna. If that's what God is like, I want nothing to do with him." He stood up and strode out through the back door.

Bennett stared at his coffee and half-eaten piece of pie. "I'm sorry, Edna."

She stared out the window but said nothing as he left the house.

He had his hand on the door of his truck when he heard the sound of chopping wood and found Earl at the side of the house. He stood and watched for a while, until Earl paused to wipe the sweat from his forehead.

"That's not what he's like."

Earl whipped around. "What?"

"God. He's not like Reverend Castor."

Earl placed the axe head on the chopping block and leaned on its handle. "How do you know?"

"Because, well, it'll take some explaining. And I'd sort of like to finish that great piece of pie that's sitting on the table."

Earl snorted and placed another piece of wood on the block. Bennett started to turn away.

"Be there in a minute," Earl said.

Bennett made sure Earl didn't see his smile as he walked away.

Edna's eyebrows shot up when she answered his knock again.

"Earl's coming back in," he explained, watching the shadow that seemed to dull the features of her face lift just a bit. She waved him to the table.

He said another fervent prayer as he sat down. *Lord, give me the words to move Earl's heart and heal the sadness in this house.*

He had finished his pie and Edna was pouring him another cup of coffee when they heard the thud of Earl's boots on the step. He went to the sink, washed his hands, and poured himself a cup. He pulled out a chair, then hesitated.

"If you're gonna preach at me, I'll go back to the wood pile," Earl said.

Bennett shook his head. "I was thinking I'd just tell you my story."

Earl sat down. "I'm listening."

"I think we're a lot alike, Earl, you and me." Bennett said. "We're men—real men who don't baby themselves and don't have much patience with people who do. Am I right?"

"You're right," Edna chimed in.

Earl's eyes flicked in her direction but he said nothing.

"I can understand why you don't want to go back to Reverend Castor's church. From what I've seen, it's the kind of place where there's not much love and a lot of condemnation. I'm guessing that suited you until now."

Earl lifted a shoulder. "I guess."

"I used to see God that way," Bennett admitted. "In fact, I used to imagine him up there with a big stick in his hand just waiting for me to blow it."

Earl stared at his hands.

"The thing is, when I did blow it, big time, the stick was in my own hand, not God's. I beat myself up so bad I figured the only way to stop the pain was to keep it all drowned in gin or vodka." Bennett looked at Earl's thick hands wrapped around the coffee mug on the table in front of him. "But there are other ways to do it. Work, for instance."

That got no response, so Bennett kept talking. "When I hit bottom, literally in the gutter, God didn't leave me there. He sent a big gruff giant of a man to pick me up and drag me into a place where I could get help. Somehow I was smart enough to recognize that I needed it. That man was a reverend, too, but he didn't preach about condemnation. He just talked about a God who cares."

Bennett took a swallow of his coffee. "I didn't believe it at first, but one day I was helping out in the kitchen at the mission when a little girl walked in. She was a teenager who came with her mom now and then to help out. We all lined up and got ready to serve the guys shuffling in. The first one to reach me was a guy I'd seen there a lot. He reeked of booze and urine and who knows what else. His hands shook so hard he could hardly hold the tray. He managed to get to one of the tables, but when he tried to eat his soup he spilled it all down the front of him. That's when that little teenager did something I'll never forget. She took a cloth, went over to that old guy, and gently cleaned him off. Then she refilled his bowl and sat there, feeding him the soup, spoonful by spoonful. I hadn't cried since I was a kid, but I cried that day. Cried like a baby. Something inside me broke as I watched that young girl and I knew, absolutely, in that moment, that's who God really is."

Earl stared at his cup for a moment, then looked up at Bennett. "Or is that just who you want him to be?"

Bennett nodded. "Yes. I want him to be like that, and so does every other human being on the face of this planet. We all long for that kind of love and compassion. Ever wonder why? Why do we need it? Why can't we just keep going like real men?"

Earl said nothing, so Bennett answered his own question. "I think it's because real men were created to be like that, too, and when we aren't we just beat ourselves up instead of turning to the only one who can help change us from the inside out. The only one is Jesus, Earl. I know, because I've seen his face in the face of a little teenager who kept on smiling while she fed an old bum a bowl of soup."

"You're getting pretty close to preachin'," Earl said, taking a last gulp of coffee and standing up. "But I appreciate the effort." He stuck out his hand and Bennett shook it. "Maybe you should stick around and tell that story to the Reverend Castor."

"We all need to get to know the real Jesus, Earl."

"Yeah, I guess we do," Earl agreed. "I just haven't seen that kind of Jesus around here much."

"Maybe that's about to change," Bennett said.

Earl shrugged. "Maybe so." He looked at Edna. "Maybe so." He then nodded to Bennett and walked away.

In a few moments, they heard the *whack, whack, whack* of the axe splitting wood.

CHAPTER SIXTEEN

A FULL MOON SPILLED PALE LIGHT INTO THE ROOM. EDNA LISTENED TO EARL'S light snoring and rolled onto her side. A soft summer breeze moved the curtain in and out, in and out. She watched it for a long time, then slowly pushed the blanket down and sat up.

Her bare feet made no sound on the wooden floor as she pushed the door to Andrea's room open and slipped inside. The diary still lay on top of the dresser. She held it in her hands and stared out the window, not seeing the moonlit yard or the slow sway of trees. She sat down on Andrea's bed and opened the book to an early entry. Andrea would have just turned eight years old when she wrote it.

Dad brought a horse home today. My very own horse! I was really surprised. He's never given me anything before. Edna is usually the one who gives the birthday presents and they're usually things I don't have any interest in. Every time she gives me something, it reminds me that she doesn't really know me. But then I guess that's to be expected since she isn't really my mother. But I guess she means well. She tries.

I'm going to call him Peso. I don't know why, I just like the sound of that word. He seems to like it, too. Dad says he was trained as a cutting horse, so he'll be really responsive and so much fun to ride. It's like a dream come true to have my own horse at last. I hope I don't disappoint Dad again. I'll make sure I take care of Peso really well.

My friend Lindsay asked me over to her house for a sleepover last week, with a couple of other kids from school. It was fun until they started to watch a video called Annie. I started crying and just couldn't stop. They all stared at me like I was some kind of freak. I don't know why I cried so much. I guess cause I could relate to how Annie felt, being an orphan. But at least I don't have to live in an orphanage. I know I should be more thankful but sometimes I just get so sad and I don't know why.

Edna closed the diary and sighed. She had failed in so many ways. If only she could go back in time and change everything. But there was no way to do that; there was only the regret. She wondered again if Andrea had read her diary and how she would feel about it. It would shock her. Would she understand? Would she condemn her as Edna knew everyone else would?

She stood up and returned the black book to the top of the dresser. It had become a habit over the past few days to come to Andrea's room, quietly at night, and read a bit more of her diary. It had become almost like a penance. She wondered if God would add it to some kind of ledger in heaven, slowly subtracting the black marks. She wondered when her pain would be enough for him.

That man, Bennett, had said God wasn't like that. But she agreed with Earl. They hadn't seen any other kind of God around here. She shuddered. God help her, she had been relieved at first that Andrea hadn't come home. She didn't think she could face their neighbours, let alone the people at church. She couldn't think of a single person who might understand and have compassion. They would all judge and condemn Andrea, or perhaps shun the whole family. Some would even gloat as they did it.

She shuddered again. They would have condemned her, too, if they'd known her secret. She had thought about leaving this place so many times, leaving Earl and the farm behind and starting again. But she couldn't see a future for herself anywhere else.

She did love Earl—as much as she could love anyone, she supposed. The truth of that had dawned on her one night as she watched him help an old cow birth its calf. He talked softly to it for hours, stroking its neck as the animal struggled to give birth. It had taken a lot of pulling to get that calf out and she thought they'd lose them both before the night was over, but both animals lived and she and Earl had smiled at one another as the baby teetered on its legs and began to suckle.

In that moment, she had dared to think Earl did love her, just a little, and she was aware of the deep, warm love she had for him. It had been slow to grow, but it was real, a love that came from living every day with a man who was kind and gentle, for all his faults. She couldn't hurt him again, especially after what she had already put him through.

And now Andrea... Tears began to flow down her cheeks. She just wanted her here, where she could see her face and touch her hand. She wanted her daughter back.

Ask and you shall receive. She remembered those words from Sunday school when she was a child. It had been close to Christmas and she'd asked for a doll with eyes that opened and closed. There was no doll under the tree that year, but... Edna pulled her shoulders up and took a deep breath. This was so much more important than a child's request for a toy.

"Please," she whispered. "Please bring her back to us. Give us another chance."

* * *

Stuffing a pillow behind her back, Andrea pulled the cover over herself and reached for Edna's diary.

Earl has decided we should go to church again. I'm not sure why. Maybe he thinks we need to do some kind of penance. I didn't want to go, but I was afraid to refuse. Once I was there, it was hard not to cry. But I managed it. I'm getting good at keeping things inside, turning my heart to stone. The service was long and the sermon was all about judgement. I wondered if Earl knew that it would be before we went. Maybe he's trying to punish me.
He doesn't look at me very much anymore. But sometimes I catch him watching me. Then he looks away as though he wasn't. I sense such sadness in

him that it's almost unbearable. I watched him cutting wood the other day and was suddenly afraid. He did it with such violence, such rage on his face. But when he came inside for coffee, he moved like a very old man, sat down, and said nothing to me. I don't know how to make it better. I don't know what to do to make up for what I've done.

Maybe he'll be content if I just keep on doing what's expected. Cook and clean and help with the animals when he needs me. I can do that. At least I can do that.

I haven't been out to the slough for some time. I hoped it would bring me comfort, but it only makes me feel more sad, more guilty. I put a stone on the place the other day, as a kind of marker. It will never have a cross or headstone as it should, but at least there's something to mark it.

Some days I just wish I could lie down and die, lie down and fade into the land. But I have to go on somehow.

Spring is here and that has helped a bit. The fields are ploughed and ready for the new crop. Earl has started the seeding, but the machinery has been breaking down a lot. I'll put the garden in soon. All my seeds arrived this week. I love the feel of the rich earth between my fingers.

This is good land, land that has kept giving back year after year. I'm a bit afraid this year may be different. I'm afraid that what we've done, what I've done, will put a curse on it. Maybe that's why the equipment keeps breaking down. I know it's superstitious, but I can't help being afraid.

Andrea closed the book. She peered into the darkness and wondered if Edna would ever talk to her about all of this, if she would tell her what really happened so long ago. She wondered what it all had to do with her. Maybe she was some kind of penance, too. Maybe she was their way of trying to get rid of their sin.

Andrea rolled over onto her side. Well, she'd never know. She'd never see her foster parents again. She let out a load groan. Why had God put her in their family? What had she done to deserve it? Why couldn't she have been born into a normal family that lived happily ever after?

She thought about some of her friends at school whose families seemed so normal. But then, they had their problems, too. She heard that two of the girls she'd known had gone to college in the city and gotten into drugs. At least one of them had also gotten pregnant. So being born into a "normal" family didn't guarantee anything. Or maybe they just weren't as "normal" as they looked.

She did know some families she wouldn't have wanted to be born into. Maybe she should just be thankful. "Count your blessings," her Sunday School teacher had always said.

Andrea sighed and closed her eyes.

Blessings is a relative word, she thought.

* * *

Benny rested his ear against Andrea's door for some time, listening. He wanted to open it and watch her sleep. Her and Benny's baby. But Evie didn't like it when he opened doors without asking, so he just listened for a while and thought about his baby. The memories of his other baby were coming back now, and he liked that, except when he remembered the bad thing.

He stepped away from the door. No. He wouldn't remember the bad thing.

* * *

Alex leaned toward Kenni as the plane banked and then levelled off for landing. The city wasn't a big one by any standard, but it was big enough for a young girl to get lost in, big enough for her to make some bad choices in, big enough to stay missing in. He sighed. Where would they even begin?

Kenni turned toward him and put a hand on his arm. He looked into her blue eyes and felt the stirring of hope again. And again, he thanked God for his wife, the wife he didn't deserve, his most precious proof of God's mercy and grace. He put his hand over hers and smiled.

They headed to the bus depot before even finding a hotel. No one there recognized Andrea's photo. Not surprising. Alex noticed that none of the bored ticket attendants even looked at the people they were selling tickets to, let alone took notice of those getting off the buses.

They found a decent hotel easily and settled in. Stan laid out a plan at dinner that evening. First, they'd contact the police and ask them to distribute the photo.

"I know a couple of guys here," Stan said. "We should be able to get them to help."

"What else?" Alex asked.

"Andrea is pregnant. That means she'll need a doctor. We won't get any information from them because of the patient/doctor privilege, but we might be able to post her photo in the offices. Walk-in clinics would be a good place to start."

"So we need to print a slew of copies of her photo," Kenni said. "And a contact number. I can make up a poster tonight."

"Good." Stan leaned back. "We might want to… uh…" His eyed flashed to Alex, then Kenni and back again. "…to contact the abortion clinics as well."

Alex nodded. "I don't like to think she'd consider that, but—"

"But she's a scared young woman without any support that we know of. It would be a logical choice, in my mind."

"Maybe," Kenni said. "She'd probably think about it, but she'd be so far along now, I don't think they'd do it."

"Let's pray not," Alex said.

* * *

They spent that first day covering different areas of the city, leaving the poster everywhere they could think of. The police hadn't been much help, but they agreed to distribute the photo and have all their men keep an eye open for her. Since she was over eighteen, even if they found her there was nothing they could do to make her contact them or her parents.

The next day was Sunday, so they decided to cover the malls on the south side of the city. They gulped down the free continental breakfast the hotel offered and headed out.

Alex was just about to flag down a taxi when he spotted the church. It was gothic in style and reminded him of the church where he had first come to understand who Jesus was. He just stood and stared at it for a while, until Kenni touched his arm.

He turned to her and pointed his chin at the old stone building. "I wonder what time their service is."

Kenni took his hand. "Let's go find out."

From the moment Alex stepped into the church, he felt something pulling at him. Half of him wanted to run back out the front door. The other half wanted to run into the sanctuary. He'd told his counsellor about that feeling once, confessing that he sometimes wondered if he was schizophrenic. The counsellor had smiled and said, "No, it's the dichotomy we all live with—our sin nature and the Spirit of God in us."

Alex turned toward the sanctuary. He knew it was his choice, and he knew which choice he wanted to make.

Someone was playing a guitar softly. Alex recognized the tune, but couldn't bring the words to mind. He and Kenni were greeted by a middle-aged couple who shook their hands and welcomed them. The woman handed Kenni a brochure about the church and told her that if they had any questions they could just ask anyone.

The church was old but had been remodelled recently. The carpet was new and the pews had been refinished and polished to a golden hue. Where once there probably had been a large altar, there was an array of musical instruments and a clear plastic pulpit to one side. The stained-glass windows spoke of days long ago, but everything else about the church told them it was keeping step with the twenty-first century.

Alex watched the people as they filed in and sat down. Some were dressed in their Sunday best—he smiled at a large lady wearing a broad brimmed hat—but many just wore jeans. More than a few were obviously street people. He relaxed as five young people joined the guitarist at the front and the entire group stood to their feet to worship.

By the time Alex sat down again, he was feeling better than he had in months. He didn't bother to wonder why. He just enjoyed the feeling. A woman with a clipboard stood at the podium and gave the announcements. She had them all laughing by the end of it, but then she got a bit more serious.

"You all know I have Scottish roots," she said. Alex watched the heads nod. "One of my favourite Scottish legends has to do with something they call thin spots." She gazed across the congregation. "They say that when you enter a thin spot, you sense you are close to heaven. I sincerely hope you all feel that you've been in a thin spot by the end of the service."

Alex smiled. At that moment, he knew without a doubt that he was in one. The music started again and by the end of the last chorus, Alex was close to tears. He barely managed to control himself.

Then the pastor took the podium. "I'm going to talk about letting go this morning," he said, "because all of us try to hold on to things we think are essential, essential to live. And they are—essential to our pride, our dignity, our sense of worth. But they are counterfeit essentials, empty essentials. They keep us from the abundant life God intends us to live, by being wholly connected to him." The pastor opened his Bible. "If you have a Bible with you, turn with me to the book of Matthew, chapter fourteen. If you don't have a Bible, there might be one in the pew rack in front of you. We'll begin at verse twenty-two."

Alex opened the Bible from the rack and leaned toward Kenni so they could both follow the text.

The pastor read the words slowly, his voice booming through the room. Then he looked up and scanned the congregation. "I think the disciples were holding on to some essentials. I think they were holding on to the safety of a boat in a storm, the safety of something solid under them. They were holding on to their own concept of reality.

"But Peter…" He chuckled. "Oh, how I love Peter! Peter jumped out of the boat when Jesus told him to come to him, but then he looked down at those wild waves and he started to sink. Peter was holding on to things, too, things that got in the way of his faith."

The man's eyes roamed the room again, and then they came to rest on Alex. At least, it seemed as though the man was looking right at him.

"What are you holding on to? What essentials are you afraid to let go of?"

Alex's mouth went dry. He'd been holding on to a few counterfeit things, like his pride, his need to get the job done on his own, to somehow put his family back together. Suddenly he recognized all of these things for what they were—sin. Tears started to flow down his cheeks. This time he didn't try to stop them.

After the service, they found a café not far away and talked for two hours. Alex apologized for being so closed and refusing to let Kenni in.

"I've been running after an imaginary world," he said, "one that would make everything seem normal and right. I guess I thought if I could just find Andrea, I'd finally have a family. I'm still holding on to that fairy tale, like a kid, afraid to totally trust God to get me through what's real." He looked up. "And I've pushed you away, Kenni. But I'm going to try hard to change that."

Kenni admitted there were things she'd been hanging on to, too. "I guess we all have to keep short accounts, every day."

Alex nodded. "Yeah. It's too easy to slip back into old patterns."

Kenni reached across the table and took his hand. "Welcome back," she said, then leaned back. "Well, shall we hit the malls?"

Alex nodded and patted his satchel. "These posters won't do any good in the bag."

* * *

They were almost finished covering the area they'd marked when Alex's phone rang. He answered, listened, made only a short comment, then flipped his cell phone closed, the frown on his face deepening.

Kenni noticed. "What is it, Alex? What's wrong?

He sighed and shoved the phone into his pocket. "That was Bennett. Cory Jacobs called him. He wants to talk to Andrea." Kenni's silence spoke volumes. "We could just ignore him."

She shook her head. "No. We can't."

Alex sighed. Just what they needed: another complication.

CHAPTER SEVENTEEN

ANDREA STARED AT THE PHONE. THERE WAS NO ONE IN THE RESTAURANT, SO it would be a good time to call. Earl, her dad, would be out in the barn working on some piece of machinery or tending to the animals. Edna, her mother, would be in the kitchen. She imagined her peeling the potatoes, scrubbing the carrots, or staring out the kitchen window as she so often did with an unsearchable expression on her face.

The phone felt cold in her hand. What would she say? "I'm sorry" would probably be a good place to start. She put the phone down, then picked it up again. She took a deep breath and dialled.

Did she just imagine the hopeful note in her mother's voice when she answered? For a moment, Andrea couldn't talk. Then the one word came out.

"Mom?"

She heard the gasp and what sounded like a sob.

"Andrea? Oh God, Andrea, is it you?"

"Yes, it's me. I'm so sorry I left without saying anything, Mom, but I just… I just had to get away. I'm sorry."

"It's okay. It's okay. Are you all right?"

"Yes, I'm fine."

"Where are you? When are you coming home?"

"I'm in Regina." Andrea hesitated. "I'm not coming home, Mom. At least, not right now. I'm working and I've made some friends here." She tried to swallow the lump in her throat.

"Please, come home, Andrea. We'll take care of you. If you want to have the baby, we'll figure it out. Please, just come home."

"I'm sorry, Mom. I'm sorry." Andrea had managed to hold on, but now the tears flowed. "I can't."

She was about to hang up when her mother almost shouted. "But Andrea, wait. There's something we have to tell you. I don't want to tell you over the phone. Please. If you won't come home, tell me where you are and I'll come to you. Please, Andrea. I have to see you. Please…" Her voice broke.

Andrea hesitated, but the anguish in Edna's voice touched her. She gave her the address and phone number and agreed to meet the next morning at the diner. She hung up and sank into a chair.

Half of her wished she hadn't told her mother where she was. The other half couldn't wait to see her. The tone of Edna's voice seemed to cling to her. She'd never heard Edna sound so… what? Vulnerable. Yes, that was the word.

She dragged herself up the stairs, fell onto her bed, and was instantly asleep.

* * *

Even though she knew it was still half an hour until Edna would arrive, Andrea kept watching the door. Evie was busy with customers, but every now and then Andrea would catch her eye. It helped just to see her smile and give a nod. She ran her hand across her swollen abdomen. The pregnancy was more obvious now. Sometimes customers commented on it, asking about the due date and if she knew whether it was a boy or girl. Some even reached out to touch her belly, but she always drew back. They were all friendly and smiling when they asked, but sometimes Andrea could see a look in their eyes that told her they didn't really approve. She knew what they were thinking. She was too young and there was no wedding band on her finger.

But she wouldn't think about all of that right now. She needed to be in control when Edna came. She couldn't show any sign of weakness or Edna might talk her into going home. Home. The word made tears form in the corners of Andrea's eyes.

No. She shook her head and wiped them away with a jerk of her hand. *None of that.*

When the clock showed it was past the agreed upon time, Andrea thought maybe Edna wouldn't come. Maybe Earl wouldn't let her. Maybe... but then suddenly she was there, hurrying toward her with her arms open. Andrea burst into tears and leaped into her mother's arms.

They both wept and held one another for some time, until Edna finally pulled away and they sat down.

"How are you?" Edna asked. "Have you seen a doctor? Is everything okay?"

Andrea nodded. "Yes. I just had an ultrasound last week and everything's fine."

Edna hadn't let go of her hand. Andrea started to stand up again.

"I'll get you a cup of coffee. Do you want anything to eat? We have some great muffins."

"No," Edna replied. "Coffee is fine."

Andrea turned toward the counter, but saw Evie already coming toward them with two mugs and the coffee pot.

Andrea introduced them. Edna ducked her head and said hello, but nothing more. Evie poured the coffee, gave Andrea an encouraging smile, and went back to the counter. Andrea noticed she was watching them. Benny was close by, too, hovering somewhere behind them.

They both sipped the coffee for a few minutes. Then Edna reached over and took her daughter's hand again.

"I'm so sorry, Andrea. I realize now we didn't handle this very well. Please, think about coming home. I, that is your dad and I, we both want you to come home."

Andrea shook her head. "I think it would be better... I just need to stay away, for a while at least. I can't go back like this." She looked down. "And I can't believe Dad would want me to."

Edna sat back and stared at her hands. "Earl... he does care about you, Andrea. I know he has a hard time showing it, but he does care."

"I think he cares more about what everyone will say."

Edna sighed and shook her head, but said nothing.

"Where are you living?" Edna finally asked.

"Here. Upstairs. I have a small room. It's comfortable and Evie has been really good to me."

"Have you decided what you'll do? When you, I mean, when the baby comes?"

Andrea dropped her eyes. "Not yet. But I've been going to a pregnancy care centre. They've been helping, helping me decide things."

"That's good. That's good."

They were both quiet for a time. Edna took another swallow of coffee. "If I can do anything to help…"

"Thanks, but…" She shrugged. "I'm doing okay now." Andrea glanced at Evie, then asked, "What was it you wanted to tell me?"

Edna opened her mouth, but closed it again. "Nothing. Nothing. I just wanted to see you."

Andrea frowned. "But you said—"

"I didn't want you to hang up," Edna lied, "without giving me your address."

Andrea knew her mother was keeping something from her, but she didn't know how to make her say it. The old frustration boiled inside her. She considered asking about the diary, about the baby born long ago, but she knew Edna would just withdraw into silence again, as she always did.

"Well, now you've seen me." She started to slide out of the booth. "I have to go."

Edna grabbed her arm. "Wait. There is something…" Her eyes darted to the corner, then back to the table. "That young Jacobs boy came to the house the other day."

Andrea let her breath out slowly. "Cory? What did he want?"

"He said he needed to talk to you. He wanted me to ask you to call him." She leaned forward. "Andrea, if you love him, don't throw that away."

Andrea stared at her. What a strange thing for her to say. Love him? She didn't even know what that word meant. "I don't want to see him, or talk to him." Her eyes narrowed. "You can tell him so, if he comes back." She stood up and waited for Edna to slide out of the booth.

Her mother's hand reached out to touch her arm, but then dropped to her side. "Can I call you? Would that be okay?"

Andrea didn't look at her but gave a quick nod. "Okay."

As she watched her foster mother leave, the tight knot growing in her stomach began to let go, leaving only a deep sadness that made the tears pour out.

Evie was at her side then, so she wiped her face and tried to smile.

"Well, I guess that went as well as I expected." Andrea tried to make her voice light, but it sounded morose.

Evie put her arm around her. "Why don't you go get some rest now?"

Andrea nodded. Yes. Sleep would be welcome. She climbed the stairs slowly, conscious of the heaviness of each step. And with each step she longed for everything to be as it had been, longed for the strange familiarity of home. But she knew it would never be the same, even if she did go home. The baby had changed everything.

Get rid of it. The words echoed over and over in her mind. *Get rid of it. That will solve everything.*

Maybe that was the better plan, after all.

* * *

Benny slipped back into the kitchen, frowning.

Benny is very good at listening, he thought. *Very good. Now Benny knows Andrea and the baby want to stay here with him. Forever. Benny likes that word. Forever.*

He finished wiping out his dishpan and put his apron in the laundry hamper where Evie had told him to put it when his shift was over. He headed for the stairs to go to his room, then changed his mind and went down to Evie's workshop.

The tumbler was whirring away. He watched it for a while, then went to the back of the room. He looked over his shoulder, then pushed open the small door he had discovered some time ago. It opened to reveal another stairway that went even further down before jogging to the right and opening into a short corridor. There were three rooms off the hall and another big door at the end.

Benny had been exploring down here for weeks. Two of the rooms were empty and the other contained a long table and a few chairs. But Benny's favourite was the room at the end with the big steel door and a humming furnace inside that felt warm when he touched it. He lifted a heavy metal latch and pushed the door open. He had dragged an old chair in here and put some pictures from magazines on the walls. He liked to just sit and look at them and listen to the hum. This was a special place. A special secret place. It was fun to have secrets.

He pulled an apple out of the pocket of his big green jacket and took a large, satisfying bite. Then he pulled a piece of paper out of the same pocket. He grinned. The Princess. He had found her picture on a telephone pole. He put a piece of tape on each corner and pressed them carefully onto the wall.

He sat in the chair and smiled at the large pillow and pile of blankets on the floor. Then he picked up one of the books he had left here. It was all about ants. Andrea had been impressed when he told her some things about them before. He would learn more things to tell her.

* * *

Alex was on a street corner stapling another poster to a pole when he got the call. Edna told him that Andrea had called and she was alright but wouldn't say where she was. Alex formed a curse in his mind but kept it from reaching his lips.

"Did you tell her? About me?" Alex asked.

There was silence for a while, then Edna's soft voice said, "No. I didn't think it was the time, Alex. She's pregnant and has enough stress in her life right now. I didn't think it would be a good idea to add any more."

Alex almost cursed out loud. "But I need to see her, to talk to her. Did she leave a phone number, anything?"

"I'm sorry, Alex, but I think it would be best if you just left us all alone right now. I have your number and I'll be in touch with you when I think Andrea is strong enough for this news."

"Strong enough? Is she sick? What aren't you telling me, Edna?"

"No, she's not sick. She's fine, but as I said, she doesn't need more stress and frankly neither do I. Please, just leave us alone."

The phone went dead. Alex stared at it for a moment, then slammed it back into his pocket. He ripped the poster off the pole and headed for the hotel.

Kenni was as stunned as he had been. She sank down onto the bed.

"But doesn't she realize how important this is to you, to us?"

Alex ran his hand through his hair. "Apparently not." He sighed. "But at least we know Andrea is okay."

"What are you going to do?"

Alex paced. "There's not much more we can do here." He threw up his hands and let out a growl of frustration.

Kenni stood up and embraced him. "I'm sorry, Alex. I wish there was something…"

Alex hugged her tight. "I know. Me, too." He pulled away, letting out a sigh. "Maybe this is part of having to let go. Maybe God just wants me to walk away.

I guess we'd better let Stan and Bennett know what's happening. No point in wasting any more time pounding the streets."

He slumped into a chair and dialled Stan's cell. They agreed to meet back at the café.

* * *

Edna stared at the phone in her hand. Her heart raced and she realized she was perspiring. Was she doing the right thing? She took a deep breath and tried to calm herself. She should tell Andrea. She had a right to know about her brother, but would it drive her even further away?

Edna needed her to come home. How could she live without her daughter? What joy would there be in life without her?

She gripped the phone and bent over, a low moan escaping her lips as she bobbed back and forth. She couldn't risk losing her forever. She would do anything to prevent that.

* * *

Alex tried to get in touch with Bennett, but he had already left for the city. Alex, Kenni, and Stan had just taken a booth in the café when he arrived.

"So, you're just going to quit?" Stan's voice was pitched with annoyance.

Alex frowned. "No. But I think maybe we should slow down a bit."

"I thought you were determined to find her, no matter what."

"I am." Alex glared at him. "But I'm trying to think about what's best for Andrea, not just me. Maybe her mother's right. Maybe this isn't the right time. She's dealing with a lot of stress right now. Maybe we should wait, for her sake. Just pull back for a while."

Stan shrugged. "She's over the age of eighteen. She doesn't need her mother's permission to see you."

Alex wrapped his hand around the coffee cup. The sounds in the restaurant were suddenly loud and distracting. He shook his head and turned away. "I don't know…"

Stan stood up and tossed a toonie on the table for his coffee. "Suit yourself. Book my flight to leave as soon as possible." He walked away without another word.

Kenni put her hand on Alex's arm. He sighed and leaned back into the booth.

"Are you sure you want to let it go, Alex?" Bennett's voice was calm and low.

"No, I'm not sure. I still feel an urgency to find her, but I don't even know her. Edna's her mother. If she thinks Andrea's on the edge, I don't want to be the one to push her over it."

Bennett nodded. "Then why don't we all sleep on it and pray?" He glanced in the direction Stan had gone. "Those of us who are so inclined. We can meet for breakfast and make the final decision tomorrow. How does that sound?"

Alex nodded. "Yeah, okay."

Bennett stood. "I think I'm going to get a little rest and maybe head over to a steakhouse I noticed yesterday. It's only a couple of blocks from here. Then I thought I'd do a prayer walk after dinner. Want to join me?"

Alex frowned. "What do you mean by a prayer walk?"

"We walk the neighbourhood and pray. Simple."

Alex shrugged.

"Sounds like a good idea to me," Kenni said.

"Good. I'll call your room when I'm ready to leave, about six o'clock."

CHAPTER
EIGHTEEN

EDNA HELD THE BOOK IN HER HANDS AND LET THE LAST OF THE EVENING sun's warmth sink into her, giving her the courage to open it. She knew the words would wound her again, but she knew she had to read them.

> *I wish I had known my real mother. I wonder so often why she gave me away. Was she sick? Did she die? Was she a drug addict or something? Edna won't tell me anything. Any time I try to ask, she changes the subject right away. She doesn't understand that I need to know. Even knowing a little bit would help.*
> *For so long I've lived as Andrea Calvert, but I'm not even legally adopted. I should have some other last name, but I don't even know what it is. It's like having amnesia or something, like half of who I am is missing.*

We had to do this project in school one time, to draw your family tree and discover your heritage. All the kids in the class did it but me. I pretended to be sick the day we were supposed to present the project. The teacher never asked me about it. Guess she figured it would embarrass everyone if she did. That's what I've been to my foster parents most of the time—an embarrassment. I guess that's why they never adopted me, never made it official. I'm a disappointment. I don't really belong to them. They would probably be happy if I just left so they could go on with their lives without me.

It seems like there's always something they're not telling me. I feel it sometimes when I see them watching me, or when I ask too many questions and they get all quiet. I understand why they wouldn't want to tell me things when I was young, but I'm seventeen now and I have a right to know whatever it is they won't tell me.

I wish there was some way to pry it out of them, but the more I try the more they close up. Sometimes Dad doesn't talk for days. I thought that was normal for a while, till I saw how other people live. I know there's no such thing as normal, but my foster parents are definitely weird.

Edna let the book slide from her hands and wiped the tears away. Andrea was right. They were "weird." Dysfunctional was a word she had read about, and she knew it applied to them. She should have known they couldn't hide the awkwardness between them from their daughter, should have known it would seep out into their lives like a poisonous gas.

She surveyed Andrea's room, noting the small details that spoke of her daughter's personality, her dreams and goals. There was a 4H ribbon she'd won for horse care when she was only eight, still pinned to a bulletin board along with a picture of her first horse. A print of ballerinas was tacked to the wall above her bed. Andrea knew the name of the artist, but Edna couldn't remember it. Andrea had told her one day, just after she'd turned ten, that she wanted to be a ballerina. The trick rider dream had faded, probably because of her failure to be able to handle Peso to Earl's satisfaction. Edna hadn't been able to understand where this new idea had come from. She'd humoured her for a while, even gave her a little ballerina Christmas decoration that year; it dangled from one of the pushpins holding up the poster. But the only dance studio was a two-hour drive away and Edna knew Reverend Castor wouldn't have approved of dance lessons anyway. Edna had always been so desperate to gain the approval of that man. She sighed. Now she wondered why. Slowly, Andrea's dream had faded away. She hadn't mentioned it in years. Swimming had seemed to take its place eventually, but the poster was still there and so were the slippers.

Then there was Andrea's refusal to play piano at church. She was good enough and they needed a standby pianist, but she had refused, refused to even talk about it. That was a disappointment. Reverend Castor would have been pleased had she been able to talk Andrea into it. She supposed she had let that disappointment show. Maybe she had let it show in other things, too. But surely Andrea knew they loved her. Surely…

She stood up and looked out the window. Earl was working on one of the tractors near the barn. She watched his slow deliberate movements, saw him stop, wipe his hands on his pant legs, then stare off across the fields. She wondered if he was thinking about Andrea. She knew he loved her as much as she did, that he had just as much trouble showing it. She also knew why. Sometimes she had tried to provoke him into showing some affection, if only a little, for the child they had brought into their home.

Now and then, she could see a kind of delight in his eyes when he watched her, but he rarely spoke about it, rarely touched Andrea, even when she had been a baby. Edna wanted to tell him not to take it out on the girl, that the pain between them was her fault, not Andrea's. But Earl remained aloof. Prickly, as her mother used to say. She'd warned her, but she never did say "I told you so." That was one of the ways her mother had shown her love—by not doing, not saying. Maybe that was Earl's way, too. And her own. Maybe that just wasn't enough for Andrea. Maybe it wasn't enough for her anymore either.

She put the book on the top of Andrea's dresser and went downstairs. Earl would be coming in for supper soon. She'd make apple pie for dessert. He liked apple pie.

* * *

The drizzle that seeped past his collar and down his neck didn't improve Alex's mood as they walked the few blocks toward the steakhouse, but the smell of food when they stepped into the restaurant almost made him salivate. The meal lived up to the smell, and by the end of it Alex was close to smiling again. Then they headed back out into the rain and started to walk.

Praying was something he'd gotten used to doing, but he'd never done it this way before. He'd been concentrating on praying for Andrea, but Bennett, and then Kenni, started praying for the city and its people in a way that made Alex realize the world was a bigger place and God had bigger plans than just his small puddle of experience. Soon he was praying with them over the businesses, the shops, the houses, and the schools and playgrounds. They prayed for the street people they saw and they prayed for Andrea.

It seemed like they had walked for hours. The rain increased as the night wore on, so they huddled under Kenni's umbrella for the last few blocks, but no one rushed their prayers.

Alex noticed a series of small beauties as they headed back to the hotel—the reflection of yellow neon in a puddle, the rim of silver in the droplets that slipped off the tips of the umbrella, the quiet laughter of a woman nestled into a man's arms as they passed. He realized he was reluctant to stop. It felt like Jesus had been walking with them, showing them that even in the middle of the turmoil they were in, there were these small things, these atoms of grace, orbits of hope they could cling to.

They agreed to end the night with a cup of hot tea and muffins at the hotel's coffee shop. Stan was sitting by himself in a corner booth. He snapped his phone shut when he saw them approach.

"I was just going to call you," he said, looking at Alex with as sheepish a look as Stan could probably manage. "Guess I was kinda out of line earlier. If you want to call it all off, it's your decision."

Bennett sat down beside him, forcing him to move over. "You're still trying to uphold your rep as an ornery old cuss, aren't you, Stan?"

"It's got me this far."

Bennett chuckled. "My point exactly."

Stan frowned but didn't reply.

"We've decided to sleep on it, Stan," Alex explained, "and, uh, pray about it some more. I'll decide what to do in the morning."

Stan nodded. "Fair enough. If you still want to cancel, we can get an afternoon flight. If not, I have a couple of other ideas up my sleeve."

"Oh?" Bennett cocked his head.

"No point spillin' the idea until I know which way you're going to jump." He waved Bennett aside and stood up. "See you in the morning."

Alex stopped him. "I just want you to know I intend on paying the fee, in total, even though technically we didn't find my sister."

Stan gave a quick nod. "I appreciate that."

They all watched him go, unspoken words hanging in the air.

* * *

Earl hung a bundle of hay in the stall and made sure the door was latched. He'd been looking after Andrea's horse every day since she'd given up trying to ride him. At first he thought maybe it was just some way he could communicate that… what? That he still loved her in spite of everything? He wanted to tell her that, but the words wouldn't come out right. Words never came out right for him.

He leaned on the stall door and watched Peso munch. He remembered Andrea's face when she'd seen him that first morning. She'd leaped into his arms and he'd laughed. A rare thing for them both. He knew the horse would be too big for her, but he thought, with some work, she'd learn to handle him. The Paint had been trained as a cutting horse and Earl had thought maybe they could enter some competitions together. He'd been wrong on both counts. The horse didn't seem to take to her and her patience ran out. He smiled briefly. Andrea always was a little shy on patience.

Then she started getting into other things at school, like swimming, and riding took a back seat. It seemed they just didn't have much to say to one another once she got into her last years of high school. When she got that part-time job, it seemed he hardly ever saw her. He hadn't been very happy about that. She didn't need to work. Her needs were all taken care of, but she'd begged and he'd given in. Now he wished he hadn't. She'd probably met that Jacobs boy at the restaurant.

Earl felt his blood heat up. He'd thought about driving over there, confronting the boy and his father. But what good would that do, especially now? It might make him feel better to give the boy the thrashing he had in mind, but what good would it do Andrea? Too little, too late, as usual. He felt the rough wood of the stall under his palm and leaned into it. He'd failed her.

Peso nickered. Earl snorted. "You agree, do you?"

The horse raised its head at the sound of Earl's voice but kept munching on the hay. Earl sighed. The horse was getting old. He hadn't exactly been a youngster when he'd bought him, and time had marched on ever since. He flexed his right hand, wincing at the arthritis that had been plaguing him for a year or more. Peso wasn't the only one who was aging.

The day was coming when they'd have to think about moving off the farm, though he hoped to delay it as long as possible. They had no son to help with the work and it was already a heavy load for the two of them. Andrea had been a big help, but now she was gone. And Edna said she wasn't coming back.

Earl scratched Peso's nose. "Guess we can't blame her, hey, old boy? What's she got to come back to? Just a couple of old geezers who can't even tell her how much she means to them."

It's not too late.

The thought made Earl's spine jerk erect. It seemed to have come from someone else. But it was a good thought. Maybe it isn't too late. *But how? God, how?*

Pray.

That word made him whirl around and look for someone standing in the doorway. There was no one there. He turned back to the stall, made sure it was latched securely, and headed for the house. Pray. He hadn't done that in years. Ever since…

Don't go there, Earl. Just don't go there.

The house was quiet when he went in. He could see Edna, sitting with her back to him in her favourite living room chair. He walked forward quietly, almost feeling like he should go on tiptoes. Then he heard her mumbling to herself. Praying, he realized, as he walked around the chair and sat down on the sofa. He was baffled by her faith. How she could still cling to God was beyond him, but he envied her that hope.

She opened her eyes after a few moments, and in a flash he remembered the first time he'd seen her. It was her eyes that had caught his attention that day—sparkling blue as a field of cornflowers. He'd asked her to go out for coffee that same afternoon.

He smiled at her now as she started to get up.

"There's muffins in the oven," she said. "They'll be ready in a minute."

He stood, stepped toward her, and put his hand on her arm. "Edna, I…"

She looked puzzled. "What?"

His hand dropped. "Nothing. I was just thinking about when we first met."

Edna's eyes widened.

"I was attracted to you, you know, from the very first moment I saw you at the hardware store."

She smiled a little ruefully. "Because I was holding a hoe and a rake?"

"That may have helped." The grin flashed, then disappeared. His hand moved. He wanted to touch her, to feel the softness of her cheek. "But it was your eyes. I know things, things have come between us and I don't tell you, but I still…"

The look in her eyes pierced him to the core.

"Do you really, Earl?" Her voice was almost a whisper.

He dropped his hand and she turned away.

"My muffins are going to burn," she said.

136

CHAPTER NINETEEN

THE RESTAURANT HUMMED WITH PEOPLE ENJOYING THEIR BACON AND EGGS, pancakes and sausages. Alex's stomach rumbled as he and Kenni were led to a booth. Stan and Bennett joined them before the waitress had time to return with their coffee.

"So?" Stan asked as he slid into the booth.

"We've decided to head home," Alex said.

Stan gave a quick jerk of his head. "You're sure?"

"Yes. I'll book the flights for this afternoon."

"Too bad. I was just getting into the feel for the hunt."

"Well, hold that feeling, Stan. If Edna refuses to tell me where Andrea is after the baby's born, we'll be hunting again."

Bennett frowned. "You think she'd do that?"

Alex shrugged. "I don't know, but she and her husband both seem pretty determined not to let anyone know what's going on. Best way to do that is to just ignore it. And that would mean ignoring me."

"Well, I guess she's going to have a few months to think about it," Bennett replied.

Kenni nodded. "Let's pray the Lord softens her heart."

Bennett turned to Stan. "Just out of curiosity, what was your next move?"

"The pregnancy centres—you know, they're usually run by religious people. I figured since Andrea was raised that way, maybe she'd go there. It'd be a good idea to put some posters up, if they'd let us."

"A good thought," Bennett admitted.

The waitress returned to take their order as their talk turned to what might be next in their lives.

"How much longer you gonna stay out in the boonies, Bennett?" Stan asked.

Bennett shrugged. "I'm not sure. My boys really loved it at the farm, which shocked me, and they said they wanted to come back, so I'm thinking I might have them out again this summer. Then we'll see."

Stan nodded. "Well, if you think you might want to get back into the PI business, I might be looking for a partner."

Bennett's eyebrows went up for a moment, then he smiled. "As a matter of fact, I've been thinking and praying about that possibility." He looked at Alex and Kenni. "What about you two? What's the plan?"

Alex glanced at Kenni. "We'll go back to work, I guess. Kenni works in a small law office where they do a lot of pro bono. It's good work—needed, you know?"

"And you?" Bennett asked.

"I'll go back to the youth centre where I was volunteering."

Stan grunted. "I guess I'll go back to looking for somebody needing to catch a husband in the act of adultery, or some other such wholesome endeavour."

Alex grinned at Stan. "I'll keep you on retainer, just in case."

Stan nodded. "Sounds good to me."

* * *

Kenni twirled the wedding ring on her finger and chewed her lip. She'd known from the beginning that being married to Alex wasn't going to be easy, but some days she really wanted to whack him on the head with a frying pan. She grinned as she thought that. It might be the only way she'd ever get inside his head.

She sighed and started to pack. She was glad in a way that Alex had decided to go home. She felt guilty about being gone from the office so long. The research, the interviews that needed to be done—it all piled up so much, putting an extra load on everyone. They needed her.

But so did Alex. She folded a shirt, rolled it, and put it in the suitcase. She knew it wouldn't be long before he'd want to come back. He wouldn't give up on finding Andrea so easily. Maybe she could bring some work back with her then, but she knew that wouldn't be very effective. She could do research on the internet, but most of her work required her to be there. It was hands on, feet on the ground kind of stuff, as her dad would say. She imagined his wink as he said it, making her think about her parents and their relationship.

She knew they had their bad days, too, but generally they were open and honest with one another and shared everything, even if it caused some raised eyebrows or raised voices now and then. That they loved each other deeply was obvious in the small things—the glances, the grins, the quick touches that could so easily be missed by a casual observer. All those small things added up to a life lived in love. That was the kind of life she wanted with Alex, but she knew it was going to take time, work, and a lot of prayer.

And it wasn't all on Alex. She had her issues, too. When he shut down, she tended to do the same. Sometimes it seemed they were like two broken clocks ticking so intermittently that both were out of sync. They both needed to be reset.

But she was afraid to push, afraid to ask questions that would probe into the painful parts of his life. Fear wasn't supposed to be there.

But perfect love drives out fear…

The verse from 1 John sang in her mind. Perfect love. She knew there was only one source for that.

She closed her eyes. *Lord, do whatever it takes to bring us together. Help us to live in your love so that it pours through us, for each other and for others.*

She smiled and folded another of Alex's shirts. With the Lord in their lives, it would be okay. It might take time, but it would be okay. Patience and trust. Alex wasn't the only one who had to learn it.

* * *

Alex shifted in the narrow airline seat and tried to relax. Kenni watched him put his head back, but noticed the tension in his shoulders.

"You okay?" she asked.

Alex opened his eyes and sighed. "It's going to be a long few months."

"For what it's worth, I think it's the right decision. To go home, I mean."

Alex squeezed her hand. "It's worth a lot, Kenni, and I know we're supposed to go home, for whatever reason, but I can't shake this restless feeling. I think there might be something more we should be doing or… I don't know." He sighed again. "Something's just not right."

Kenni rested her head on his shoulder. "The Lord will show us."

Alex nodded again. "I just hope it doesn't take nine months."

"She's a few months pregnant now. It won't be more than four or five, at the most."

"Five months." Alex said it with a groan.

Kenni snuggled into him. "Lots of time to learn about patience and trust."

"Yeah. Patience and trust." He leaned his head to the side so his cheek rested on the top of her head. "This isn't going to be easy."

Kenni sighed. "I know," she said, more to herself than to her husband.

* * *

Back home, Alex scanned the information Stan had given him about his parents for the hundredth time, hoping to glean something more, something new. He couldn't shake the feeling that there was some essential piece of information missing. He folded the papers and stuffed them back into the envelope. He remembered Stan's suggestion that he try to obtain the medical records. And he remembered Kenni's thought, that it would be good to know his family's medical history if or when they decided to have kids.

Kids. Alex shook his head. He couldn't even consider that right now. But the medical history was probably a good idea. At the very least, it would give him something to do. He pulled a phone book out of a drawer in the kitchen and flipped to the section listing medical clinics.

* * *

Dr. Rossiter's office was located in a large building downtown. Alex told him why he was there.

"This is a bit unusual, Mr. Perrin," the doctor said. "Medical records are usually only requested if there's a question about a patient's medical condition. Do you have reason to suspect you have some kind of disease?"

"No, I just thought it would be a good idea to have some medical history. I just got married and…"

The doctor sat back and adjusted his glasses. "I understand. Can I see your identification please?"

Alex showed him his driver's licence. He had brought along his birth certificate as well, just in case. He also gave him his parents' health insurance numbers and birth certificates. The doctor examined the cards, then handed them back.

"I'll need copies of these. Have my receptionist do that before you leave. It will take a few days to have the records faxed to me."

Alex stood up and shook the man's hand. "Thank you."

He headed for the door, but the doctor stopped him. "When was the last time you had a medical examination yourself, Mr. Perrin?"

Alex frowned, remembering his stay in hospital just over a year earlier. "Uh, it's been a while."

"Perhaps you should make an appointment. My receptionist will be happy to do that for you."

Alex shrugged. "No need. I'm healthy."

"Are you sure?"

Alex hesitated, then put his hand on the doorknob. "Thanks for your help," he said, and left the office.

* * *

Bennett opened his Bible and read for half an hour. When he closed it again, he was smiling. It was good to get back into his own routine, back to the quiet after the noise and pace of the city. He closed his eyes and prayed for Kenni, Alex, and Stan and their search for Andrea, then stared out the window for some time.

The crops were coming along nicely. The farmers would have their hands full in another month, getting the first hay crop in. He looked forward to seeing his kids, glad they could come for part of the summer, glad they were excited about it. He could imagine what Edna and Earl had been going through—the longing to see their daughter, to be sure she was all right.

God, if I can help...

Visit.

Bennett smiled again. "Right," he said out loud, and headed for his truck.

* * *

Edna and Earl seemed surprised to see him but invited him to stay for lunch. Bennett noted that Edna didn't make eye contact, and after a bit of superficial conversation she suddenly blurted, "I'm not going to tell you where Andrea is. I already told her brother that she's got too much stress in her life right now and—"

Bennett held up his hand. "I understand, Edna. We don't intend to pressure you or Andrea into anything. In fact, Alex and Kenni have gone back to Vancouver."

"They have?"

"Yes. Alex wants what's best for her, too."

Edna's shoulders relaxed. "I don't want to keep them apart forever, but, I just feel this is for the best right now."

Bennett nodded. "I know." He watched as Earl finished his pie, downed the last of a huge mug of coffee, and nodded to his wife. "That was good."

She nodded back to him and took the plate away. Bennett stood up with Earl.

"Anything I can give you a hand with?" Bennett asked.

Earl hesitated, his hand on the doorknob. "Nothing I can't handle myself," he replied, "but if you want to get your hands dirty, suit yourself."

Bennett followed him out to the barn.

Earl pointed to a large bin. "You can scoop some of those oats into that small bucket, there," he said. He went over to a large stack of hay bales, pulled one down, and wrapped a net around it. He hefted it into the stall and hung it on a hook.

Bennett held the pail for the horse, who dove into the treat.

"He likes his oats," Bennett commented.

Earl nodded and stroked the horse's neck. "I've been spoiling him a little since Andrea left. He misses her."

"I imagine you do, too."

Earl took the pail from his hands and dumped the last of the oats into his hand. Bennett watched him as he let Peso nibble.

Earl's next words came out in a mumble. "Guess we should have expected it."

"Why is that?" Bennett asked.

"She wasn't our own. Guess she never felt like she was. Can't blame her for leaving."

"But it seems like you gave her a good home."

Earl shrugged. "Not good enough."

"Kids sometimes run away from the best of homes."

Earl pulled his hat off, wiped his brow with his sleeve, then put the hat back on. "I guess she was looking for something she didn't find here."

"Got any idea what?"

Earl turned away and latched the door to the stall. He mumbled something that sounded like the word love, but Bennett wasn't sure.

"What was that?" Bennett asked.

Earl turned and faced him. "You ever hear the old expression, there's an elephant in the room?"

Bennett nodded. "Sure."

"Well, we've had an elephant living in our house for over twenty years. I think it got in the way of a lot of things."

"Want to tell me about it?'

Earl lifted his chin and used it to point to the stack of bales. "You might want to take a seat. This could take a while."

Bennett listened without commenting until Earl was done. Both men were silent for a moment.

"Well?" Earl said. "Got any suggestions?"

"Just one," Bennett said. "Talk about it."

Earl snorted. "Easier said than done."

"I know, but there's no other way to get rid of the elephant than to point to it and say, 'I know it's there and I want to deal with it.' Until then it'll always be there and it will always be in the way of everything you try to do."

Earl nodded. "Maybe so. Maybe so."

CHAPTER TWENTY

Andrea stared at the boy she was serving. He was so much like Cory that it almost made her gasp. He tilted his head the same way, and when he looked at her, his eyes had that same glimmer of mocking that she hated and loved at the same time. His hoodie could have been Cory's. His blond hair stuck out the same way from under the same kind of ball cap.

"Well?" he said. "Do you have yam fries or not?"

Andrea dropped her eyes and said yes, finished taking his order, and walked away.

She couldn't get Cory out of her head for the rest of the day. She kept imagining his smile, remembering his voice. When she almost gave four plates of food to the wrong table, she told herself to get a grip. But it didn't help.

At the end of her shift, she trudged up the stairs and sat on the edge of her bed for a long time. She had talked herself out of thinking about Cory before, but it wasn't easy. He was the only boy who had ever shown any interest in her. Maybe he was the only one who ever would. But he'd left her, found someone else. And now he wanted to talk to her? She wrapped her arms around herself and groaned. Seeing him again would only make things worse.

She went into the washroom and turned on the shower. Letting the hot stream pour down, she turned her face up toward it and let the tears mingle with the water.

* * *

It was two weeks after his appointment with the doctor when Alex got a phone call.

"Can you come to our office this afternoon? I can squeeze you in at about two o'clock," the receptionist said. "You may have to wait a while, but Dr. Rossiter does want to see you as soon as possible."

"Can you tell me why?"

"No, sir. I'm afraid you'll have to wait to speak to the doctor."

Kenni insisted on going with him and he was glad she was there. It kept him from pacing but didn't keep him from continually picking up a magazine and putting it down again. It was almost the end of the afternoon before they called his name. The nurse ushered them into an office and waved her hand at two padded chairs facing a large desk.

"The doctor will be right in," she said.

Kenni reached over and took Alex's hand. It felt soft and warm and made him aware that his was ice cold. She squeezed it and he smiled at her.

With a light tap on the door, the doctor swooped in and sat down behind the desk. He opened a manila envelope, scanned the papers, and slipped them back inside.

"Do you know what haemophilia is, Mr. Perrin?"

"Haemophilia? That's what they call a bleeder, isn't it?"

The doctor nodded. "Yes, that's right. These records indicate that your mother was a carrier of the disease." He handed the envelope to Alex and adjusted his glasses. "I suggest you be tested immediately, though if you haven't shown any signs of it by now it's highly unlikely that you have it."

Alex's hand shook a bit as he opened the envelope and scanned the information. He couldn't make sense out of much of it. He frowned at the doctor. "How dangerous is it?"

"It's quite rare," the doctor explained. "The medications used to treat it have come a long way in the last couple of decades, but it isn't a condition to be ignored."

"My mother was a carrier? That means she didn't have the disease herself?"

"That's right. But it means that any of her male offspring would have a fifty percent chance of having it. As I said, it's unlikely you do—it's usually detected when a child is quite young. Any small bump can be dangerous. Assuming you had a normal childhood, any time you fell or had a small injury you would have bled profusely. I'm assuming that didn't happen?"

Alex glanced at Kenni. "No," he said, with an ironic tone in his voice. "I didn't exactly have a normal childhood, but I did have a number of injuries. And I didn't bleed to death."

"Again, I do suggest you get tested, just to be sure."

"So, how do I go about doing that?'

"You can have it done at any lab." He swivelled his chair to face a computer and began typing. "I'll print out the requisition. My receptionist will give you the information and make an appointment for you."

Alex nodded. "Okay." He and Kenni stood as the doctor handed him the form. Alex stared at it, then looked at the doctor again. "How dangerous would this be if… for my sister?"

"It's possible she may be a carrier as well. It can be potentially life-threatening for a woman during pregnancy, more so if there's any chance of a termination for some reason. But in a normal pregnancy, with proper care, everything would be fine."

Alex was aware of Kenni's hand on his arm. "A termination? You mean an abortion?"

"Yes, that's right. But as I said, with proper care in a normal pregnancy…" He frowned. "Is your sister pregnant?"

"Yes." Alex shifted his eyes. "But I don't know where she is." He looked up at the doctor's frowning face. "We were separated when we were kids. I've been trying to find her and… well, we sort of did but I haven't actually met her yet."

"I see. Well, if I were you, I wouldn't waste any time with that. This could be critical information for her to know."

Alex held out his hand. "Thank you, Doctor. I appreciate you getting me the information so quickly."

Dr. Rossiter shook his hand. "Glad to help. My receptionist will make the appointment for you at the lab."

* * *

Alex dialled Edna's number while Kenni drove. The phone rang several times before she finally picked up. She was quiet while Alex explained.

"It's important, Edna." Alex hoped she would hear the urgency in his voice. "This condition is serious and Andrea needs to see her doctor right away."

There was silence for a moment, and when Edna finally spoke, her voice sounded far away. But she agreed to tell Andrea as soon as possible.

"I'm on my way back to Regina as soon as I can get a flight." Alex's voice deepened. "And I want to see my sister."

The only reply was the buzzing of the disconnected phone.

* * *

Andrea wasn't sure she wanted to see her mother again, and she was sure she didn't want to face her father, but Edna had been so insistent. "There's something important we need to tell you, Andrea," she'd said.

Evie poured her a large glass of milk and manoeuvred herself up onto the stool beside her at the counter. "What is it, hon? You look worried."

"My mother called this morning. She and my dad…" Andrea sighed. "They're coming to see me. They say they have something important to tell me. Her voice sounded so intense. I'm just wondering what it could be."

"I'm sure it's nothing serious. When are they coming?"

"This afternoon, at about three."

"Well, then we'll just have to make sure we're ready."

"I'm pretty sure they're going to try and talk me into going home again."

Evie put a hand on Andrea's arm and leaned toward her. "Would that be such a bad idea?"

Andrea shrugged. "No. Yes." She sighed. "Yes, it would be a bad idea." She looked into Evie's face. "Will you stay with me, Evie?"

Evie patted her arm. "Of course I will. Of course."

Benny popped his head around the corner. He looked frightened half to death. "Andrea can't go home," he said, shaking his head wildly. "No, no, no. Andrea can't go home."

Evie stood up and put her arm around his broad shoulders. "Calm down, Benny. Andrea's going to stay right here with us. She's not going anywhere. Don't worry."

"That's right, Benny. I'm staying right here in the diner, with you and Evie."

His big shoulders dropped. "Okay," he said, relief visible in his face. "Okay. Benny has to take care of his baby."

Andrea caught Evie's eye. She didn't look happy but steered him back toward the kitchen without saying anything more.

* * *

Andrea checked her watch again. They were five minutes late. She drummed her fingers on the table. Her foot had started to tap out its own rhythm when Evie squeezed into the booth across from her.

"Girl, you're more nervous than a long-tailed cat in a room full of rocking chairs."

Andrea laughed at her attempt at a southern accent.

"How about a nice cup of tea?" Evie asked.

Andrea nodded. "That would be great."

Evie had just stood when she noticed Benny wiping the table across from them. "I think that one is clean enough, Benny," she said. He turned toward her just as the bell on the door rattled and Edna and Earl walked toward them.

Andrea reached out and caught hold of Evie's sleeve, pulling her down beside her. "Don't leave," she whispered.

Evie took her hand and squeezed. "I'm not going anywhere."

Benny went back to wiping the table, over and over again.

Edna slid into the booth and took Andrea's other hand in hers. "How are you, dear?"

"I'm okay," Andrea replied. She didn't look at her father. He sat slowly but said nothing.

Edna glanced at Evie. "We need to talk to our daughter. In private, please." Her voice sounded tight.

Andrea tightened her grip on Evie's hand. "No. I want her to stay. What's so important? Just tell me." Andrea's voice rose a notch above normal.

Edna stared at her hands. "We've been given some information about your biological family."

Andrea's pulse quickened. "What?"

"Your mother was a carrier of a disease, Andrea, a disease called haemophilia. Do you know what that is?"

Andrea shook her head but couldn't speak. Her mouth had gone dry.

"It's a disease that could be dangerous for you, because of the…" Edna glanced at Earl. "Because of your condition." She reached for her hand again.

"You need to tell your doctor."

Andrea nodded. "Okay," she said softly.

"We were told that everything will be fine as long as they take the necessary precautions. They'll have to do some tests. So the doctor needs to know, as soon as possible."

Evie stood up. "I think we all need some tea," she said, heading for the counter.

Edna scooted toward Earl, forcing him to stand. She sat beside her daughter and put her arms around her. "It's going to be okay. I'm sure it will. I'll go to the doctor with you and explain."

"You'd do that?" Andrea's eyes were wide.

"Of course I will. Your dad and I have taken a hotel room here in the city for the next couple of days. We'll stay as long as you need us to."

Andrea looked at her father out the corner of her eye. "What about the animals?"

"I can make the drive in the morning and evening," Earl said, his tone flat.

The look on his face was at once anxious and somehow pleading. She could tell he was struggling for control.

Andrea burst into tears. "I… I'm so so… sssorry," she sobbed.

Edna drew her into her arms. "Shh, shh. It's all right. Everything will be all right."

Andrea managed to get herself under control just as Evie returned with four mugs and a teapot. She poured the steaming liquid into the mugs and padded away. Andrea gripped the mug hard and sipped the soothing tea slowly.

They didn't say much more. Andrea promised to let her mother know when the appointment was scheduled so she could go with her. As they stood to leave, Andrea suddenly thought of a question.

"How did you find out about this?"

Edna glanced at Earl and let out a puff of breath. Earl nodded and they both sat back down.

Edna fussed with her purse for a moment. "We decided we wouldn't tell you unless you asked." She swallowed. "A young man came to the house a while ago. He was looking for you. He said he was your brother."

Andrea's eyes widened. "My brother?" Perhaps it had been Cory, but why would he say he was her brother?

"He had documents to prove what he was saying. We believe he was telling the truth." Edna's eyes shifted away. "He looks a lot like you."

Andrea's breath came in short bursts. Her heart raced. "Where is he? When can I meet him?"

Edna dug in her purse and brought out a small notebook. She tore out a page and handed it to her. "This is his phone number. His name is Alex."

Andrea stared at the slip of paper. Alex. Her brother. Oh God, she had a brother!

Then she frowned at her mother. "How long have you known about this? Why didn't you tell me right away? Why were you keeping this from me?" Her voice rose in volume with each question.

"We were concerned, Andrea. With all this stress, we thought it might be too much for you to handle right now."

"Too much? But he's my brother." She breathed out the words.

Edna's eyes shifted. "We just thought, well… but now you know." Her voice dropped a notch. "He's on his way here. He wants to meet you."

Andrea stared at the numbers on the slip of paper. "Excuse me," she said, drawing her lips into a tight line. "I have to make a phone call."

She scrambled out of the booth and headed into the back room. As she dialled the number, she glanced out through the long slot in the wall from the kitchen.

Edna and Earl sat for a while, then finally stood up and started to leave the restaurant. As they passed the doorway into the kitchen, Andrea saw Earl hesitate. He put his hand on Edna's arm, then turned on his heel and walked through the doorway.

Benny blocked his way. "No," he said.

Earl took a step back. "I want to talk to my daughter."

Benny shook his head hard. "No. You make Andrea cry."

Evie squeezed past Benny and put her hands on his shoulders. Andrea could tell they were bunched with tension. "It's okay, Benny. It's okay. Let him pass."

Benny scowled but did what he was told.

Andrea returned the phone to its cradle and turned as her foster father approached. Before she could react, Earl's big arms engulfed her in a tight embrace.

"We're at the Brighton Arms Hotel," he said gruffly, then released her, turned, and walked away.

Andrea sank into the small chrome chair, tears streaming, and watched him go. Then she dialled the number again.

The automated message, sounding maddeningly efficient, said the phone number wasn't available. Andrea slammed the receiver down for the third time. Evie put her hand on her shoulder.

"Just keep trying," Evie said.

"But what if I can't get through? I don't even know where he lives. How will I ever find him?"

Evie's hand slipped to Andrea's back and rubbed it slowly. "I believe the Lord is leading him here, Andrea. And the Lord's plan will unfold."

"I can't believe they didn't tell me," she said, the exasperation making her voice hard with anger.

"I'm sure they thought they were doing the right thing. They were only trying to protect you."

Andrea sighed and picked up the phone again. She got the same automated response.

* * *

Benny frowned and banged the pots as he put them away. He didn't like the idea of Andrea's mother and father coming here, and now there was a brother coming, too. They couldn't take care of Benny's baby. That was Benny's job.

He banged another pot. The baby had waved at him. Benny had to show them he could take care of this baby.

CHAPTER TWENTY-ONE

ALEX AND KENNI WERE IN A TAXI ON THE WAY TO A HOTEL BEFORE HE THOUGHT about turning his phone back on. The message waiting for him made Alex gasp.

"What is it?" Kenni asked.

Alex faced her. "She called."

"What?"

"Andrea—she called." Alex grabbed her hand. "We've found her, Kenni!"

Kenni's face lit up. "Where is she?"

"Here, in Regina. Not far from where we were staying."

"Praise God," Kenni said.

Alex squeezed her hand and let out his breath. "I'm almost afraid to believe it." He turned to the taxi driver and asked if he could drive any faster.

"You betcha," the man replied and put his foot to the floor.

Kenni and Alex burst out laughing.

* * *

The few customers watched with curiosity as the three men and a woman rushed into the restaurant. Andrea slid off the stool at the counter, conscious of her swollen belly. She stared at the man extending his hand to her. It was like looking in a mirror. She shook his hand, then flung herself into his arms as their tears started to flow. Alex introduced her to Kenni and they embraced, too. Then the tears turned to laughter.

Bennett elbowed Stan and they retreated to the far end of the bar.

Evie bustled around from behind the counter and ushered them to a large circular booth at the back of the room. "You'll have more privacy here," she said and started to leave.

Andrea grabbed her arm and introduced her. "This is Evie. She's my boss, and my friend."

They shook hands all around as Evie asked if they wanted coffee. Kenni asked for tea.

Evie winked at her. "A girl after my own heart." She almost skipped back to the kitchen.

Andrea couldn't take her eyes off Alex's face. It was at once strange and thrilling to be looking at someone with such a strong resemblance to herself.

"How did you find me?" Andrea asked.

Alex explained about the safety deposit box their parents had and the photos he'd found in it. He slid them across the table. "When I realized I had a sister, my one goal in life was to find you."

She picked up the two small photographs and studied them for a long moment. Kenni and Alex waited quietly, giving her time to absorb it all.

"We've met your foster parents," Alex said. "They seem like good people."

Andrea shrugged. "I guess. They have their flaws, but I had a pretty good childhood, really. How about you?"

Alex dropped his eyes. "Maybe I'll tell you about it someday. For now, let's just say it wasn't ideal."

"I'm sorry."

Alex shrugged. "I survived, and the Lord has blessed me in all kinds of ways." He smiled at Kenni and squeezed her hand.

"You're a Christian?"

Alex nodded and cocked his head.

Andrea stared at her hands. "You must think I'm—"

"We think you're a beautiful young woman," Kenni interrupted, "and we love you already."

Andrea couldn't keep the tears back. Evie arrived just in time with the mugs, a coffee pot, and a box of tissues. They all smiled when she plopped it in the middle of the table and said she'd be right back with Kenni's tea. When she returned, Andrea tugged on her sleeve and shifted over.

"Sit," she said, her eyes pleading.

Evie squeezed in beside her.

"How far along are you, Andrea? Have you been to the doctor yet?" Kenni's eyes were filled with concern.

Andrea nodded. "Yes, a couple of times, and I've had one ultrasound, but I haven't talked to her about the haemo, haemoph…"

"Haemophilia," Kenni finished.

Andrea nodded. "I have an appointment in a couple of days."

Alex opened the large manila envelope he had with him. "This is the medical information. The doctor will want to see it."

Andrea scanned the paper. "This is our mother's information?"

Alex nodded. "I have other information about our parents, which I copied for you. It isn't much, but at least it tells us a little about them."

Andrea reached inside and pulled out the papers, newspaper clippings, and other documents.

"This is their life," she said.

"A small part of it, at least," Alex answered.

"So they're…" She looked up at Alex. "They're both dead?"

Alex nodded. "In an accident. The details are there."

Andrea stared at the newspaper article about the accident. "I always wondered."

Alex frowned. "I always knew they were dead. You weren't told?"

"No. I wasn't told anything." Andrea shook her head and looked up. "Edna and Earl thought that was best."

"Well meaning, but misguided," Kenni said.

"I suppose," Andrea answered. "Any time I asked questions about them, they just wouldn't answer, so I finally gave up. I always thought I'd go looking one day." She stared at the photos again. "I guess now I don't have to."

"Andrea," Alex said in a gentle voice, "we want to help you in any way we can."

Andrea smiled and grabbed a tissue from the box. "Thanks."

"You don't have to work," Alex continued. "I mean, we have money."

"But…" Andrea looked at Evie. "I like it here."

Evie smiled and patted her hand. "We'll take good care of her, and she can stay as long as she likes, even if she doesn't work."

"I just don't want to lose touch again," Alex said, "now that we've found one another."

"Me neither," Andrea replied.

"Well," Kenni said, smiling, "let's just take it one step at a time. I think the priority right now is to make sure you and the baby stay healthy."

Alex nodded. "Absolutely."

"Edna and Earl want me to go home," Andrea admitted. "But I'd be such an embarrassment to them and to myself. I don't think I could face going back. Not right now anyway."

Kenni reached across the table and took her hand. "We just want whatever is best for you."

Andrea pulled another tissue from the box, then laughed softly. "I didn't know there could be so much fluid in one body."

Alex chuckled, then pushed a small card across the table. "You can call me anytime you need anything, Andrea, or even if you just want to talk. Anytime."

"I will," Andrea promised. She put her hand on the papers still scattered on the table. "Can I keep these for a while? I'd like to read through them all."

"I made those copies for you. You can keep them," Alex explained.

She drew them toward her and slipped them back into the envelope. Then she smiled at Alex. "It's strange. I sort of feel like my life is beginning all over again."

Alex nodded. "In a way it is, for both of us. We have a lot to catch up on. Can we see you tomorrow, or the day after? How about we take you out for supper tomorrow night?"

They all jumped at the loud rattle of dishes being dropped into a bin. Evie frowned at Benny, but he just turned his back to her.

Andrea turned back to Alex. "I'd like that," she said.

"Okay. We'll pick you up at six."

They stood up together and embraced again. Kenni glanced around and waved at the two men who had come into the diner with them. They left their seats at the counter and Alex introduced them.

"Stan and Bennett have been a big help in finding you," Alex explained.

Bennett, whose smile couldn't have been wider, pulled a camera out of his pocket. "Let's immortalize the moment," he said.

Kenni stepped aside and drew Andrea between she and Alex. They put their arms around her and Bennett held the camera out. He was about to snap it when Benny bumped him from behind. Evie grabbed his arm and ushered him toward the kitchen.

"Benny," she scolded. "What's gotten into you?"

Bennett took the picture. "I'll have a copy made for you," he told Andrea.

She shook his hand. "Thanks again, for helping us to find each other," she said.

"My pleasure," he replied.

There was another round of hugs, and then they were gone.

* * *

Benny watched them leave from behind the kitchen slot.

"Go away," he mumbled. "Go away."

* * *

The restaurant Alex and Kenni took her to was in the heart of downtown. Traffic zoomed around them as they stepped out of the cab and Andrea felt a little like a country bumpkin, watching all the well-dressed women being escorted inside by their handsome men. She had never been to a place like this before. The tables were spaced apart, with barriers of green foliage between them. The lights had been dimmed and a smiling waiter held her chair as she sat down. The white tablecloth really was made of cloth and the array of cutlery gleamed in candlelight.

"I feel a little like a traitor, not eating at Evie's," Andrea confided, "but this is nice."

Kenni gave her a warm smile that helped her relax. They chatted about Andrea's childhood as they ate. She told them about Peso and how much she missed him.

"I miss the farm," Andrea said. "Cities aren't really my thing."

Kenni glanced at Alex and smiled. "Your big brother here would live as far into the boonies as I'd let him."

Andrea cocked her head. "But you live in Vancouver."

Alex nodded. "I was raised there, so it's familiar ground. And we have work there—work we both love. For now, we know that's where God wants us to be."

He glanced at Kenni. "But maybe someday… we'd like to raise our family in a smaller community."

Andrea's eyes widened. "You have kids?"

Kenni laughed. "No, not yet, but we do want kids eventually."

Andrea dropped her eyes. She was glad when Alex changed the subject.

"So, what looks good on the menu? Are you into steak or seafood?"

"Steak sounds good," she said. "I've never had lobster or crab."

"Well, maybe this should be the night to try it," Alex answered. "I'll order some."

Andrea smiled and nodded. She watched as they put their heads together to study the menu. It was obvious they were in love with one another. Andrea forced the tears back and hid behind her menu. Would she ever find anyone to love her that way?

The food came and they chatted their way through it as they coaxed her into trying the seafood. When she said she thought she'd stick with steak and potatoes, Alex's laugh made her smile.

"Another checkmark in your favour," he said. "I'm a meat and potatoes man myself."

"Did your family raise beef?" Kenni asked.

Andrea nodded and started talking about the breeds they had raised over the years. She chattered on until she realized they were staring at her with blank faces. She stammered again.

"Uh, sorry. I was in 4H for years and I can get a little carried away with all the animal husbandry stuff."

"No need to apologize," Kenni said. "I had no idea breeding cows could be that complicated."

Andrea opened her mouth to tell her she should say cattle, not cows, but thought better of it and took a sip of water instead.

"You'll have to educate us city slickers." Alex winked at her.

She smiled at him again. When he smiled back, she was stunned once more by their resemblance. Her brother. She still couldn't believe she was sitting here talking to her flesh and blood brother.

They lingered over dessert and chatted more about their hopes and dreams. Alex talked about doing that river trip in the Yukon and Andrea told them she had thought about going to college someday, but had given up on that idea.

"And now, well, I guess those things will never happen now."

"Don't be so sure," Alex said. "You never know what God might do."

I haven't seen him do much, Andrea wanted to say, but again stopped herself. They obviously had a strong faith in God. She didn't want to give them the impression that hers was any different.

She was sorry to see the evening come to an end, but when she started to yawn Kenni said they should get her home so she could rest.

Her concern brought Andrea close to tears again. *I'm going to like having her for a sister-in-law,* she thought.

Andrea said goodnight at the back door to the diner. She was surprised to see Benny sitting on the top stair as she started to climb.

"Benny, what are you doing here?" she asked.

"Waiting," he said. "I wanted you to come home sooner."

"Well, I'm home now. You should go to bed. It's late."

"I'm not tired," Benny replied.

Andrea was a few stairs down from where he sat. "Well, I am, so I'm going to bed."

Benny didn't move. She couldn't read his expression in the dim light, but she could see the tension in his body.

"Benny? Let me get by please."

He shifted slowly and stood up, towering over her.

"Andrea should take better care of the baby."

She stepped past him. "The baby's fine, Benny. We're going to sleep right away. You go to your room now, okay?"

"Okay," he mumbled, but he stayed there, watching her until she went into her room and closed the door. For the first time since she'd arrived at Evie's diner, she flipped the bolt lock into position.

* * *

Alex scraped the palm of his hand along the wall. *There must be a light switch here somewhere,* he thought. The concrete felt rough and cold as he moved his hand up and down. The darkness seemed like a black hood covering his head. He panted beneath it, panic causing bitter bile to rise in his throat. He had no idea where he was, but Andrea was here. He knew it and he knew she was in danger. He had to find her quickly, had to find a way to shed light in this cold dark place.

He heard a humming sound and froze. It was a man's voice, or a boy's maybe, coming from somewhere further into the darkness. He moved forward, keeping one hand on the wall and waving the other into the air around him. He came to a corner and turned, came to the end of that wall and turned again. The humming was a bit louder. He kept moving, turning corners, following the walls, but there seemed no end to it.

The humming stopped and Alex held his breath. Then he heard weeping. A woman, or a girl. Alex's heart beat hard. He called Andrea's name, but there was no answer, just soft whimpering. He hurried along the wall again, slamming into another corner. He put his hand to his head and felt something wet. He was bleeding, but he didn't care. He had to find Andrea.

"Andrea!" He screamed her name. "Andrea!"

Then someone was shaking his shoulders, calling his name. He jerked away as a light came on and he opened his eyes. Kenni was leaning over him, her eyes full of concern.

Alex sank back onto the pillow, wiped at his face with both hands, and took a few deep breaths. He turned to his wife. "Sorry," he said.

"It's okay," Kenni answered, reaching for his hand. She snuggled closer to him. "We've found her, Alex. It's all going to be okay now."

He turned toward her and kissed her forehead. "I know," he said, "but these dreams, they seem so real." He shivered.

God, he prayed, *keep her safe. Please. Keep her safe.*

CHAPTER TWENTY-TWO

EDNA AND EARL ARRIVED ABOUT HALF AN HOUR BEFORE THE DOCTOR'S appointment, so they were early when they arrived at the office. Andrea could tell Edna was concerned. The frown didn't leave her face and her hands were never still. Earl's face was stony, as usual, and he didn't look at her.

Andrea introduced them to Dr. Hardisty. Earl then retreated to the waiting area as they entered the examination room.

Andrea watched the doctor's face closely as she studied the papers. The doctor frowned, too, but her voice was light as she said, "It's very good that we have this information, Andrea." She sat down at the computer and started to type. "I suggest you have some tests done immediately to tell us whether or not you are a carrier and whether or not you're symptomatic. That will help us to know if this is an issue to be concerned about, especially if you're still thinking of—"

"What kind of tests?" Andrea cut her off.

"First of all, a blood test. There are two possibilities—you may be symptomatic, which means you are susceptible to bleeding yourself, but that's not likely if you haven't shown symptoms before now, and it's very rare for a female to have the disease. But you could be a carrier. That's what I suspect is the case, so if you are carrying a boy, he has a fifty percent chance of having the disease. We'll do another test, kind of like an amniocentesis. Do you know what that is?"

Edna nodded. Andrea shook her head.

The doctor explained that they would take a sample of the baby's amniotic fluid, which would tell them if it was a boy or a girl.

"If it's a boy, we'll do a blood test to determine if the haemophilia is a factor." The doctor reached out and touched Andrea's arm. "Don't worry. These tests are done by qualified surgeons. There is some risk, but very little."

"Do we have to do it?" Andrea asked.

"I highly advise it, yes. If there's a high risk of bleeding during delivery or…" She looked from one to the other. "Well, we'll want to know, for the baby's safety and yours."

Andrea nodded and sighed. "Do I have to go into the hospital?"

"Only for a short time. The test doesn't take long." She stood up. "I'll schedule the procedure right away. I'd like to make copies of this information for your file, if that's all right?"

Andrea nodded again and the doctor left the office. Edna took Andrea's hand in hers and patted it. "Everything will be fine, dear, I'm sure of it."

Andrea gave her a weak smile. "Thanks for coming with me, Mom."

The doctor returned and gave the papers back. "My receptionist will make the appointments for you and let you know when to be at the hospital."

Andrea stood up. "Thanks, Dr. Hardisty."

She put her hand on Andrea's shoulder. "I would like to speak with you for a moment, privately."

Edna frowned but nodded. "I'll wait with Earl."

Andrea sat back down and the doctor closed the door. "I just want to make sure you realize that this information is crucial if you're still thinking of terminating the pregnancy. You would have to inform—"

Andrea shivered. "No. No, I'm not."

Dr. Hardisty sighed. "Good. Under these circumstances, it would be quite dangerous. But there's no need to worry about all this, Andrea, it's a bit of a complication, but it's very easy to deal with now that we know."

The ride back to the diner was silent and seemed to take forever. Andrea didn't invite them in when they arrived. She thanked them for taking her and got out of the car. She could feel their eyes on her back as she walked away.

* * *

Back in their hotel room, Kenni asked, "So what are you thinking, Alex? What's the next step?"

Alex ran a hand through his thick hair. "I think I'll rent an apartment here for a while. Andrea might not want to move in right away, but eventually, if she's going to keep the baby, she'll need a place."

Kenni nodded. "But we, or at least I, need to get back to the office soon."

"I know. I should let them know what's happening at the youth centre, too. I feel guilty about not being there, but I want to get to know her, Kenni. I want to be here for her."

She put a hand on his arm. "Then you should stay as long as you need to."

Alex leaned forward and kissed her. "I love you."

Kenni smiled. "I know." She picked up her purse. "I'll go find a newspaper so we can see what's available to rent."

Alex stared at the closed door, feeling a little guilty that he hadn't told Kenni the whole truth—that the dream he'd had about trying to find Andrea in the darkness still plagued him.

She's safe.

He kept telling himself that. Why couldn't he believe it?

* * *

They found a three-bedroom apartment in a good neighbourhood and furnished it simply. Alex wanted to buy a crib and other baby paraphernalia, but Kenni cautioned him about going slow. She helped him purchase other things needed for an apartment, then flew home the next day.

* * *

Alex roamed the apartment, straightening the furniture and wiping the kitchen counter for the fourth time. He opened the refrigerator and stared. Kenni had left it well-stocked, but nothing in it looked appetizing. He hated eating alone. He shut the door and dug his phone out of his pocket, glancing at the time as he dialled.

Evie sounded out of breath, but she was gracious and let him talk to Andrea.

"Hey, I know it's lunch time, so I won't keep you, but I just wondered if you'd like to come over for dinner tonight, to see the new apartment."

There was silence for a moment. Alex could hear the hum of the busy diner in the background. He realized he'd been holding his breath when she finally said yes.

When he hung up, he opened the fridge again. A cheese sandwich would do for now.

* * *

Alex set a plate in front of his sister and smiled. "I'm not much of a cook, but it's pretty hard to ruin mac and cheese."

Andrea smiled back. "My favourite."

"Really?" Alex sat down and picked up his fork.

Andrea chuckled. "No. I was just trying to make you feel better."

Alex laughed. "I confess, it is one of mine. A holdover from my foster days. Mac and cheese and hot dogs. Couldn't have survived without 'em. You'd think I'd never want to see them again, but I crave them sometimes."

Andrea grinned, then got more serious. "You said you had a pretty rough time in foster care. How bad was it?"

Alex felt the familiar darkness that still cast a shadow too often. "Bad." He put a big forkful of macaroni into his mouth. "I had the stereotypical foster parents from hell."

"You were abused?"

Alex nodded. "It's taken time, counselling, and a lot of God's grace to get over what I went through." He swallowed. "There are some things, well, I'm still dealing with some of it."

Alex decided to change the subject. "So, when do you think you'd like to move in?"

Andrea's head jerked up. "Move in?"

Alex nodded. "Yeah." He waved his hand around the room. "This place is for you."

"But I don't think I could afford…"

Alex put his hand up to stop her. "This is my gift to you, no rent needed."

"I don't know what to say. This seems like too much."

Alex put his fork down and was quiet for a moment. "Andrea, I told you our mother left me an inheritance and I intend to share it with you, but there's a detail about that story I need to tell you and it's not a very pretty one."

When she didn't reply, he continued.

"When George—he's the lawyer who came to see me in the Yukon—told me I'd inherited just over a million dollars, I didn't believe him. I knew nothing about my biological family except that they'd abandoned me to foster care hell. I didn't believe they would have left me anything, let alone that much money." He played with his fork, staring at it for a moment. "But George's story was intriguing enough to get me to go to Seattle, where our parents had lived, to find out what it was all about. What I found wasn't pretty."

Alex stood and poured himself a glass of water. "They gave me a bunch of documents filled with a lot of legalese, but the bottom line made my blood run cold. The inheritance was in a trust fund in my name. It had been put there by my mother—our mother—after she tried to abort me."

Andrea put her fork down. Her eyes were wide, but she still said nothing.

"It was a shock that made me run back to the Yukon as fast as I could. But then Kenni discovered there was a letter that had gone missing. When they found it, Kenni made it her mission in life to get it to me, even though I made it pretty hard for them to find me."

He grinned. "I'm glad Kenni is as tenacious as she is. She just wouldn't give up, and God didn't either." Alex noticed Andrea's head tilt a little.

"You really believe God cared, that he made it all happen?"

"Well, I know he engineered an encounter especially for me—a grizzly encounter." He tugged on a black cord around his neck and revealed a long, curved bear's tooth.

Andrea leaned forward as Alex pulled the necklace over his head and handed it to her. "I wear it to remind myself."

Andrea held the tooth in her hand. "What happened?"

"The grizzly ended up in a stew pot and then, well, I guess you could say we became one flesh." He grinned at Andrea's frown. "The meat was full of trichinosis, parasites. I still have it. I'll have it for the rest of my life."

"But how? What did that have to do with how Kenni found you?"

"I ended up in hospital and police custody—that's another part of the story I'll tell you some time. But anyway, when I finally recovered and the charges were dropped, Kenni gave me the letter. It changed everything."

Andrea blinked. "But our mother… she really tried to abort you?"

Alex nodded. "Apparently the doctor wasn't very skilled. That's where the money came from. She sued him and won."

Andrea strode away from the table. She stood with her back to him, staring out the window at the city lights below. Alex left her alone for a few minutes, then walked quietly up behind her. He reached out and touched her shoulder, turning her gently toward him.

"Andrea, have you… did you think about having an abortion?"

She didn't look up. "Like mother, like daughter," she said softly.

He took her in his arms and just held her for a while. "Our mother had a lot of courage. In the end, she admitted how wrong she'd been and gave her life to Christ." He felt his sister stiffen in his arms. "I don't have the letter here, but I think you should read it someday." He gave her a squeeze and tried to lighten the mood. "Mac and cheese isn't very good when it's cold."

That got a bit of a grin and they returned to the table, eating in silence for a while.

"Take your time. About the apartment, I mean," Alex said. "There's no rush for you to move in. I'm sorry if I seem to be pressuring you. It's just that I want to help."

"I know," Andrea replied. "And I'm grateful, but I'm just not sure about things yet."

"How did the appointment go at the clinic?" Alex asked, trying to find a topic that didn't make either of them feel uncomfortable.

Andrea tensed as her head jerked up. "The clinic?"

"Yeah. You had an appointment with the doctor, didn't you?"

He noticed her shoulders drop. "Yes," she said quietly. "Everything's fine." She played with the food on her plate.

"Want some ketchup?" Alex asked.

She shook her head, letting her hair hide her face. She put the fork down. "Alex, I need to tell you something that you're probably not going to like."

Alex waited, trying to read her face. He saw her take a deep breath, but she didn't look up as she spoke.

"I've been going to a pregnancy care centre. They've been really good, you know, to help me sort things out."

"That's good," Alex said quietly.

"They gave me a bunch of information." She looked up. "On adoption."

Alex's stomach twisted as she continued.

"And I've decided, at least, I think, maybe that's what I'm going to do, when the baby comes. I'm going to give her, or him, to someone who really wants a baby and can take care of it."

Alex felt his throat constrict. "I see." He sank back into his chair.

Andrea didn't look at him and neither of them said anything more as they finished the rest of the meal. When he was done, Andrea took Alex's plate to the sink and started washing the dishes. Alex took a dish towel from the drawer and they worked together until everything was cleaned up.

Alex had just moved away when he heard her almost whisper.

"Please don't hate me."

He whirled around, took her arm, and turned her toward him. "I could never hate you, Andrea. It's just a bit of a shock, that's all. And, well, you're right. I don't like it."

Andrea sniffed. "I don't like it either, but I just think it's the best thing for the baby."

Alex drew her to the table and they sat down. "You don't have to worry about money, you know, because of the inheritance. There's more than enough for all of us. There won't be any problem, at least financially, taking care of a baby for as long as it takes."

"But you're married and I just… I don't think I can take care of a baby by myself."

"But you're not alone. Kenni and I will help."

She shook her head. "I just don't know what to do."

"Well, you don't have to make any decisions right away. You have a few months yet."

Andrea nodded. "But the woman at the pregnancy centre said I should decide soon, so they can start arranging everything." She hung her head and tears came again. "I'm sorry, Alex. I've made such a mess of everything."

Alex squeezed her hand. "Let's just keep praying about all this, and don't make any decisions until we're sure it's what's best, and what God wants. Okay?"

She nodded again and brushed the tears away. "Okay."

"Hey."

Andrea looked up.

"How about some ice cream to top off that mac and cheese?"

She gave him a weak smile. "That *is* one of my favourites."

* * *

Alex lay in bed staring into the darkness. The more he thought of Andrea giving the child into the hands of strangers, the more his stomach tied itself in knots. He knew there were some good foster homes and lots of adoptions that worked, but he also knew the negative statistics. He knew them because he had been one.

He wouldn't let it happen. He just would not let her do it. But how could he prevent it? Could he and Kenni raise it themselves? Would Kenni agree to raising the child? Did he even have the right to ask that of her? Question after question circled in his mind. Most of them only raised more.

God, he prayed. *Please, show me what to do.*

He got up and looked at the clock. It was late, but Kenni's time zone was two hours behind his. She might not be in bed yet. He threw on a shirt against the chill and felt around for his cell phone. Kenni answered on the first ring. The words spilled out, and with them his anguish. He had to choke back the emotions more than once. He wished she was here with him. He needed to hold her, needed to feel her comfort and hear her voice.

When he hung up, he sank onto the bed and buried his face in his hands. *God. Please. Please!*

* * *

Kenni lay awake through most of the night after her conversation with Alex. She knew it was killing him to think Andrea would even consider giving the baby away. She understood why they would counsel a young woman like Andrea in that direction, but that was before they'd known she had family. Real family. She prayed that Andrea would reconsider. The thought of losing touch with the baby made a lump form in her throat that she couldn't swallow.

The next morning, she stumbled out of bed, her head heavy from lack of sleep and her heart aching for the man she loved. She showered and had a cup of coffee before making the call she had wanted to make in the middle of the night.

The phone rang only once and she heard her mother's soft voice—a melodic voice tinged with a southern drawl. She felt better almost immediately. Kenni's parents knew what was going on and she knew they'd be sympathetic to how Alex would take this latest bit of news.

"The Lord has a plan, Kenni," her mother said. "Let's just keep praying. I'm sure it will all work out in the end."

"But what if it doesn't, Mom? It'll kill Alex if she gives the baby to strangers. After all he's been through in foster care..."

"Then we'll pray for grace and mercy for him, Kenni. Grace and mercy and a huge dollop of trust."

"Would you pray for some of that for me, too, please? I have a feeling I'm going to need it as much as Alex."

"The Lord knows, sweetie. The Lord knows."

It was hard to say goodbye.

CHAPTER
TWENTY-THREE

Kenni dressed slowly in the morning and headed to work. She loved the walk through the city to their street level office. Her morning ritual made her feel secure as she stopped for a latte and croissant, but she missed Alex. He would have teased her about watching her weight while she ordered her morning pastry. She enjoyed watching the other people as she made her way to the office, but the heaviness of last night wouldn't go away.

A woman pushing a stroller caught her eye. The mother had stopped to push a soother into the crying child's mouth. Kenni smiled as she watched her tease the little one into laughter. Kenni had never been one to babysit much. She liked kids but felt a bit awkward around babies. They seemed so vulnerable. She was always afraid she'd do something to hurt them.

The office was already buzzing with people when she arrived and checked her desk for messages. She sighed at the stack of files waiting for her. She knew being away for so long had been hard on the others in the office. It looked like they seemed determined to make her pay for it.

Brent, one of their most in-demand lawyers, strode by and tossed a "Good morning" over his shoulder. "Hope you can get going on that Halliday case right away, Kenni," he said. It was more a statement than a question.

She sat down and searched through the pile until she found it. A child custody case. Kenni sighed. There were a lot of them these days. She opened the file and was soon lost in the details. The father was alleging that the mother was unfit due to a history of drug and alcohol abuse. The mother had come to them desperate to keep her children, swearing that she had been to rehab and was clean.

Kenni picked up the phone. That would be easy enough to check. Then she'd talk directly to the mother to get a feel for what she was like and determine whether or not they could trust her.

After a short conversation, Kenni agreed to go to her apartment for the interview. The woman had two preschoolers and an infant. It wasn't easy for her to get out.

The woman's apartment was small but clean and tidy except for a scattering of toys on the living room floor. A dark-haired boy and girl peeked out from behind the young woman's legs as she opened the door and invited Kenni in. The baby cried just as they sat down, so the woman got up and came back into the room with a small bundle wrapped in a soft white blanket. Then the little boy started to whine.

"Mommy, I hafta go," he said, looking at his mother with pleading eyes as he pulled at his pants.

With a smile, she sighed at Kenni and stood. "We're just starting to potty train," she explained. "I'll be right back." She started to follow the boy, then turned back. "Could you… would you mind holding the baby for a minute?"

Kenni took the infant and sat down in a small rocking chair. The little girl watched her for a moment, then ran after her mother.

Kenni opened the blanket to see two bright brown eyes staring up at her. Then the child's face crinkled into a smile and her small hand reached out. Kenni put a finger into the tiny palm and the baby took hold, gurgling softly. Suddenly the room disappeared and Kenni was captivated by the tiny face, the tiny hand wrapped around her finger. Tears sprang to her eyes as love like she'd never known before swelled up inside her.

When the mother came back into the room and moved to take the baby, Kenni sat back. "I'm okay with her, if it's alright with you," she said.

"She seems to be okay with you, too." She watched the baby for a moment, then stood back. "Would you like some tea?"

Kenni nodded and watched as the woman went into the small kitchen behind the living room. She came back a while later with a tray holding a teapot and two cups. The cream pitcher was chipped but the china was real.

She poured Kenni a cup of tea, then gently lifted the baby from her arms. "You have the magic touch," she said. "She's fast asleep."

She took the child into the other room and came back immediately.

"I've tried to be a good mother to my kids," she said. "I've been clean and sober for more than three years, since Colby was born. I have a good support system and I have a stack of letters from people who know me and will testify for me, including my employer and my pastor." She laid the pile on the table. "My ex is just being vindictive. He doesn't want the kids. He just wants to hurt me. I've met someone." She leaned forward. "He's a good man, and my ex has been causing trouble ever since."

Kenni took out a legal pad and started asking questions and taking notes. The two toddlers interrupted now and then, but Kenni just smiled and chatted with them, too. By the time they were finished, the little girl was snuggling beside her.

"Do you have kids?" the woman asked as Kenni finished and slid her pen into her purse.

"No." Kenni shook her head. "Not yet."

"You should. You'd make a great mom."

Kenni smiled. "Thanks. I'm convinced you are, too, and I'm sure we can help."

The woman seemed relieved. "I have a little money, but…"

"Don't worry about that. Our office will cover the costs." She stuffed the letters into her briefcase and shook the woman's hand. "We'll be in touch," she said and started to leave. She hesitated and turned back. "Could I have a peek at the baby again?"

The woman cocked her head, then nodded and led Kenni into the bedroom. It, too, was clean and neat. Half of the room was taken up by a cradle and change table. Diapers were stacked on shelves with various baby clothes, blankets, and other baby accessories. The woman's bed was pushed up against the far wall.

They tiptoed in and Kenni peered down at the sleeping child. Tears came again, but she brushed them away and slipped quietly back out of the room.

* * *

Kenni was almost all the way to the office before she realized she was driving on autopilot. She couldn't get that tiny face out of her mind. She had a hard time concentrating on writing her report, but finally finished it just as Brent was locking up. She handed it to him as she headed for the door.

"Good luck with this one," she said. "I think this woman deserves to keep her kids and the evidence makes me believe it wouldn't be a good idea to grant custody to the father."

Brent nodded. "Thanks. Your opinion counts. I'll do my best. Have a good night, Kenni."

She was on the street when she turned back.

"Brent, I may have to leave again. Soon."

The lawyer frowned and sighed. "Well, I can't fire you, so I guess if you have to, you have to. Just try and make it quick, okay?"

"I will, but, well, I can't promise anything."

Brent sighed. "I guess you gotta do what you gotta do."

Once in her apartment, Kenni went right to her computer and booked her flight to Regina for the next day. Then she called her mother and asked her to pray.

* * *

Kenni called Alex from the airport and told him she'd take a taxi to the apartment.

"That was fast. Did you miss me that much?" Alex asked.

Kenni could hear the smile in his voice. "Didn't you miss me?"

"Can't wait to see you."

"I have something I wanted to talk about that we can't do on the phone."

"Oh?"

"I'll be there in a bit. Love you."

"I love you, too, especially when you're so mysterious."

Kenni laughed and hung up. She prayed all the way to the apartment, realizing that she could have been doing more of that all along.

Alex swept her into a warm embrace before she could even say hello. "I did miss you," he said, and kissed her again.

Kenni pulled away and tossed her coat onto a chair. "Is Andrea here?"

Alex shook his head. "She's still insisting on working at the diner and doesn't want to move in yet."

"Good," Kenni said.

Alex cocked his head. "What's up?"

She took his hand, led him into the living room and pushed him down onto the sofa. She pulled an ottoman close and sat facing him, her knees touching his.

"Alex, I've been thinking."

"That's a good sign," he joked.

She slapped his knee. "Be serious."

"Okay, what have you been thinking?"

She took a deep breath. "I've been thinking we should adopt Andrea's baby."

Alex sank back into the sofa and stared at her without saying a word. She waited, but when he still didn't respond she rushed on.

"I know it's a crazy idea and we had decided to wait a few years before having kids, but I think I'm ready, Alex, and I really think we should do this. I think that baby needs us, and so does Andrea."

Alex leaned forward, reached out, and touched her cheek. Tears began seeping out the corners of his eyes. "You're sure?"

"Yes, I'm sure." She cocked her head. "What do you think?"

"I think you're the most amazing woman in the world." Alex looked away.

Kenni cocked her head. "But?"

Alex stood. "I've been praying about this ever since Andrea told me what she was planning to do, Kenni. I've been thinking about talking to her about adopting the baby, too, but..." He pushed his hands through his hair. "I don't know. I can't stand the idea of letting her give it away to strangers, but I just don't know if we're, if *I'm*, ready to do this. I mean, it's a good idea, but raising a kid..." He sighed. "That scares me. It scares me a lot."

Kenni stood and pulled his hands down. "Then let's just keep praying."

Alex pulled her to him. "Disappointed?"

Kenni let her face snuggle into his neck. "It's okay. You're right. This isn't something we should rush into, and maybe Andrea wouldn't even agree to it."

Alex frowned. "You think she'd rather adopt it out than give it to us?"

Kenni shrugged. "I don't know her well enough yet to know how she'd react. But I've noticed that she's not quick to make decisions about anything."

Alex sighed. "Well, we shouldn't mention it until we're sure."

Kenni rested her head on his chest for a moment. They sat together and prayed.

* * *

Alex woke up the next morning happy to see his wife beside him. She was lying on her side, her face turned toward him, her breath gentle in sleep. His eyes traced the curve of her cheek and the upturned lift of her nose that always made him smile.

God, he thought, *I hope you don't ever get tired of me thanking you for bringing this woman into my life, because I don't think I'm ever going to stop.*

He rolled over onto his back.

So. About this baby. I'm scared. Nothing new, hey? I'm scared to think I could be a father in a few short months. And I'm scared that Andrea will give it up and it will disappear from our lives forever. I'm scared it might end up with a story like mine.

But look where you are.

Alex was so surprised that he pushed himself up on his elbows. *But what I went through...*

But look where you are.

He dropped back onto the bed. *Okay. I'm here, talking to you. I get it. You'll take care of the baby. Is that what you're saying?*

Suddenly the room seemed full of light and Alex felt as though he might float right off the bed. He almost laughed out loud.

Kenni murmured and shifted beside him. He rolled onto his side and watched her wake up.

"Morning." She stretched and reached for him.

It was a while before they finally made their way into the kitchen for breakfast. Alex couldn't stop grinning.

"What?" Kenni finally asked.

"I think we should talk to Andrea."

Kenni sat down across from him. "Really?"

Alex nodded. "It doesn't matter, Kenni. Whatever happens to that baby, it's in God's hands. If Andrea is okay with us adopting it, God will help us raise it. If she gives it up for adoption, God will be there, too. Whatever happens, I'm okay with it—or at least, I know I can be okay with it, with God's help."

Kenni reached across the table and intertwined her fingers with his. "Trust," she said, smiling.

Alex nodded. "Yeah. Trust."

CHAPTER TWENTY-FOUR

BENNY BATTED HIS EARS AND SCREAMED. HE HOPPED FROM ONE FOOT TO THE other as soapy water spilled over onto the floor and Andrea slid slowly down into the middle of the puddle. Joe came up behind them, reached around, and turned off the tap. Evie rushed in and helped Andrea to her feet.

"What happened?" she asked, taking Benny's arm. "Are you all right, Andrea?"

Andrea nodded. "I'm fine. I just slipped on the water."

Evie had her arms wrapped around Benny and was talking softly to him.

"It's okay, Benny, it's okay. It's just water. We can mop it up. Did you forget to turn the tap off?"

Benny stopped hopping, but his hands still flapped in the air as he nodded.

"I'm sorry," he said. "I'm sorry. There's too much water. Too much water." He stared at Andrea with wide eyes.

Evie took his arm and steered him toward the staff room.

"It's okay. Joe and I will clean it up. You just go sit down for a minute, okay?"

Andrea started toward them. "I'll help you, Evie."

Benny leaped at her, grabbed her arm, and pushed her back. "No, no, no! There's too much water for the baby. Too much water."

Andrea staggered back. "Okay, Benny, okay. I won't help. I'll sit at the table with you, okay?" She took his arm and led him to the staff room.

Evie frowned, then heard Joe rummaging in the closet and mumbling to himself. "I'll be right there," she said. She glanced at Benny and nodded at Andrea. "It's okay, Benny. We'll get it all cleaned up."

Andrea got him to sit down and put her hand on his arm. "The water won't hurt anyone, Benny. Evie and Joe will have it cleaned up in no time."

He batted his ears, jumped up, and ran out of the room. When Evie came back, they went out into the alley and called his name, but he was nowhere to be seen.

Evie sighed. "He'll be back when he calms down. He probably went up to the roof. This isn't the first time." She shook her head as they went back inside. "Benny sure has a thing about water."

* * *

Andrea leaned heavily against the counter watching Alex and Kenni walk toward her. She was surprised to see them, especially Kenni, but the sight of them both somehow made her feel better.

"I thought you were going to be gone longer."

"She just couldn't stay away from me." Alex winked.

Kenni rolled her eyes. "Let's find a booth, shall we?"

They slid into the big booth where they'd first met.

"Have you eaten?" Andrea asked, looking for Benny. She jumped a little when she realized he was right behind them. When Kenni said no, Andrea asked him to bring them some menus. He kept wiping the table, ignoring her.

"Benny," she said again. "Would you bring us some lunch menus please?"

He returned a few minutes later with one menu, which he placed in front of Andrea.

She frowned at him. "We need two more, Benny. You know everyone has to have a menu."

Benny made a sound that indicated he didn't really care and walked away.

Andrea rolled her eyes and stood up. "I'll be right back."

She got the menus, then sat down again, rubbing her swollen belly.

"Joe makes a great steak sandwich." Andrea started to get up again. "I'll get us some glasses of water."

Kenni put her hand on her arm. "You stay put. I'll get them."

She returned in a minute, holding three glasses between both hands.

"Want a job?" Andrea teased.

"Isn't it about time you quit working?" Kenni asked. "What are you, six months now?"

Andrea nodded and took a sip of water. "Six and a half, and yes, I'm starting to think about quitting. Evie hired a new girl yesterday, so once she's trained I won't be needed as much. I do get awful tired by the end of a shift."

"You know you can quit any time, Andrea," Alex repeated.

She smiled. "You've only told me that about a hundred times, Alex."

"I mean it. You don't have to work."

"I know. It's just, well, I guess I want to be independent at least a little bit, and I do like working here. Evie and Benny have become my best friends."

"Benny is Andrea's friend." They were all startled by Benny's loud voice. He had stayed right behind them.

"Everyone knows that, Benny," Andrea told him.

Benny glared at Alex, then went back to wiping the table.

Alex leaned forward and whispered. "I don't think he likes me."

Andrea frowned as she glanced over her shoulder and replied in a soft voice. "Benny has been acting funny lately. But he's harmless."

Kenni put her hand on her shoulder. "We're here for you, too."

"I know and I'm thankful. For both of you."

Kenni glanced at Alex. He gave his head a bit of a shake.

Andrea looked from one to the other. "What is it?" she asked. "You both kind of look like the cat that ate the canary."

Alex smiled. "We have something we'd like to talk to you about, but right after lunch."

"Right," Kenni said, cocking her head at Alex. "Let's eat first."

"Well, I have some news, too," she said.

Kenni leaned forward. "Oh?"

"The doctor called with the results from the amnio. I'm having a girl."

They both beamed. "That's wonderful. Then the haemophilia isn't an issue?"

Andrea shook her head. "No. The doctor said I'm not symptomatic, so there's no danger of excessive bleeding, though she said it's good that they know about it."

"That is good news," Alex said.

"A girl," Kenni said. "Have you thought about a name?"

"Lots, but I haven't picked anything yet. I have a few ideas, but I can't decide. I think I'll wait until she's born."

Kenni smiled and looked at Alex. Andrea noticed but didn't say anything.

Benny had moved over by the door to the kitchen. She saw him peek around the corner into the kitchen every few minutes. When Joe called out that the order was up, he scooted over to take the plates and delivered them to their table. Then he took his cloth and started wiping the table right behind them. Again.

They ate in silence for a while, then Andrea put her fork down. "Okay you two, spill it. I can see you can hardly contain yourselves. What's going on?"

Alex and Kenni exchanged a look, then Kenni began. "I came back so quickly, Andrea, because there was something I wanted to discuss with you. Alex and I have talked about it and agreed, so now, well, we were wondering…" Kenni took a deep breath. "How would you feel if we told you we want to adopt the baby?"

Andrea's eyes went wide. She gave a little gasp and then tears began to spill out. She opened her mouth to speak but leaped as Benny dropped a pan of dishes right behind them.

She turned to see him picking up the pieces. "It slipped," he said.

Andrea shifted back to Alex and Kenni. "I don't know…"

Alex put his hand on hers. "It's entirely your decision, Andrea. We don't want to pressure you in any way." He glanced at Kenni. "We haven't talked much about the details yet, but we would probably want to take the baby with us back to Vancouver. You could move there, too, of course, or stay here in Regina if you like and come visit any time you want. We'd be happy if you wanted to be involved in the baby's life, as much as you want, but we do think it would be best if we legally adopted it."

Andrea put her face in her hands and sobbed.

Kenni stood up and put her arm across Andrea's shaking shoulders. "We don't want to upset you, Andrea, but we really think this is a good solution, for all of us. We hoped you would, too."

Andrea started to nod as she got herself under control. "I just don't know what to say."

Kenni gave her shoulders a squeeze. "Take all the time you need to think about it."

Andrea pushed her hands through her hair. Kenni almost smiled at the gesture that was so much like Alex.

"I… I'm just not sure," she said.

Kenni embraced her.

Alex stood and wrapped his arms around the two women. "Then let's keep praying."

* * *

Benny muttered as he took the pan of broken dishes into the kitchen and dumped them noisily into a large trash can.

God can't take Benny's baby away, he thought. *Not again. This is Benny's baby. Benny's baby. He'll show them he can take care of this baby.*

* * *

Andrea's eyes darted from spot to spot as she told Evie what Kenni and Alex had proposed. The woman sat heavily in one of the chrome chairs at the staff table.

"How do you feel about this?" she asked.

Andrea paced. "I can't decide what I feel. On one hand, it makes sense—it's a good solution, and Alex is my only real family, but when I think of giving up the baby, even to them, it just makes me ache all over. And really, I hardly know them. What if I sign the papers and then we don't get along? What if they get a divorce or won't ever let me see the baby once they move to Vancouver? What if…"

Evie took her hand. "There are a million 'what ifs,' sweetie. But you have to trust God to give you peace about it. If he doesn't, don't do it."

Andrea frowned. Peace? How could God give her peace? How would she know he had given it to her if and when he chose to? What was Evie talking about? She sighed.

"Well, I'll be moving into the apartment Alex rented next week. I thought I'd make the decision after that."

Evie nodded. "Good. One thing at a time."

Andrea nodded. "I want to have the baby here," she said softly. "But whatever I decide, whether I let them adopt her or I keep her, it might mean moving to Vancouver pretty quick after she's born. Alex and Kenni said they would help me find an apartment. I suppose… I was thinking maybe I could go to college after all, Evie."

Evie smiled up at her. "That's wonderful, sweetie. It's a good plan, a good plan."

"I'll miss you."

Evie took her hand. "I'll miss you, too, but you can't let that affect your decision. You have to think of what's best for the baby and for you."

Andrea sat down across from her. "If I do decide to do this, how are we going to tell Benny?"

Evie frowned. "We'll have to think of a way. It will be hard for him, but he'll get over it."

Andrea sighed. "I wish I could transport you all to Vancouver, restaurant and all."

Evie chuckled. "I don't like the rain much, I'm afraid."

"But you would come and visit us, wouldn't you? You and Benny, too?"

"Lord willing, of course we would. And you can visit us here as often as you can." Evie winked. "We can always use another good waitress."

"I don't know how to thank you for all you've done for me, Evie."

The woman waved her hand. "All in a day's work, my girl, all in a day's work." She heaved herself up. "And speaking of work, I'd better get back at it." She swiped at her eyes and embraced Andrea. "Come put some coffee on for me, will you? I have pies to bake." She headed for the swinging doors, then turned back suddenly. "Have you talked to your mother, Andrea, about all this?"

Andrea shook her head. "Not yet."

"You call her," Evie said. "Today."

Andrea nodded. "I will."

She swallowed, wondering how her mother would take the news.

* * *

Benny leaned hard into the wall of the walk-in freezer.

Andrea should live in Benny's house, he thought, *not go away. Benny's house is better. Benny has a special place where Andrea could live.*

He smiled. Andrea would stay here with Benny's baby. Benny would make sure of it.

* * *

Edna sat down heavily at the kitchen table. Andrea's voice sounded so far away. "How do you feel about the idea?" she asked.

"I'm thinking it's a good solution," Andrea said. "I was leaning toward giving it up for adoption. At least this way I'd know who was raising her, and she'd still be with family."

"Yes, but it could be complicated, Andrea, to stay so closely connected."

"I know." Andrea's voice went soft. "But at least I could still see her and know what was going on in her life."

"Yes, that would be good." Edna stared out the window. Earl was working on the tractor in the yard. "But I had hoped..." He wiped his hands on a rag and turned toward the house.

The silence felt pregnant. "Mom? Are you there?"

Earl was on the doorstep. "I have to go now, but I'll talk to you later, okay?"

"But..."

Edna hung up the phone just as Earl stepped into the room.

"Who was that?" he asked.

"A telemarketer," Edna said and went to the counter to pour him a cup of coffee.

CHAPTER
TWENTY-FIVE

ANDREA STOOD BESIDE THE WASHING MACHINE, HER JEANS IN ONE HAND AND a slip of paper in the other. Her hand shook as she stared at the phone number written on it. She knew the number by heart. She'd been trying to forget it. Cory was with someone else now. It had taken him exactly three weeks from the time he'd left to find someone else.

"What's that?" Benny's voice startled her.

Evie was right behind him. "Oh, we didn't know you were down here, Andrea." She peered at her, glanced at the piece of paper in her hand, and turned to Benny. "Just leave the basket here, Benny, and go see if Allan needs help, okay?"

Benny dropped the basket of clothes and trudged back up the stairs, grumbling to himself as he went.

When he was gone, Evie turned to her. "What is it? You kind of look like you've seen a ghost."

"Cory's phone number," she said, showing her the piece of paper. "Alex said Cory wants to talk to me."

"But you haven't called him."

"I don't want to talk to him," she said.

"I understand," Evie said, "but he is the baby's father, and if he wants to help…"

Andrea brushed hair away from her face and stuffed the slip of paper into her pocket. "I don't need his help."

Evie reached out and touched her hand. "But he is the baby's father," she repeated.

"He got another girlfriend as soon as he left. What does that tell you?" She bit her lip and shook her head hard. "No. I don't want to talk to him."

Evie pulled some clothes out of the dryer. "Okay," she said, "but I'm going to pray about this."

Andrea took a t-shirt from the pile and folded it. *Go ahead,* she thought. *Prayers don't seem to work where I'm concerned.*

But when she lay in bed that night, Cory was all she could think about. Cory holding their baby. Cory smiling down at their baby. Cory tickling their baby. She rolled over and groaned. The small glowing numbers on the alarm clock told her it was after midnight.

She flicked on the bedside lamp and got out of bed. The cold floor gave her a chill. She found her housecoat and wrapped it around herself, then pulled on a pair of heavy socks and went downstairs. The phone's small light glowed in the dark as she picked it up. She dialled the numbers quickly and let it ring several times before hanging up. She was halfway up the stairs when the phone rang. She almost fell as she ran back down to grab it.

"Hello, Cory."

"Andrea? God, where are you? Are you okay?"

She held her breath for a moment. "Yeah, I'm fine. How are you?"

"That guy, Bennett, he said you were in the city."

"Yes. I'm working at a diner on Raymond Street."

"Can I come and see you?"

"You want to?"

"Yes. I want to if… is the baby mine?"

"You have to ask me that?" Andrea could feel the heat rising up her neck.

Silence for a moment.

"No. I guess I don't."

Andrea heard him sigh.

"I'll do whatever I have to do. Just tell me what you want, Andrea."

"What about your girlfriend?"

"It's not that serious. I was thinking of breaking up with her anyway. So this timing is good in a way, you know?"

"Don't feel that you have to help."

"But I want to. I mean, I should. If I'm the father."

Andrea tried not to cry, but the tears started and then she couldn't control them.

Cory's voice sounded funny as he tried to comfort her. "It'll be okay, Andrea. I'll be finished this course in just a few more months. Then I can get back to work and look after us. It's going to be okay. Please, stop crying. Please."

"Evie's Rocky Road Diner," Andrea managed to get out. "On Raymond."

"I'll be there first thing tomorrow morning," Cory said.

Andrea slumped down to the floor and let the sobs come.

Suddenly Evie was there, pulling her into her arms. She held her for a long time, then gently sat her down and bustled into the kitchen. Andrea knew she was making tea.

"Do you want this boy in your life, Andrea?" Evie asked as they sipped.

"I thought I loved him, when we were together," Andrea said. "But now I don't know. I don't know if he loves me. He said he had another girlfriend, but now he says he doesn't. I don't know what to believe."

Evie sighed. "Then I'd be very cautious."

"He says he'll get a job and look after us. But I'd almost decided to let Kenni and Alex adopt her. Now my mom wants me to go home and…" She dropped her head. "This just complicates everything. I shouldn't have called him. It's such a mess." Andrea groaned.

Evie patted her hand. "But God makes beautiful things out of messes, when we let him."

"Cory isn't a believer."

"All the more reason to pray," Evie said.

Why? Andrea thought. *What good will it do?*

They finished their tea and Evie tucked her into bed. It made her feel like she was six years old again. She kind of liked the feeling. The big woman leaned over and planted a kiss on her forehead.

"Sleep tight," she said.

Andrea clutched the blanket and closed her eyes. *Don't let the bed bugs bite.* She could hear Edna's voice as she slipped into sleep.

* * *

Evie returned to her room and sank thankfully into her bed. She was weary but stayed awake for some time, talking to the Lord, asking him for help, as usual. She felt so inadequate to help this young girl. She knew Andrea needed to know Jesus. He wouldn't suddenly make everything rosy, but knowing him would bring the joy and peace that was missing in her life. Evie knew it, because it had happened to her.

That long ago day was still bright in her mind, the day she realized God not only existed but loved her enough to give her the desire of her heart—a baby of her own. She remembered the look on her husband's face when she told him. He was so stunned that he'd almost fallen over. Then he'd grabbed her and danced her around their small kitchen. She smiled, remembering it.

A tinge of sadness came whenever she thought of Jake. She missed him still, even after twelve years. But the Lord always soothed that pain. She knew she would see him again someday and it would be all the more wonderful because they would be in the presence of Jesus.

Evie sighed. There were some days when she wanted that to happen right now, but she knew God had work for her to do here on his good earth for a while yet. She closed her eyes and prayed again for Andrea.

* * *

Andrea slept late the next morning and was surprised to see the clock show 10:25 when she finally got up and dressed. Her head felt heavy and her eyes stung. She went into the bathroom and laid a warm cloth over her face for a moment, then went downstairs, holding her stomach as she went. She wondered if Cory was already here.

She had only taken a couple of steps into the diner when he was suddenly in front of her. Cory looked at her swollen belly, then embraced her. It felt good to feel his arms around her, but she felt a kind of awkwardness, too. She tried not to cry, but the tears started to flow again. He kissed both her cheeks as tears slid down them.

"It's going to be okay," he said over and over again.

Andrea took a deep breath and pulled away, conscious of curious eyes looking their way. "Let's sit down," she said.

Cory was quiet when she told him that Alex and Kenni had offered to adopt the baby.

"Is that what you want?" he asked.

"It's a good plan," she said. "I know they'll take good care of her and I can see her whenever I want."

"But…"

"But it's my baby." She touched her swollen abdomen. "I don't know if I can give her away, even to my own brother."

Cory was quiet again. He reached out and took her hand. "Maybe we can make this work, Andrea. I've got a pretty good job, and when I'm finished this course I'll be making even more money. It'll take a while to save up enough for a house, but we can get our own apartment here in the city. Once the baby comes, you can work, too."

She frowned. "But who'll look after the baby?"

Cory shrugged. "Daycare. That's what everybody does."

Andrea searched his face. "You really want to be with me?"

"I want to do the right thing," he replied.

Andrea pulled her hand away. "I need to think about everything. I just need time to think."

Cory sighed. "Okay. Okay." He stood up. "But don't think too long. I'm either in or I'm out. I have to get focused on my course. I can't afford to blow it."

Andrea nodded. He leaned down and she thought he was going to kiss her, but instead he just squeezed her arm. "I'll call you later."

Andrea watched him walk away. Tears started coursing down her cheeks again. She put her head on her arms. *God,* she prayed. *Please help me decide what to do.*

* * *

Benny shoved his dish bin onto the table and sat down. "Andrea is sad again," he said.

Andrea sniffed and wiped the tears away as she nodded. "Just a little, Benny."

He looked over his shoulder. "Who was that boy?"

"Just a friend."

"Friends don't make you cry."

Andrea gave him a weak smile. "I wish that was true," she said, "but sometimes they do."

Benny shook his head. "Friends don't make you cry," he repeated.

* * *

Hoping it would be a good opportunity to bond, Kenni called the next day and asked if Andrea wanted to go shopping for some baby furniture. Kenni picked her up in a rented car and they drove to a nearby mall where she'd seen sale signs. Andrea wasn't terribly interested in looking at all the cribs and change tables, so they selected what they needed quickly. When Kenni suggested they have a look for some maternity clothes, however, Andrea seemed grateful.

"Most of what I've been wearing is getting tight," Andrea admitted.

Kenni tried her best to make the shopping fun, commenting on how fashionable the clothes were and how good Andrea looked in them. After trying on several outfits, she noticed Andrea starting to run out of steam. She helped her choose two pairs of jeans with tops and one dress she had lingered over. She seemed reluctant to buy it, but Kenni insisted. It was obvious that Andrea was pleased even though she said she had no idea where she'd ever wear it.

Two and half hours later, they sat in a café sipping lattes and watching the shoppers scurry by.

"Thanks, Kenni," Andrea said.

"For what?"

"For all of this," she said. "I don't get to go shopping very often and I really needed these clothes."

Kenni smiled. "I confess I love to shop. But don't tell Alex."

Andrea laughed. "He told me how you two met. It's a pretty wild story."

"Tracking him down was an adventure, all right," Kenni said. "All the way to the Yukon! Then he came to my dad's law firm. That was the first time I saw him."

"He told me about the inheritance and the letter. He said I should read it someday."

"I think that would be a very good idea."

Andrea watched a young family walk by. "So, you worked for your dad?"

Kenni noticed the change in subject but took a sip of her drink and nodded. "Ever since getting out of college. I did an undergraduate degree at Seattle

University, but still didn't know what I really wanted to do, so I took a paralegal course after that. I never wanted to be a lawyer but my dad's firm hired me as a researcher and I found my niche."

"That's what you do now?"

"Yes. I volunteer at a small street firm that does mostly pro bono work and advocacy for those who can't afford the normal legal fees."

"So, when you saw Alex, was it love at first sight?"

Kenni laughed. "Not at all. Well, I admit I did find him attractive, in a ruggedly handsome sort of way."

Andrea grinned. "But…"

"But we were like oil and water at first. He made me so mad at times that I never wanted to see him again. And I did the same to him. But then we started to get beyond the issues and, well, I knew I was in love with him. It scared me half to death."

"Why?"

"Because I was aware of his background and the pain he'd gone through. I knew it wasn't going to be an easy road ahead."

"But you chose to get involved anyway."

Kenni nodded. "I prayed a lot about it before I knew it was what God wanted, too. Then I couldn't help myself, and I haven't been sorry." She winked. "Most days."

"It's obvious Alex loves you."

Kenni noticed Andrea's shoulders drop. "Do you think Cory loves you, Andrea?"

She looked away and shook her head. "No. I don't think so."

Kenni could see she fought to keep the tears back but didn't succeed. She reached across the table and took her hand. "Have you decided what to do?"

"No. But Cory is the baby's father so maybe I should marry him so we can take care of her."

The pleading in her eyes broke Kenni's heart.

"I just don't know what to do."

"Have you prayed about it?" Kenni asked.

"I've tried but…" Andrea sighed. "I'm just not sure God would really listen to me now. You know, after, well, now that I've made such a mess of things."

"We all make messes, sweetie."

Andrea looked up. "You really think he forgives us?"

"I know he does. Forgiveness and mercy are what Jesus is all about." Kenni took another swallow of her latte. "Do you know the story in the Bible about the woman who was caught in adultery?"

"The woman they wanted to stone?"

Kenni nodded.

Andrea smiled wryly. "I remember our pastor preaching about that story."

"Then you know how compassionate Jesus was."

Andrea frowned. "I don't remember that. I think Reverend Castor emphasized the fact that the woman had sinned so bad, they were ready to stone her. I don't remember him talking about Jesus forgiving her."

"But that's the point of the story! When the men threw her to the ground at Jesus' feet, he took a stick and wrote something in the sand. We don't know what he wrote, but when he stood up again not one man was there. What he said to them gives me wonderful hope."

"What did he say?"

"Let he who has no sin throw the first stone." Kenni smiled. "He was telling us that we all need him. None of us is without sin. I always imagine him taking that woman's hand and pulling her up from the ground. He gave her a second chance at a new life that day. I'm pretty sure she took it."

"I sort of feel like you and Alex have offered that to me, too."

"We can offer you all kinds of help, Andrea, but only Jesus can forgive you and offer you eternal life."

Andrea sipped her drink. "I never heard Reverend Castor talk like that. He was always talking about how bad we are and how we have to purify ourselves all the time. I don't think he thought anyone was good enough for God."

"Well, at least he got that right. No one is good enough, but Jesus makes us good. That's what he did when he died on the cross. He took everything wrong we've ever done on himself and paid for it with his life. So when the Father looks at us, he doesn't see the messes we've made. He just sees Jesus. And he's standing with open arms, waiting for us to come to him."

"But what if… what if I'd decided to have an abortion? Would he have forgiven me for that?"

"It would have hurt him deeply, but yes, if you accepted the sacrifice Jesus made for you, he would accept you as an adopted child. He has already forgiven all of us. All we have to do is say yes to that forgiveness."

Andrea shook her head. "It's all kind of confusing."

Kenni put her hand on her arm. "Then just ask him to make it clear to you. He will."

Andrea sighed again. "I don't know if even he could get through my thick skull."

"Hey, he got through Alex's!"

Andrea laughed. "I guess we Perrins are all pretty stubborn."

"Don't worry. He never gives up on anyone."

Andrea stretched. "He sure does make active babies."

Kenni scooted her chair closer. "Can I feel?"

Andrea took her hand and placed it on her swollen belly. The baby kicked hard and they both laughed.

"She's a Perrin, all right," Kenni said.

CHAPTER
TWENTY-SIX

EDNA WALKED THE PATH TO THE KNOLL BY THE SLOUGH, FOLLOWING THE small creek, her mind restless, her heart heavy. None of the relationships in her life were healthy. Her husband barely spoke to her, and now her only child seemed a million miles away. She sighed. How could she mend it?

She stopped at a bend in the creek and knelt down. Sometimes you could see tiny minnows swimming here. She let her hand trail into the cold water, then reached for a small colourful stone. It was round and smooth to the touch, gleaming with the water still on its surface.

Andrea had often come home with stones in her pockets. Edna would find them when she went to do the laundry, and she usually scolded her. But she understood. There was something in her, too, that wanted to bring home what was beautiful, even tiny bits of nature.

She tossed the stone back into the water and continued along the path to the knoll.

Sinking to the ground, she began the litany she had recited here for so long.

"Forgive me," she cried. "Please forgive me."

She wondered if the tears she had shed on this spot for so many years counted for anything to anyone. There had never been an answer, so now she just appealed to her dead child. But she knew the child could not answer. Yet still she prayed into the air, hoping, longing. Did anyone anywhere care? Was there someone somewhere who could grant the forgiveness she longed for? She touched the stone. Was there a god who cared?

"Are you there?" she moaned. "Please, please show me."

The grasses swayed and a soft breeze touched her. She raised her head. It felt warm, almost a caress as it lifted a tendril of her fine, greying hair.

Then the very air seemed to form itself into an embrace. Edna sucked in her breath and stood, wrapping her arms around herself, wanting to hold onto whatever it was that was surrounding her. She sank to her knees and rested her forehead against the stone, the sobs coming freely, not wrenching her soul, now, but healing it.

New words came to her mouth and she cried them out in a loud voice.

"Thank you. Oh God, thank you."

* * *

It was past suppertime when Earl came home. Edna took the casserole from the oven when she heard the truck door slam. He stopped in the doorway and seemed surprised to see her there.

She smiled at him. "Sit down, Earl," she said. "I made your favourite chicken casserole. And I have something to tell you."

Earl devoured the food while she tried to describe what had happened at the slough, how she had been comforted and forgiven.

She reached for his hand. "I'm not explaining it very well, I know, but he's real, Earl. For the first time in my life I truly believe God is real, and he has forgiven me."

Earl stared at his plate for some time, then gave a jerk of his head. "That's good," he said. "That's good." He stood up and shrugged into his old jacket. "I'd better check on the animals."

Edna watched him go, the sadness in her almost enough to make her weep again, but then she smiled. It would be okay. Whatever happened now, it would be okay.

* * *

"I don't think this is a good idea." Alex frowned as he pushed his hands through his hair.

Andrea glanced up at him, then down again.

Kenni put her arm around her. "But we know it's your choice, Andrea, and we'll be here for you, no matter what you decide." She tossed Alex a look. He sighed, but said nothing.

Andrea gave Kenni a weak smile. "Thanks." She glanced at Alex again. "I haven't completely made up my mind, but Cory wants us to try to be together, and I…" She hesitated. "I'm thinking maybe that would be best. I do want to keep my baby, and Cory has promised…" She let out a deep sigh but didn't finish the sentence.

Alex started to pace, then came and put his hand on her shoulder. "Just promise you'll keep praying about it, okay?"

She nodded. "Okay."

Her voice was so soft and Alex knew she had little understanding of what praying could do or how God could guide her.

* * *

That night, as Andrea reached for the small lamp by her bed, her eyes fell on the brochure lying next to it. She picked it up and scanned the photos again.

The size of a football, she thought, *but it can open its mouth and move its arms and legs spontaneously.*

Her hand slipped to her belly and the image of that little hand waving filled her mind. She smiled, put the brochure down, and reached for the light again. But again she hesitated. She lay there for some time, then slipped out of bed onto her knees. She hadn't prayed on her knees since she was a little girl, but somehow she thought this prayer required a kneeling posture.

Her mind went blank for a while, then she remembered a Sunday school teacher telling her it was always good to give thanks to God before you asked for anything. That seemed like a good place to start.

"Thank you," she prayed. "Thank you for this miracle. I don't understand why you would let it be a miracle considering how I've messed things up, but somehow I know you have. So thank you." Tears coursed down her cheeks onto the blanket. "Please help me to make the right decision."

She threw herself back into bed.

As she reached to turn out the light, she thought she heard a soft scraping noise by the door. She lay still and listened, but heard only silence and the soft ticking of the clock. She pulled the blanket up to her chin and closed her eyes.

* * *

Kenni flew back to Vancouver two days later. Alex saw her off at the airport and promised to call.

"You're sure you don't mind that I stay?" he asked.

"No. I understand."

He could feel the sadness in her, but he didn't know what to say, what to do. It made him angry, but he tried not to show it.

She touched his cheek. "I'll call when I get home."

They hugged and then she was gone.

Alex kept noticing the bars along the way as he drove back to the apartment. The palms of his hands started to sweat and he licked his lips so much that they started to feel chapped. But he made it back to the apartment without stopping. He thought about thanking God but couldn't bring himself to do it.

He sat in the living room and stared out at the twinkling lights of the city. So many people with so many messed up lives. After touring around in the boonies looking for Andrea, he knew things weren't much better out in the country.

Alex sighed. Life was never easy. But there was someone he could turn to. Someone he could talk to. He'd been a bit on and off with God lately, but he knew it was his own fault. This whole mess with Andrea still had him tied up in knots, as much as he had tried to give it to God. Bennett had suggested he was holding onto something. But what?

Control.

The word hit him like a kick in the gut and he knew it had hit the mark. He wanted—no, *had* to control his life, every detail of it. This was the same issue he'd been battling for years. So much of his life had been out of his control for so long. The abuse and intimidation had left him determined to control. He realized it was a kind of security blanket, one that took the place God should have in his life. The counselling had taught him that. As long as everything was going as he thought it should, as long as everything danced when he pulled the

194

strings, he felt safe. He knew that was illegitimate. Nothing and no one could keep him safe but God. And God would not be controlled.

This situation with Andrea wasn't going the way he wanted it to and it seemed like God wasn't doing a very good job of keeping things together. Alex didn't think it was a good idea that Cory and Andrea try to raise the baby on their own, but could he and Kenni really do any better? Raising a child... he was terrified of that idea, too. That's what he was mad at God about. He'd led them right to his sister, but right into a pile of stress and trouble.

Thanks a lot, Lord. Nice to have a friend like you.

Alex put his head in his hands.

Listen to yourself, Donnelly.

He snorted. *Donnelly.* He wasn't a Donnelly anymore. He wasn't a scared little kid who was powerless to do anything to help himself or anyone else. He was a Perrin—Alex Perrin, the name he'd been given at birth. That was his identity. But who was that person? A grown man who was just as impotent as that little boy?

He sat back and stared out the window again, almost laughing out loud. Yes. In a way, he was just as powerless as he'd been then, but now he was a grown man who could live in the strength and power of Jesus Christ. A grown man who could humble himself before his God and ask for forgiveness for being so full of pride and slow to obey. He sank to his knees.

He prayed for almost an hour before finally reaching that point of peace he needed. Once again, he gave up and knew that whatever happened, it would be okay. God was God. He was in control and he would take care of them. Alex could accept the idea of Andrea and Cory raising the baby, if that's what they chose, and he'd do what he could to help them, trying not to be too much of a hovering brother and uncle. He stood up and paced.

Maybe they'd come and live in Vancouver. He could help them get settled, buy them a house, get Cory a job.

Control.

He shook his head and grinned. Maybe it was going to be harder not to hover than he thought. He laughed out loud.

Okay, Lord, I'll try and keep my hands off, if that's what you want. I trust them all to you, and I thank you again for what you've done in bringing us together, even if it isn't exactly the ideal situation I had in mind. Thank you. Thank you. Thank you.

* * *

Andrea stared at the phone after Edna hung up. She sounded so different. Almost happy. Andrea frowned. Well, she'd find out soon enough. Her mother insisted on coming to see her right away.

When she arrived, Edna almost ran to her, and when they embraced Andrea thought Edna would never let go. Edna now sat across from her, her face beaming, holding Andrea's hands between her own.

"I can't explain it, Andrea, but something has happened. Something wonderful. And I just wanted to tell you that I love you. I love you so much."

Andrea couldn't keep the tears from coming. She pulled her hands away and covered her face as the tears became sobs.

Edna slipped out of the booth and Andrea felt the seat cushion sink as she sat down beside her. She leaned toward her and rested her head on her mother's shoulder. Edna wrapped her arms around her and rocked her like a small child.

When the sobs subsided, Andrea took a shuddering breath. "I don't think you've ever said that to me before."

Edna's arms tightened. "I know. I know and I'm so sorry. It was because I didn't even realize I could love you. But now I know I do, Andrea, because I know God loves me." The sound that came from her mother's mouth then made Andrea think of a little girl, giggling as her father played with her. "And I really do want you to come home. I want… I suppose I want to try and get back all the years we lost, Andrea. I know we can't do that, really, but we can begin again, can't we? With the baby, we can begin again. Everything will be all right, you'll see."

The longing Andrea had known all her life pulsed inside her. She wanted to accept her mother's offer, more than she would have thought, but she was afraid. Afraid of being hurt again.

"What does Dad think about that?"

"He wants you home as much as I do. He loves you, too, Andrea. He just has a hard time showing it, like I did."

Andrea straightened and pulled away. "I'll think about it."

Edna sat back. "Okay, okay. Just know you can always come home, any time, no matter what."

Andrea held her breath as Edna embraced her again.

CHAPTER TWENTY-SEVEN

THE RECEPTIONIST SMILED AT ANDREA WHEN SHE ARRIVED AND EXPLAINED that Nicole would be with her in a moment. It was always good to see Nicole's smiling face. Andrea heaved herself up and followed her into the small room.

"How are you doing?" Nicole asked. "You're getting big."

Andrea smiled. "No kidding." She sat down and sighed.

Nicole came right to the point. "So, have you decided about your brother's offer?"

Andrea looked at the wall. "I've decided, I think…" She lifted her face. "My boyfriend is back in the picture."

Nicole sat back. "Oh?"

"He wants us to be together. He wants us to raise the baby ourselves."

"And how do you feel about that?"

Andrea rubbed her eyes. "I don't know what to do. I'm more confused now than ever. I know it's our responsibility—I mean, the baby is ours, so we should take care of it, right? And I thought I loved Cory, but now I'm not sure. I don't think Cory really loves me. He said he wants to do what's right. Maybe he's just worried about what everyone will think. Maybe it's all about appearances, just like my parents." Andrea shook her head hard. "And my mother—my foster mother—came to see me and, well, I could go home. She wants me to. I just don't know what to do." She let her head fall into her hands.

Nicole was quiet for a moment, then said, "Well, maybe it will help to talk about all the pros and cons." She stood up, opened a drawer in the cabinet against the wall, and came back with a pad and pen. "So, what are the positive things about letting your brother and his wife take the baby?"

For the next half hour, they listed the good and bad of every possibility. By the end, Andrea wasn't any closer to a decision but she was a bit clearer on what each decision meant. She felt more confident being able to make a decision for the good of the baby and for her. She just had to do it.

On the way back to the diner, she decided that the first thing she needed to do was talk to Cory again. She wanted him to meet her at the diner the next day, but he claimed to be busy. Two days later, she sat in the corner booth, watching the clock tick past the time when he was supposed to be there.

Half an hour later, she saw his truck pull up in front of the diner. She told herself to keep it together. No tears. Just straight talk. As soon as he sat down across from her, she got right to the point.

"Would you still want to be with me if there wasn't a baby?"

Cory frowned. "But there is a baby. Unless you're thinking of…"

"No. I'm not going to have an abortion. It's too late for that now. I am going to have the baby, but, Cory, I don't want to live in a relationship that's only about duty. I've seen firsthand what that's like. If you don't love me… I don't want to live like that."

Cory sighed. "So you want to give the baby to your brother?"

"Maybe that would be best," Andrea said softly.

Cory nodded. She noticed his shoulders drop.

"Okay," he said. He stared out the window for a while, then back at Andrea. "It sort of feels like I've just been let out of prison." He leaned forward. "You're sure this is okay? I can really just walk away and you won't hate me?"

Andrea nodded. "That prison would have choked the life out of all of us, eventually."

Cory nodded again and stood up. "Then I think I'll stay out of it from now on."

"You can still see her, if you want to. I won't stand in your way. You are her father."

Cory shook his head. "I'm an all or nothing kinda dude." He leaned down and gave her a quick kiss on the cheek.

"Goodbye, Andrea. Have a great life."

Andrea sat for a while, letting the tears come. But as she watched Cory saunter away, she felt like a weight had lifted.

* * *

Andrea helped Evie and the new girl for a while first thing in the morning, then spent the next hour sorting her belongings and getting ready to pack. She was supposed to make the move tomorrow, but she hesitated. The new girl was still a bit shaky and could use another day or two before having to be on her own.

She picked up the phone and dialled the number at the apartment. There was no answer, so she left a voicemail message and hung up. She had thought of telling Alex and Kenni that she'd made her decision, that she wanted them to raise the baby, but something kept her from saying the words.

Benny was standing outside her door when she went to leave. Andrea smiled at him.

"Look, Benny, I have some new clothes." She held up one of the colourful tops.

Benny frowned. "Benny can buy clothes, too."

"I know, of course you can. Maybe we can go shopping together some day. Would you like that?"

He nodded. Andrea slipped by him and went into the washroom. She listened for his footsteps but heard nothing. When she came out, he was still standing beside her door.

"I'm really tired, Benny. I'm going to rest now, okay?" She stepped around him into the room.

He didn't move, so Andrea started to close her door. "I'll see you in the morning."

The door was almost closed when Benny suddenly lunged forward and grabbed Andrea's hand.

"You have to see," he insisted, pulling her out of the room and down the back stairway.

Andrea sighed. "Benny, slow down. I can't move this fast. My belly's too big."

Benny stopped and stared at her, then nodded. "Okay." He let go of her hand but clamped his long fingers around her wrist. "Then we'll go slower." He pulled her along beside him.

When they were at the bottom of the stairs, Andrea tried to pull free.

"Let go, you're hurting me."

His grip weakened a bit but still held firm as he headed toward the basement stairs.

Andrea tried to pull away again. "I don't want to work with the stones right now, Benny. I have packing to do."

He didn't respond but pushed her gently ahead of him. She had no choice but to descend the narrow stairway. When he pulled her toward the far end of the room and through another doorway, she tried again to wrench her wrist free.

"Benny, please, you're hurting me. Let go."

Benny said nothing but nodded and let go of her. "There's something important. You have to see it."

Andrea rubbed her wrist. Something inside her told her to run, but she pushed it away. Benny was just a little upset. She knew he was harmless. "Okay, but only for a few minutes."

Benny grinned. "Benny will take care of his baby."

Andrea shook her head and sighed, but followed him through a doorway into a long corridor. She hadn't realized there was so much more to the building than she had seen.

He stopped and opened another door. "Okay." He pointed inside the room. "Come and look what Benny did."

Andrea leaned forward and glanced in as Benny flicked the light on and stood back. The proud look on his face made her smile. The walls of the room were covered with what looked like pictures torn out of magazines. There was a pile of blankets on the floor and a large pillow. Andrea turned and smiled at Benny again. "You've been making yourself quite a little nest here, haven't you?"

He beamed. "Andrea will be warm. Benny will bring more blankets."

She frowned. "But I can't sleep here, Benny. You know that."

Benny giggled. "Benny will take care of his baby."

Andrea's frown deepened and she made a move to leave. Benny laughed and blocked her way.

* * *

Kenni was unpacking her clothes as she listened to the voicemail message one more time. She frowned. She thought Andrea had been planning to move in right away. She replayed the message again.

"I'll bring the last box over in a couple of days," she said. "I'll let you know when."

Alex came up behind her. "Hey, was that Andrea?"

"Yes. It sounds like she's not moving today after all."

Alex frowned. "Oh? I thought today was the day."

"Me, too. I guess she's hesitating a bit. Maybe we should call her."

Alex cocked his head. "I don't know. Maybe we should give her some space. Let her go at her own pace with all this. It must be kind of overwhelming for her."

Kenni replaced the phone on its cradle. "I suppose. It just seems a little odd. Yesterday she was ready to go."

"We'll call her tomorrow, if she doesn't call us first." Alex wrapped his arms around her and kissed her neck. "Maybe we should take advantage of this. This could be the last night we'll be alone for a while."

Kenni twisted around in his arms. "So, what did you have in mind?" She laughed as he kissed her again.

* * *

Andrea banged on the door again. "Benny! Benny, let me out!" She heard him push the bolt across the doorframe.

"Andrea is safe now," he said. "Benny will get more blankets."

"No! Benny, please, let me out! Please."

She heard his heavy footsteps lumber away.

She started to cry, but then calmed herself. Evie would find her soon. She sank down onto the blankets, then cried again when she realized Evie might not even notice she was gone. She was supposed to move to the apartment. What if Evie thought she had left?

Oh God, she prayed. *If you're out there somewhere, please help me.*

* * *

Evie saw Benny stuff a sandwich into his pocket. She was surprised at how well he had accepted the idea of Andrea moving over to the new apartment. They hadn't told him yet that she planned to leave for Vancouver right after the baby was born. She hoped he accepted that as well.

She tapped him on the shoulder. He jumped back.

"If you're hungry, you know you can just ask Joe to make whatever you want, Benny."

He giggled but didn't respond.

She looked at his pocket. "Is that a midnight snack?"

"Benny gets hungry sometimes."

"Oh, I'm well aware of that!"

Benny giggled again and headed for the stairs. Evie watched him go and sighed. He was going to miss Andrea. So was she. She had expected her to come and say a last goodbye before leaving in the afternoon, but the bus had arrived and she'd gotten so busy that she didn't realize Andrea was gone until she started to clean up and get ready for the supper hour. Andrea probably hadn't wanted to interrupt her in the middle of the busy rush.

Evie picked up a cloth and gave the counter another swipe.

She'll probably call tomorrow.

* * *

Benny hurried to his special place. There was no sound from inside, so he thought Andrea must be sleeping. That was good. Andrea needed to rest. He slipped the bolt over slowly and opened the door just enough to slip the sandwich inside. Then he closed it softly and remembered to move the bolt back. He'd bring her some tea later. Tea would keep her warm.

* * *

Andrea tucked another blanket around her feet and shivered. The night had been long and damp, even though the furnace had come on twice. She knew Evie always turned it way down at night.

She had to get out of here. She had given up trying to get Benny to let her out and she'd screamed until she was hoarse, but no one came. She started to cry again, then sniffed and stopped.

Think, she told herself. *What can I say to Benny to make him let me out?*

Nothing came to mind.

God, please help me. Please.

She hugged her tummy and peered at the walls. There were pictures of animals and birds of all kinds and a few of ocean scenes in tropical countries. She scanned them, twisting around to see what was on the wall behind her.

She caught sight of something there that was unlike the other glossy pages and stood up to see what it was. She found herself staring at her own blurred photograph. She reached up and pulled it down, reading the words under the photo: "Have you seen this girl?" The phone number wasn't local, but it was in the province.

This must have been the poster Alex and Kenni and their friends put up all over the city. She sank down against the wall, pressed the poster to her chest, and let the tears slip down her cheeks. They had been looking for her, seeking her, wanting her.

So am I.

Andrea brushed the tears away. "God," she whispered, "I'm here."

Words began flowing through her mind. Words she had learned in Sunday school. They hadn't meant anything to her then, but now they were like a balm to an open wound, flowing like a river in a swift stream.

Surely I will be with you always. Fear not, for I have redeemed you. I have summoned you by name. You are mine.

Her hand went to the stone around her neck. Evie had said God's word acted like water on stone, to smooth and polish our lives. She'd thought of it as a painful process, but what she felt right now was peace and joy. Joy was a word she hadn't ever thought about before, because she had no idea what it meant. But now she knew. Joy was something beyond happiness. She wasn't happy. She was still in a damp, ugly basement and had no idea how to get out. But the joy was there. The joy was real.

"Because I know now that God loves me."

She remembered her mother's words. Her mother. Andrea let the sobs come. Yes. Edna was her mother and Earl was her father and they did love her.

So do I.

"I know," she whispered again. "I know."

CHAPTER
TWENTY-EIGHT

EARL SAW EDNA LEAVE THE HOUSE AND HEAD ACROSS THE FIELD, A SMALL dark form against a powdering of white. He watched her for a while, then wiped his hands on a rag and followed, staying far enough away that she wouldn't hear him. She never turned around, just made a beeline for the slough. Earl's heart started to beat fast, but he kept walking.

He saw her sink to the hard ground, then wrap her arms around herself and start swaying back and forth, as he had seen her do before. He crept closer, telling himself to stop, but he couldn't. Edna's head jerked up and her eyes went wide when she saw him. She leaped to her feet and said his name.

He didn't stop until he was standing right in front of her. Close to her. He put his hands on her shoulders and opened his mouth. For a moment, nothing came out. Then he blurted, "I forgive you."

She staggered back. "What?"

"I forgive you," he said again, taking a step toward her. "Can you forgive me, for all these years? Can you, Edna?"

She shook her head. "There is nothing to forgive, Earl. It's all my fault."

Earl reached for her. "No. It's my fault, too. I should have said those words twenty years ago. But I was too hurt for a while, and then, I don't know. It just seemed better not to talk about it. But that was wrong and that was my fault. Please, Edna, I need you to forgive me. Please."

Tears started streaming down Edna's face. "I do," she said. "Of course I do."

He pulled her to him. She wrapped her arms around him and put her head on his chest.

She gulped for air. "I love you, Earl. I always did love you, but I just… I was so young and my head was full of foolishness. I got swept away for a while, that's all. I never meant to hurt you."

Earl felt something give way inside him and tears started streaming from his eyes, too. "I know," he said. "I know."

They stood for a long time, rocking back and forth, holding each other in the swirling snow. When he felt Edna shiver, he slipped his arm around her shoulders and guided her back to the house.

"C'mon," he said. "I'll make you a nice cup of tea."

* * *

When Andrea didn't show up or call by noon the next day, Alex called Evie's diner. She was surprised to hear that Andrea wasn't there.

"I thought she moved to the apartment yesterday, Alex. She told me she just had one more small box to take and would be back to say goodbye later. When she didn't come to say goodbye, I just thought I must have been busy with customers."

"She's not here," Alex said. "Are you sure she's not there? Did you check her room?"

Evie's voice came in bursts of air. "I'm on my way up the stairs right now," she breathed.

Alex heard her gulp for air between each word. "The box is still here," she told him. "I'm worried, Alex. Where could she have gone?"

"I'll be right over," he answered and jammed the phone into his pocket.

Evie was talking to Joe when he arrived. Both of them were frowning.

"I just don't understand it." Evie kept shaking her head. "Where would she go?"

Alex glanced at Benny's stooped back. "Have you asked Benny if he's seen her?"

Evie nodded. "Yes. He just giggles and shakes his head."

Alex stared at the boy's back for another moment, then whirled on his heel. "I'm calling the police."

* * *

Benny poured the tea into a small thermos, slipped it into the big pocket in his jacket, and plodded to the basement stairs. He glanced back at Evie, Joe, and the bad man huddled by the counter. That man wanted to take Andrea away. But now he couldn't. Now Andrea and the baby were safe.

He giggled and pushed open the door.

* * *

The rattle of the lock woke Andrea. She sat up as Benny entered the small room, pulling a thermos and another sandwich out of his pocket. She pushed herself up, her back to the wall, and smiled as Benny handed them to her.

"Thanks, Benny. We'll eat this together, okay? Then I need to go and help Evie in the restaurant, just like always."

Benny frowned. "Another girl helps Evie now. She's nice, too."

"That's good," Andrea said. "But I need to help, too. You know there's always lots of work to do and I don't want Evie to get sick. Do you, Benny?"

Benny shook his head and frowned.

Andrea handed him half of the sandwich. He ate it slowly, the frown never leaving his forehead.

She took another sip of the tea and stood up, handing the thermos back to him and taking a step toward the door.

"Thank you, Benny," she said, inching around him as he fumbled to put it in his pocket. "That was good. Let's go see if Evie needs help now, okay?" She reached for the door but his large hand caught her wrist.

"The bad man is still here," he said. "Benny will keep you safe here. The bad man will see you if you go upstairs."

Andrea frowned. "What bad man, Benny?"

"The man who wants to take Andrea away, and Benny's baby." He pushed her back from the door. "Benny has to take care of the baby."

"But it's not good for the baby down here, Benny. It gets cold at night and the baby needs to be warm. Let me go up to my own room, okay? The baby will be safe there."

Benny shook his head. "Benny will bring another blanket," he said, pulled the door open, and shut it quickly behind him.

Andrea pounded on it. "Benny, let me out right now!"

She heard him shuffle away as he called out, "Benny will be back later."

* * *

The police were in the kitchen talking to Joe when Benny returned. He pulled his jacket off and wrapped the apron around him the way Evie had taught him to do it. One of the policemen was watching as he picked up his cloth and put a clean pan of water and bin on his cart. He started to leave but the policeman blocked his way.

"Who are you?" he asked.

"Benny has to wipe the tables now," he said, trying to push his cart past the uniformed man. He put his hand on it.

"Just hang on a minute. I'd like to ask you some questions."

"Benny has to clean the tables now," he repeated in a loud voice.

Evie burst through the doors. "It's all right, officer. Benny doesn't know anything about Andrea. Do you, Benny?"

"Benny has to wipe the tables," he repeated again.

"I'm sure this nice policeman will let you do that now," she said, raising her eyebrows at the policeman. He gave Benny a look, but stepped aside.

"Benny helps Evie," he said as he pushed the cart forward. "Andrea doesn't have to help now. Benny helps."

The policeman watched him go.

"You're sure about him?" he asked Evie.

"Yes, I'm sure. He's totally harmless and he loves Andrea. He would have told me if he knew anything."

The man's partner appeared and said he was finished questioning everyone. "We'll talk to her parents. Maybe she decided to go home after all, or took off to visit the boyfriend." He slipped his notebook into his shirt pocket. "We'll circulate her picture, of course, and do what we can. We'll contact you if we learn anything. If you hear from her, let us know immediately."

Evie nodded. "Of course."

Alex slipped off the stool as the officers walked by him.

"We'll be in touch," one of them said.

Alex nodded and watched them leave. He ran his hand through his hair as Evie came out of the kitchen shaking her head.

"They seem to think Andrea has just run away again," Evie said. "I don't think they'll do much."

"I know. But they'll still circulate her photo and put out a bulletin about her." Alex sighed and shook his head. "I don't think she'd go home, but I'll call Edna right away."

* * *

Alex was on the phone with Edna when one of the police officers returned. Alex told Edna he'd call her back and turned as the officer held up a red woollen glove.

"Do you recognize this?" he asked Evie.

Evie's face went pale as she nodded. "It's Andrea's. Where did you find it?"

"In the back alley," he answered.

"Oh God." Evie sank down into a booth. "Oh God, something's happened. I know something must have happened to her."

Alex stepped to her side and put his hand on her shoulder.

The officer sighed. "We'll have a K-9 division come by as soon as possible."

"K-9?" Evie asked.

Benny pushed his cart closer.

"Dogs," Alex answered.

The officer nodded. "If she was out in that alley, they may be able to track where she went."

* * *

Kenni had spent the evening praying. She knew Alex's frustration was reaching a dangerous level, so she prayed that Andrea would be found, safe and sound and quickly. Bennett and Stan had both arrived that afternoon and were scouring the streets, looking for any clue. The K-9 team had arrived, but could find no trace of Andrea other than a few feet from the back door of the diner. The police thought she must have gotten into a vehicle that was parked there, but there were no tire tracks, no clues at all. None of them could understand why anyone would kidnap a pregnant girl who had no money. Unless...

Kenni stood up. What if it was someone who knew about Alex's inheritance? But no one knew except the few people they trusted. She couldn't imagine any of them would do this.

"Oh God," she prayed again, "Please help us find her."

She heard the key in the door and went into the foyer as Alex stepped inside. He looked worn out.

"Anything?" she asked.

Alex shook his head and tossed the keys onto the table by the door. Kenni embraced him.

"She seems to have just vanished," Alex said, pulling away from her.

Kenni slipped her hand into his and drew him into the kitchen. "I just made some coffee," she said.

"Stan and Bennett are on their way. We thought we should touch base and try to put together some kind of plan."

Kenni put a mug on the table. "Alex, I was wondering, do you think… could it be someone who knows about the inheritance?"

Alex shook his head. "I've thought of that. But there's no one, unless you think your parents or George might be involved." He grinned at her and she smiled back. "Not likely, huh?"

Kenni shook her head.

Kenni placed two more mugs on the table and poured the coffee as Stan and Bennett arrived.

It was Stan who brought their attention to Cory.

"What do we know about him?" He looked at Bennett.

Bennett frowned. "Not much, but from my conversation with him earlier, I really don't think he's involved. You think he might have taken her?"

Stan shrugged. "Maybe he was angry, feeling rejected. Maybe he feels he has a right to make her do what he wants, since he's the father of the baby."

Bennett shook his head. "It doesn't fit. He seemed more concerned about how to get out of being involved. I can't see him doing this."

"Maybe nobody did anything," Alex said.

Stan frowned. "You think she disappeared on her own?"

"Maybe I've been pressuring her too much," Alex said. "To decide what to do, to move into the apartment. Maybe it all just piled up on her and she needed some space."

Kenni put her hand on his. "She wouldn't just disappear, Alex. I'm sure she would have said something to Evie or to you."

Alex nodded. "You're right, I guess. I just don't want to think about other possibilities."

They had all downed most of their coffee when Stan stood up and started to pace. "Okay," he said. "We're obviously missing something. Let's start at the beginning again. Who was at the diner when Andrea disappeared?"

"Evie and Joe," Alex answered. "The new waitress didn't start her shift until four in the afternoon."

"And Benny," Kenni said.

Bennett looked up. "Benny is always there, isn't he? But you sort of don't notice him."

"What do we know about him?" Stan stopped pacing.

"Nothing, really." Alex cocked his head. "Except he doesn't like me."

Stan pulled his jacket off the back of the chair. "Maybe we should find out more."

CHAPTER TWENTY-NINE

EVIE FROWNED, HER EYES FLICKING FROM ALEX TO KENNIE TO BENNETT, THEN Stan, and back again. "Well, I don't know much about Benny either, really." Her frown deepened. "But Benny can't have had anything to do with this. He's harmless and he loves Andrea."

"Where did he come from? How did you happen to hire him, Evie?" Stan asked.

"Well, he just wandered in off the street one day. He was sort of lost and forlorn looking and had nowhere to go." She looked at Alex again. "So I taught him how to be a busboy. That was almost two years ago."

"Did he ever tell you where he came from? Does he have family?" Bennett leaned forward.

Evie shook her head. "No. I tried to get him to tell me at first, but it just seemed to upset him and he'd get all confused and flustered, so I quit trying. I did contact social services at the time, but they didn't even come by to talk to him." She shook her head again. "Benny has never been any trouble. I can't believe he'd do anything to hurt Andrea. He's really bonded with her and he's so excited about the baby…"

Bennett's eyebrows went up. "Excited about it?"

Evie nodded. "Yes. In fact, ever since we took him with us to see the ultrasound, he's called it his baby and talked about how he has to take care of it." She was smiling, but the smile faded at the look on Bennett's face.

"Where is he right now?" Bennett asked.

"Probably in the kitchen," Evie said, waving her hand toward the door.

Bennett looked at Alex and Kenni, then back to Evie. "I want you to ask Benny something, Evie. We'll all wait here so we don't spook him. I want you to ask Benny what happened to the baby."

Evie frowned. "I don't understand. What baby?"

"What are you thinking, Bennett?" Alex asked.

He held up his hand. "I'm just acting on a hunch. Just ask him that and come back and tell us how he reacts."

Evie sighed and heaved herself up. "Okay. I'll be right back."

As soon as she was out of the room, Bennett explained. "Just over two years ago, I remember hearing about a case on TV where a woman died after slipping and hitting her head on a bathtub. She was pregnant and for some reason the baby didn't survive either. It was a tragic incident that captured the news for a while."

"But what does that have to do with Benny?" Alex asked.

"There was an older sibling, a boy who was mentally challenged in some way. He was having a bath when his mother fell. The report said he lapsed into an almost catatonic state. A few months later, the story was back in the news because he had disappeared from an institution. As far as I know he was never found."

Kenni's hand flew to her mouth. "You think Benny could be—"

"Yes, I think it's possible. And if he is that same boy, Andrea's pregnancy could have triggered something that made him overly protective. Maybe protective enough to want to hide her."

* * *

Benny was wiping out his dish bin when Evie put her hand on his shoulder and asked him to sit down at the staff table. She sat opposite him and smiled.

"I just have a question to ask you, Benny. Okay?"

He nodded and smiled back at her.

"Benny, can you tell me what happened to the baby?"

His eyes darted around the room and he started to shake his head hard. His hands flew to his ears and he batted them with his fingers. Evie reached out and took his hands. She forced herself to speak slowly, calmly.

"It's okay, Benny. It's okay. You can tell me. What happened to the baby?"

"Benny was having a bath," he said. He looked at Evie with pleading eyes. "Mommy said it was important to have baths." He started to rock back and forth. "But there was too much water." He pulled one hand free and started batting at his ear again. "Too much water," he repeated.

"What happened then, Benny?"

"Mommy went away and Benny had to go away for a while."

"Where did you go?"

"To the big house." He stopped swaying. "Benny liked the doctors there."

Evie smiled. "That's good. Did the doctors let you leave after a while?"

His eyes darted around again, but he didn't answer.

"Benny?" Evie squeezed his hands. "Do you know where Andrea is?"

"Benny has to take care of the baby."

"I know, Benny, but I have to take care of the baby, too, and Andrea. Is that okay? I've taken good care of you, haven't I?"

Benny nodded.

"Can I help you take care of Andrea? Please? I really want to help you take care of her and the baby. Do you know where Andrea is, Benny?"

"Andrea is warm now."

Evie held her breath. She knew there were hallways and rooms in the depths of this old building where no one ever went.

"Is she here, Benny, somewhere in this building?"

"Benny has a secret place," he whispered.

"Will you show me?"

Benny looked at her but said nothing.

"Please, Benny?"

"Okay," he said, and pushed himself out of the chair. "But the bad men have to go away first."

"What bad men?"

"The bad men who want to take Andrea away."

"Okay." Evie nodded. "I'll tell them they have to go away, and then you can take me to the secret place, okay?"

Benny nodded and followed Evie to the door into the diner. He peeked around it as Evie spoke to the four people whispering together. They hurried from the diner and Evie waved for Benny to come out.

"See? They're gone now."

Bennie shuffled toward the back of the diner with Evie on his heels.

As soon as they were out of the room, Alex, Kennie, and Bennett stepped back in. Stan got on the phone to call the police.

Benny led Evie to the furnace room. He pushed the bolt back and Evie called Andrea's name as she pushed the door open.

The girl flew into her arms and began to sob.

"It's okay, sweetie, I'm here now," Evie assured her. "It's okay." She led Andrea back into the diner where the others waited.

Benny started batting his ears and pacing. "No. The bad men were supposed to go away." He made a beeline for Andrea. "Benny has to take care of Andrea and the baby," he said, lunging for her arm.

Bennett and Stan grabbed hold of his arms and held him back.

"Don't hurt him," Andrea said. She put her hand on Benny's chest. "Benny, these aren't bad men. They want to help me and the baby, too."

"They want to take Andrea away."

"Only for a little while, Benny. We'll always see each other. I promise."

"And the baby, too? Benny can see the baby?"

"Yes, of course you can." Andrea smiled. "We'll bring the baby to see you often, okay?"

Benny nodded but looked nervously over her shoulder as the police arrived.

Evie took his arm and Bennett let go. "We're going to go with these nice policemen now, Benny. They're going to help you go back to the big house where those good doctors were, okay?"

"Benny liked the doctors."

Evie smiled and walked him toward the door. "The doctors will take good care of Benny."

* * *

Alex and Kenni took Andrea to the hospital at the urging of the police, to make sure she was all right. They kept her overnight and did a battery of tests to make sure she and the baby were fine. Everyone was relieved to find out they had suffered no lasting ill effects.

Andrea moved into the apartment the next evening. As she lay down on the

214

soft warm bed, she breathed a prayer of thanks, a prayer that was more from her heart than any other she'd ever prayed. Then she prayed for Benny. And she knew who was listening.

* * *

Three days later, Andrea asked Kenni and Alex to sit down at their small kitchen table. She was amazed at how calm she felt, how totally sure that she was doing the right thing. She smiled to herself. The peace Evie talked about—now she understood what it felt like.

"I've made a decision—a final one—about my baby." She put her hands flat on the table. "I want to thank you both for all the help you've already given me, and for offering to adopt her." She took a deep breath. "I know this is going to be hard for you both to accept, but I've decided I should be the one to raise her. Cory won't be in the picture. At least, not right now, but my mom and dad have asked me to go home and I think that's what I need to do. We have some rebuilding to do and I think it's what God wants. In fact, I'm sure of it." She smiled and looked at Alex. "Everyone deserves a second chance."

Her brother stared at her for some time, then nodded. "Okay," he said quietly. "Okay."

Kenni reached out and put her hands over Andrea's. "We'd still like to help, Andrea, if you'll let us."

Andrea nodded. "Every little girl needs an auntie and uncle."

Alex cleared his throat. "Then we'll be the best ever."

"You're not mad at me?"

Alex shook his head and looked at Kenni. "No. I think you're right, Andrea. I think this is what God wants."

* * *

The next few months flew by. Andrea's pregnancy progressed normally and the doctor assured them all that the haemophilia wasn't an issue unless something went wrong during delivery. Since they knew the family history, they would be prepared, but she anticipated that everything would go well.

As the due date grew closer, Andrea got more and more nervous, but Evie was always there to help her stay calm—and even her own mother was a help. They spoke on the phone every day and her parents both visited often. Andrea was a little mystified, but also thrilled, at the bond forming between them all.

She and Evie were in the staff room pouring over a baby name book when Andrea suddenly looked at her friend and said, "I know I keep saying this, Evie, but I don't know what I'd have done without you these past months."

Evie waved her hand in the air. "Not to worry, hon," she said. "I've loved having you here and being part of your life, and the baby's, if only for a little while."

Andrea glanced down at her swollen belly. "Well, it's not over yet."

"Are you still a little scared?"

She nodded. "A little."

Evie smiled and patted her hand. "That's perfectly normal. But everything is going to be just fine. You're going to have a beautiful, healthy baby girl. I just know it."

Evie squeezed her shoulder and leaned forward to look at the book.

"What have you chosen so far?" Evie asked.

"Emily Alexandra."

The baby gave a strong kick, making Andrea heave herself up from the chair. She leaned back and laid her hand on her stomach. "I think she liked it," she laughed.

"Alex will like it, too. Have you told him yet?"

Andrea shook her head. "No. I want to surprise him and Kenni, after she's born."

"It will please him for sure. And I think Kenni will like it, too."

Andrea turned toward the kitchen. "I think I'd like some more tea. Do you want…" Her eyes suddenly went wide and she grabbed the edge of the table.

Evie was at her side immediately. "What is it?"

She stared down as fluid trickled down her legs. "I think my water just broke."

Evie helped her back to the chair. "I'll get our coats. You just stay put."

By the time they reached the hospital, Andrea had had several contractions. The first few were weak, but they gradually gained in strength. The doctor admitted her immediately and Evie called Alex and Andrea's mother to let them know. Within an hour, the waiting room was full of anxious people. Evie and Edna took turns in the birthing room and giving reports on her progress to everyone waiting.

Just after sunrise, Edna came to tell them that a healthy little girl had been born without complications. She had a full head of dark curly hair.

Alex and Kenni were the first into the room. Andrea smiled as she opened the blanket so they could see her more clearly.

"Emily Alexandra," she said.

Alex stared at the tiny baby. "Emily Alexandra," he repeated and beamed.

"Beautiful," Kenni answered. "She's just beautiful."

Andrea lifted her up and Kenni took the tiny bundle in her arms. They were all weeping and laughing at the same time.

Andrea noticed her parents standing in the doorway. She waved them in.

Kenni handed the baby to Edna. "Congratulations, Grandma."

Evie bustled in. "It's my turn," she said, taking the infant in her arms. "Just look at all that black hair!"

Andrea looked at Alex. "It must be a Perrin thing," she said.

Alex nodded but couldn't speak.

CHAPTER THIRTY

As Andrea began to make plans to move home, she told Evie she wanted to see Benny before she left. Evie called to ask Benny's doctor about bringing Andrea and the baby to see him. Dr. Vallier said he thought it would be a good idea, so they made arrangements to visit the next day.

Jameson House was a big home built in an older subdivision of the city. The house was old but had been well-maintained. Evie told her that eight people lived in the residence, all of them like Benny, people who needed supervision.

Benny jumped up and clapped his hands when they came into his room.

He waved at the baby, then frowned when she didn't wave back.

"Doesn't she like me anymore?" he asked Evie, a distressed look on his face.

"Of course she does, Benny, but she's still a tiny baby. She hasn't learned to smile and wave yet."

"Oh," Benny said. "Nobody's mad at me now?"

"No, Benny," Andrea assured him. "We're not mad at you."

He took Evie's hand. "I do jigsaw puzzles. Come see."

He led her to a large table in a corner of the room. Two other people were sitting there, working on the puzzle. Benny sat down and was immediately engrossed in searching for a piece that would fit. Evie moved away and joined Andrea and the doctor.

Dr. Vallier smiled. "Benny's been doing well," he said. "But we're not sure he'll ever progress to a place where he's able to live on his own."

"Has his family been to see him?" Evie asked.

"Yes, his father and an aunt come regularly."

"I'm glad." Evie glanced over at him. His head was still bent over the puzzle. She sighed. "I miss him at the diner, but I guess it's better that he's here."

The doctor nodded. "We can't be certain that he wouldn't do something again to hurt someone else, or himself. It's best that he's here, where he's under constant supervision."

"He's barely even looked at me," Andrea said.

"Don't be offended," the doctor said. "It's been weeks since he's seen you. Go and talk to him. He'll probably respond to your voice more than your face."

Andrea approached, leaned over, and said something softly in Benny's ear. He didn't look up but nodded vigorously. They could tell he was chatting on about the puzzle. Andrea stood beside him for a while, then came back and joined them.

"He seems happy," she said.

Evie nodded.

"Autism has its positive side," the doctor commented. "As long as his needs are met and he has people around him who understand and accept him, he'll function quite well."

They talked a bit more, then Evie looked at her watch. "I think it's time to go."

They approached the table and Evie put her hand on Benny's shoulder. "Benny, it's time to say goodbye," she said. "Andrea and the baby are leaving now."

Benny looked up for a moment, said "Okay," and went back to the puzzle.

Andrea gave his shoulder a squeeze and they left the room.

Once outside, Evie wiped her eyes. "That was harder than I thought it was going to be."

Andrea strapped the baby into her car seat and nodded. "But he is happy, and he has his family back."

"Yes," Evie said, "and we know how important family is."

Andrea slid into the driver's seat and took Evie's hand. "You'll always be family to Benny, Evie, and to me, too."

Evie patted her hand. "I know. I know."

* * *

Andrea handed the last box to Alex. "That's it," she said, scanning the room to make sure she wasn't leaving anything behind. She took a step toward the door, then glanced down at the small bedside table. Edna's black diary lay beside the small lamp. Andrea picked it up and slipped it into the side pocket of the diaper bag.

* * *

Earl was in the barn when they arrived. He stood at the door watching them all come toward him. Andrea cradled the baby in her arms and watched as her foster father took a deep breath and seemed to steel himself.

"Hi, Dad," she said.

He nodded and said hello. He acknowledged Kenni and Alex, saying, "Morning."

"Your mother…" He stared across the field in the direction of the slough. "Your mother went for a walk."

Andrea looked across the snow-patched fields. She handed the baby to Kenni, took the small black book from the side pocket of the diaper bag, and handed the bag to Alex. "Go ahead inside," she said, "I'll be right back."

Earl stepped forward and grabbed her arm. "Maybe you should just let her be for a while, Andrea. Come inside. She'll be back soon. "

Andrea put her hand over his and shook her head. "No, Dad. We need to talk." She felt his hand release its grip. "We all need to do more of that," she said. He nodded and let go. Andrea headed across the fields.

Edna was on her knees, facing away from her, toward the slough, so she didn't see Andrea coming. Andrea watched the breeze move the tall grasses that stuck up out of the snow. She pulled her jacket tighter and stood at a distance for a while, waiting.

Finally, Edna stood and turned to leave. She stopped when she saw Andrea. Her eyes flitted to the black book in her hand, then back to Andrea's face.

Andrea approached, holding the diary out in front of her. "I found it in that box of old books. I didn't mean to take it. I thought it was mine."

Edna's smile was weak. "I know. I found yours." She took the diary and peered into Andrea's face. "Did you read it?"

Andrea nodded. Edna's eyes dropped to the smudged drawing of the earring. She held out her hand and drew her daughter toward the knoll and the round stone at the base of the trees. She stared down at it.

"It all happened about six years after Earl and I were married. He had hired a young man to help with the harvesting."

"Roy," Andrea said.

Edna nodded. Andrea saw her swallow hard.

"He was very handsome and charming." Edna's eyes focused on Andrea's. "The harvest was almost over when Earl fell off the barn roof and broke his arm and a leg. The arm healed pretty quick, but the leg was bad. It took almost a year before he was able to get out and do any work. So Roy stayed to help and I worked alongside him. He had travelled a lot and he told me about all the places he'd been—Italy and Spain, England, too. He knew a lot about so many different things. We would talk for hours sometimes."

She looked off toward the tall brown reeds swaying in the wind. "Then one day he told me I was beautiful and that he loved me." Tears began to slip down her cheeks. "No one had ever said those things to me before. Not even Earl." She swiped at the tears. Her hand waved in the air. "It happened so easily, so naturally." She was silent for a while. Andrea waited.

"Of course I was terrified when I discovered I was pregnant. Earl and I, we just weren't able to have a child and, well, we'd given up. Then, just before my belly started to swell, Earl decided we didn't need Roy anymore. I think maybe he knew." She took a deep breath. "He never said anything to me, just looked at me one day and said, 'He's gone.' After that, it was a long time before he would even look me in the eye.

"Once the pregnancy was obvious, I stayed on the farm. I was afraid someone would somehow know what I'd done. I was so ashamed. It was easy then. There weren't many neighbours in those days and we didn't go to church at all. Earl went to town alone if we needed something. He never asked me to go with him, so no one knew."

Edna's voice softened. "Then the baby was born dead." She reached out and touched the stone. "We buried her here."

"That must have been awful," Andrea said quietly.

Edna wiped her eyes. "It was awful for several years, until you came." She smiled. "You were my sunshine then, and you still are." She touched Andrea's cheek. "It was Earl's idea, you know? To have a foster child."

Andrea nodded. "You wrote about it."

Edna smiled and ran her hand across the book. "My mother used to get upset with me because I was always scribbling something or other instead of doing chores. It's my way of coping with things I guess." She looked off into the distance. "After you came, things got better. Not totally good, but better. Earl and I sort of lived in a state of truce for a long time, until, well, your pregnancy brought everything back. So we've had to talk about it, deal with it."

"But didn't you ever want more, Mom? All those years, didn't you want more than just a truce?"

"Yes, but I never thought I could have more." She shook her head. "I didn't believe I deserved more. I've been grateful for what I've been given. I don't deserve any of it."

"But living with the guilt... how have you been able to do it?"

Edna looked into her face for a long time before answering. "I'm afraid I didn't do it very well, and that hasn't been fair to you, Andrea."

"To me? What do you mean?"

"I had to shut down so much, to keep the pain and guilt from overwhelming me. The easiest way was to just not feel anything at all, not even love." The tears started to course down her cheeks again. "I'm afraid it kept me from loving you as I should have."

Andrea hugged her tight. "I always knew you loved me, Mom, in a way." She drew away. "But why didn't you ever adopt me, legally?"

Edna shrugged. "It was just something we never discussed. I was always afraid to bring it up, afraid it would be going too far, somehow, and Earl would be upset. I just didn't want to do anything more to upset him."

"I was always afraid to ask, too," Andrea admitted.

Edna sighed. "We've all lived with too much fear in our lives. Not enough love. But that's going to change."

Andrea smiled as her face began to glow.

"When you left, when all of this started to happen, I thought God was punishing us, punishing me." Edna smiled. "But one day I came out here and asked him to forgive me, and I know he did. I understand what they mean about a relationship with God now. I never thought such a thing was possible, but now I know it is. Then I started to see all of this, your pregnancy and everything, as a mercy. Pure mercy. And now here you are, safe and sound." She hugged her again. "He's given us all a second chance."

Andrea took her hand. "Come and see the baby," she said, tucking her mother's arm in her hers.

Edna pulled away. "Wait," she said, turning back to the knoll and laying the diary by the stone. "This is the past."

They walked together across the fields, their closeness banishing the chill of the day.

When they walked into the kitchen, Kenni was pouring Alex a cup of coffee and Earl was holding the baby. Edna stopped and stared. Earl looked up at her and smiled. Andrea was still holding Edna's hand. She gave it a squeeze.

"You look pretty good with a grandbaby in your arms, Dad," she said, beaming at him.

Earl nodded. "Feels good," he said. "It feels real good."

PILOGUE

EDNA PUSHED THE WORKSHOP DOOR OPEN. EARL WAS STANDING WITH HIS back to her, bent over the bench.

"Lunch is ready, Earl. Are you almost done out here?" She approached the bench as he turned toward her. She could see two pieces of wood about two feet long laid at a ninety-degree angle to one another and held in a vice. She stared at the small cross.

"I was going to varnish it today, but then I wondered…" He stepped aside so Edna could see the whole of it. "I wondered if you wanted some words on it, or a name?"

"Pearl," she said softly. "Baby Pearl."

Earl took a step toward her and she fell into his arms. "We'll put it on the grave tomorrow," he said. "The ground is soft enough now."

ALSO BY MARCIA LEE LAYCOCK

Fiction:
One Smooth Stone

Non-fiction:
Spur of the Moment
Focused Reflections
A Traveler's Advisory
Abundant Rain

Anthologies:
Hot Apple Cider
A Second Cup of Hot Apple Cider
Stories for a Woman's Heart
Christmas God's Way
Christmas Miracles

CPSIA information can be obtained
at www.ICGtesting.com
Printed in the USA
LVHW011401220221
679637LV00006B/782

9 781770 694552